1

BEN

When Gemma Charles smiles at you, rest assured you're fucked. And she's been smiling since she entered the courtroom.

Her client, Victoria Jones, is about to lose her three children. The prosecutor has provided his evidence, and you can make anything sound believable if you know how to tell a story.

Unfortunately for him, Gemma tells a better one.

She begins by proving the grounds for the welfare check were baseless. She plays bodycam footage showing a gross abuse of power by both the police and the social worker.

She proves the letter notifying Victoria of the visit was mailed *after* the visit. She's blown up the social worker's photos of the dirty kitchen floor—the only specific complaint made about cleanliness—and asks the social worker to demonstrate how, exactly, Victoria was supposed to get the floor clean while confined to a wheelchair.

And Gemma, naturally, has brought a wheelchair and a broom with her for the demonstration.

The court is laughing, the judge is getting irritated, and Gemma is in her element. She has the face of an angel—high cheekbones, wide mouth, almond-shaped eyes—but she's too goddamn argumentative and short-tempered to do anything but fight for a living. She's gliding across the floor like a dancer and turning the courtroom into a circus, one in which the arresting officer and social worker are the clowns. She's clearly proven her case, but she's still going strong because she's so fucking mad. She wants every single person in this room to see how ludicrous and unfair the situation is.

"Miss Charles," grouses the judge as Gemma begins to push the wheelchair out, "put that away. This isn't drama class." He turns to the state's attorney. "Motion is denied. This was a disgusting abuse of power on the part of social services, and I won't forget the way you just wasted the court's time."

Victoria and her family cheer. Gemma hugs them all before rushing toward the exit. I'm hidden at the back of the court-room, but I catch a glimpse of her eyes just before they disappear behind sunglasses.

She's crying. And I'm not sure they are happy tears.

2

GEMMA
Two Years Later

The devil on my shoulder is summoned every other Monday.

This morning, as I prepare for the all-staff meeting, he's dancing like a flame in my chest, and I can't seem to put him back in his place.

I flat-iron my dark hair until it hangs sleek and shiny, just past my shoulders. I spend extra time on my makeup and put on my good luck heels, which will only bring me to my nemesis's shoulder, but will at least level the playing field a bit. When we enter today's meeting it'll feel less like David versus Goliath, and more like Churchill versus Hitler.

To be clear, *I'm* Churchill in this scenario.

I rush out the door and into the bright September sun, reaching my building with only moments to spare. Fields, McGovern, and Geiger is on the fifteenth floor of the most sterile, soulless building in LA, and that's fitting. They're also LA's most sterile, soulless law firm. It's why I chose them.

The conference room is already full when I arrive, and I'm aggrieved to discover *he* has beaten me in. His head—a foot higher than any other—is positioned directly across from the seat saved for me by my assistant, Terri. Has he done this on purpose? Undoubtedly. Ben Tate lives to irritate me. And he barely needs to try—the sight of his smug face is enough.

Behave yourself, Gemma, I think as I cross the room. *For once, don't stoop to his level.*

I'm not normally so restrained, but it's a big day for me. FMG is excruciatingly stingy with partnerships, and aside from Ben—who came here as a partner two years ago—someone either needs to retire or die before I can step up. Fortunately, two partners plan to retire next spring. Perhaps I can stop hoping tragedy strikes.

Terri slides me a latte as I take the seat beside her. "You're wearing the good luck shoes," she says with a nod at my profoundly expensive baby-blue Manolos. I've never lost a case wearing them. "You think this is it?"

"It had better be after they amped it up the way they did," I growl.

Though other associates have been at the firm longer (including Craig, Ben's bland favorite) none of them bring in anywhere near the amount of work I do, nor have they garnered the kind of publicity I have.

Gemma Charles, Junior Partner. FMG's *only* female partner. It has such a nice ring to it, and God I'm going to love watching that smirk on Tate's mouth fall away when he hears it for the first time.

He's been my sworn enemy since his first week here, when he somehow managed to steal Brewer Campbell, a prospective client I'd spent six months courting. I'm alone in my hatred, however: the other women on staff don't care that he's a smug bastard and stealer of clients. They don't care that he barely seems to notice they exist. Apparently, all you need to be forgiven around here are broad shoulders and a winning record.

Although his face doesn't hurt either.

Even I will admit he has a face that's hard to look away from. His features shouldn't work together—sharp cheekbones, a nose that appears to have been broken at some point, intense brown eyes. His would be a *stern* face were it not for that upper lip, which is slightly fuller than you'd expect and turns him into the kind of man you think about a little too long. The kind you see when you close your eyes after swearing repeatedly to yourself that you have no desire to see him at all.

Nicole, the generically pretty blond associate sitting to his left, watches him run a hand through his thick hair, which is somehow always perfect and a little fucked-up at once, as if it was professionally done but then mussed when he banged the hairdresser afterward. Beneath the table, my foot taps with impatience.

"Ben," Nicole says, after clearing her throat, "I was at Adney's Tavern this weekend. I thought you might pop in." The words sound practiced, as if she rehearsed them in the mirror all morning. She's so fucking infatuated that she probably did.

Behave, Gemma. I pick up my phone and start looking at shoes online.

Ben's distractedly flipping through a file. "I went home for the weekend."

"Home?" I murmur, glancing at him. "I didn't know humans were allowed to jaunt back and forth over the River Styx like that."

His eyes raise to mine. His mouth twitches. "There's a small toll. It's really quite civilized."

Don't laugh, Gemma. Do not laugh. I look down at my phone, ignoring the box of donuts someone's shoved in front of me.

"Live a little, Gemma," says Caroline Radner, who isn't well-placed to provide advice, given she passed fifty a while ago and is never going to make partner. I'd planned to get some of the strawberries they always have at these meetings, and now I want to refuse even that on principle.

"Gemma can't have sugar," Ben says, his eyes alight. "She likes to keep her teeth sharp."

"I imagine everyone familiar with dental hygiene hopes to keep their teeth sharp, *Ben*," I retort.

"Ah, but you've got more than average, right?" he asks.

I narrow my eyes. The running joke, among pretty much everyone here, is that my vagina has teeth. The Castrator, they call me. In theory because I often represent women in custody disputes, and in truth because I won't play the game—I don't bake cupcakes and make cooing noises over pictures of everyone's kids. If a man doesn't bake cupcakes and make cooing noises, you know what they call him? *Senior Partner.* Ben hasn't made cupcakes once. But men expect *you* to be more thoughtful than they are—softer, more accommodating. And when you are paid less than your peers, or assaulted on a date, or lose a promotion, they'll tell you it was your fault—you were *too* soft, *too* accommodating.

They think it's a slur when they refer to me as a castrating bitch, but all it says to me is that they've finally realized I'm not someone to fuck with. I was someone who was fucked with a lot, once upon a time. It won't happen again.

Fields' assistant, Debbie, steps to the front of the room and beside me, Terri discretely sets a timer. We have a running bet about how long Debbie will speak, because even the simplest statement can take thirty minutes in her capable hands.

I text Terri.

> Three minutes, thirty seconds.

TERRI
> Three minutes, forty seconds.

"So, I shouldn't have to say this again," says Debbie, "but I really need everyone to label food in the break room."

It's going to be a long one—I can already tell. I go ahead and slide Terri a five-dollar bill.

"So many containers look the same," she continues. "I don't want to accidentally eat your escargot when I brought in a tuna sandwich."

I consider pointing out that you would have to be a fucking idiot to confuse escargot with a sandwich of *any* kind, but it would just give Debbie something more to talk about, which is the opposite of what I want.

"Anyway," Debbie says, "you really need to label and it's not hard to do. I like to use a piece of masking tape, and then I just write my name on there with a Sharpie."

Debbie continues to explain, to a group of grown humans, how food is labeled. I sigh quietly, and Ben's eyes flicker to mine, as if he finds my irritation amusing.

One day I'm going to light him on fire—we'll see how much laughing he does then.

When she says *labeling is really important* for the third time—repetition is Debbie's favorite conversational gambit—I have to tune her out and go to my happy place...Shoes. Shoes I will buy. Shoes I wish someone would make. Right now, I'm thinking about green suede heels I saw at Nordstrom. Some people might argue that a kelly-green suede shoe has limited usefulness, particularly when it costs five hundred dollars, but with enough rationalization, I can make the math work in my favor.

"You're thinking about shoes again, aren't you?" whispers Terri.

I give her a sidelong glance. "What else would I think about?"

"You're young and gorgeous. You should be thinking about a hot guy walking out of your shower."

"What hot guy? There certainly aren't any here."

Her eyes flicker toward Ben, but she knows better than to suggest him to *me*.

"Chris Hemsworth," she replies, and I laugh quietly.

The statistical probability of Chris Hemsworth walking out of my shower is almost zero, and if it *were* to happen, I know exactly how it would end, because every attempt at a relationship since Kyle has ended in the exact same way: with him accusing me of being 'dead inside' or obsessed with work, which is what men say if you work harder than they do. Unlike shoes, which just exist to cradle you in their green suede bosom.

"Care to share the conversation?" Debbie snaps at the two of us.

"We were talking about Sharpies, for labeling the food," I reply smoothly. "I just asked Terri to order some."

"It's weird, then," says Ben, eyes glinting with malice, "that she'd respond by saying *Chris Hemsworth*."

For a single moment I picture whipping one of my heels across the table—his cry of pain, the brief triumph I'd feel before I remember I've done this in front of the most litigious people in LA.

Fortunately, Arvin Fields, managing partner, enters the room before I can act. Arvin is approximately one million years old, but shows no signs of retiring, and he's still younger than McGovern, who likely remembers voting for John Adams in our nation's third election.

"As you know," he begins, "there are changes coming." His speech is gratingly slow, which isn't a product of age but more a tactic to wind us all up. He likes his underlings to be like a swarm of angry bees, fighting for dominance, stinging anything in their path.

Which is why Ben and I have both done well here. We were already angry bees when we arrived.

"At the end of this year, two of our partners will be retiring." I sit up straighter. *The announcement.* "We're hoping one of you can step up to the plate."

My head jerks. "One?" I ask, my voice sharper than I'd like.

"Just one. Over the past decade, we've seen a lot less work from certain sectors, and it's cut into our profits. We'll be watching you very closely this winter, so may the best man, or woman, win."

It feels like someone just put a hole in my lungs and all the air is escaping. I deserve to make partner, and instead of just *giving* it to me like they should, they're going to turn it into a fucking competition. One Ben will go out of his way to make sure I lose.

My phone vibrates in my lap and I glance at it.

BEN

Uh oh :-(Sorry about the bad news.

God, I hate him so much. He has my number thanks to the company directory. He's only used it abusively, thus far. As I have, in turn.

Bad news for whom?

I thought that was obvious. It'll be fun watching you on your best behavior for a few months, though.

Best behavior? The standards here are pretty low. As long as I'm not caught in the bathroom with a client's spouse, I should be in the clear.

Ben had a little *incident* at his first holiday party with FMG, during which he got caught with a client's drunk wife. It's the only thing he's ever seemed embarrassed about.

I try to reference it whenever possible, obviously.

That devil in my chest is cackling maniacally while Ben

reads the text, but he merely leans back in his seat, a casual smile on his generous mouth, eyes gleaming behind absurdly thick lashes.

> BEN
>
> You sure bring that up a lot. It's almost like you wish it was you.

The skin on my neck tingles, as if he's whispered those words in my ear—his voice soft as velvet, dark as the grave. I turn my phone facedown, ending the conversation. I wonder if I can report him, but as I go over what was said, I realize it doesn't make me look great either.

Whatever.

I'm about to be FMG's first female partner, at which point I will begin crushing the boys' club here under my very expensive heels. And Ben Tate is where I'll start.

3

My father calls more often than I'd like, which is to say he still calls on occasion when I wish he'd drop off the face of the Earth. He's a man who always wants something from you, a man incapable of a genuine gesture. If he gives you a gift, a smile, a compliment... rest assured he is about to ask for far more in exchange.

What he wants, *always*, is my time and attention. None of this is done out of love—it's simply his innate need to win at all costs. He still wants to win a divorce that took place nearly fifteen years ago, during which he stole everything from my mom but custody of me, and then he came back and stole that too.

I'm twenty-nine, way too old to be a pawn, but he still does his best, offering extravagant vacations, timed to hurt my mother—on her birthday, or Mother's Day—and claims it's a coincidence. When I was younger, he said he'd pay for college, but only if I spent the summers with him and his new wife on Nantucket. Law school? Sure. But I'd have to give him every Thanksgiving and winter break in exchange.

I take a vicious sort of pleasure in being the one thing he can't buy.

"Tell him I'm busy," I say to Terri when he calls.

She gives me one of those heavy sighs of hers, the kind that says she doesn't approve of ignoring a parent, even if he's an asshole.

"Gemma," she says, "just talk to him. He's called so often even *I'm* starting to feel bad for him."

I love Terri, but sometimes I wish the other associates kept her busy enough that she'd have less time for scolding me into responsible adult behavior.

Internally groaning, I hit the speaker button, my voice civil and nothing more. "Hi, Dad."

"I've been trying to get ahold of you for a while. FMG must be keeping you busy."

"They are." I turn to my laptop and start clearing out junk mail.

"So, have they made you partner yet?"

His timing is impeccable. "It won't happen for a few more months."

"You know if you came to my firm, you'd already be a partner. You might be an equity partner by now."

"So you've mentioned. Repeatedly." And I might not always love the work I do at FMG, but I'd *hate* the work I'd do for my father. I doubt there's ever been a time when his firm wasn't on the wrong side of history.

"Speaking of work," he continues, "I was thinking I might make a donation to that charity you like. That women's thing... the domestic abuse one."

So generous, Dad, to give money to a charity you don't even know the name of. Surely, no strings attached there.

"The Women's Defense Fund."

"Is fifty thousand enough, you think? If so, I'll probably

throw a little party to celebrate. And since you've inspired the donation with your work, I'd love to have you there."

Fifty grand to charity for a few hours of my time—he makes it sound so simple, so clear-cut, but it never is. If I agree, it will suddenly involve *other* events, or will be taking place on Christmas day, somewhere far from my mom. With my father there's *always* a catch.

"Well, let me know when it is. I'm pretty busy here."

"I was thinking February," he says. "Maybe we'll do it in conjunction with Stephani's birthday."

My irritation coalesces into a tight ball of rage. Stephani is his wife, the one with whom he cheated on my mother, the one who now lives in my *mother's* house.

What he's saying is he is willing to pay fifty grand for me to attend Stephani's birthday. He wants *The Washingtonian* and *Town and Country* to show us together as a family, and he'll make sure the press refers to me as *their* daughter, cutting my mother out of the picture entirely, as if she never existed.

"I'm definitely not available then, Dad," I reply. "I'd better go."

I stare out the window after I hang up, trying to see LA the way I did nine years ago, back when it seemed like a fresh start, a break from my family's chaos. I was so different then—someone who smiled simply at the feel of the sun on her face, someone with big dreams. Would I still be her if I hadn't worked at Stadler during law school? Who would I be if I'd been able to stay?

I guess the question is pointless, since staying wasn't an option.

But I miss those other versions of myself anyway.

～

FIELDS ASKS to see me in his office that afternoon, a turn of events Terri is expecting too much from. She thinks he's going to tell me I've made partner, except the principals here don't give anything away freely—partnerships, bonuses, praise. If it was up to them, they'd pay us in nickels thrown at our feet while we dance. And if Fields didn't announce my promotion at the meeting, he's sure as hell not going to hand it over privately.

I walk down the long hall to his corner office, with its sweeping views of downtown LA, but stop short when I realize Ben Tate is already there. If Ben and I are being called in at the same time, it means one of us is here to get scolded, and this time it's probably me. I may or may not have recently encouraged people to call Ben "the Undertaker". If he doesn't want unbecoming nicknames, maybe he shouldn't go after a client's ex-wife for funeral expenses.

I plaster a smile on my face and stride to the available seat. I will laugh this off, apologize, and then make whichever associate ratted me out wish he'd never heard my name.

This is already the case for most of them.

Ben and I eye each other. I scoot my chair an inch farther from his.

"What am I going to do with you two?" Fields asks, glancing between us. "You always look like you're one step from a knife fight."

"To be fair, Gemma looks like that with everyone," says Ben with one of his glib smiles.

"*Au contraire*," I reply. "I'm thrilled to see you here, as it means you're not off getting a homeless mother evicted from a shelter somewhere."

"That was an accident," he growls.

I smile; his irritation delights me. "Hmm."

"Anyhow," sighs Fields, who is now fondly remembering the days when you could just call a mouthy woman a witch and have her drowned, "as I've just been discussing with Ben, a gender discrimination suit is being brought against Fiducia, one that may prove lucrative."

I sit up a little straighter. Fiducia—a well-known investment capital firm that gives lots of lip service to ideas about diversity and acceptance and workplace equality—is *big*. They would generate press, and that's what I need. My long-term goal is to exclusively practice family law, but it takes a while to build a name. Walter, my favorite corporate client, is giving me enough work until that happens, but I wouldn't mind taking the fast track, and a newsworthy discrimination suit would provide it. Plus, if I win, it will be impossible for them to not make me partner afterward.

"Margaret Lawson, the plaintiff, is fifty-four years old and was with Fiducia for well over a decade. She was passed over for promotion nine years in a row and was let go when she complained about it."

This case is sounding better and better. I will dance on Fields' desk and let him throw nickels at my feet to get my hands on it. I will fight Ben to the death for the chance, though that implies fighting Ben to the death is a disincentive, which it is not.

"I'd like you and Ben to work on it together," Arvin concludes, and my spine crumples. "You've handled gender discrimination cases before, and Ben's an expert at negotiating a settlement."

"*Together?*"

Ben, Stealer of Clients and Evictor of Homeless Mothers, is no one I want to work with, and I don't think he's ever even handled this kind of case, so why the fuck should I take direction from him? He'll obviously make me do all the work and steal every ounce of credit.

"We're not being given a choice, slugger," Ben says with a sigh, scrubbing a hand over his stupidly pretty face. He does not want to work with me any more than I do him. In the two years he's been here, he hasn't brought me in on a case even *once*. "And it might amount to nothing, for all we know. We've got to talk to her first."

He'll undoubtedly find a way to screw me over, but it looks like I'm not being offered the opportunity to turn it down anyway.

I stumble, shell-shocked, from Fields' office and take a glance at my feet to assure myself I'm actually wearing the good-luck shoes.

I am. Apparently, their luck just ran out.

IT'S WELL AFTER DARK, and I'm only halfway through drafting a custody agreement when Ben arrives at my office door. "Knock knock," he says.

I raise a brow. "You realize saying *knock knock* is redundant when you *actually* knock."

He leans against the door frame. "I mostly said it to annoy you."

"You shouldn't have expended the effort." I open a new document on my laptop. "You standing there is enough to annoy me."

He takes the seat on the other side of my desk, though I don't recall inviting him to sit.

"Gemma..." His voice is gravel wrapped in velvet; a voice made for giving orders you can't resist.

Reluctantly, I stop to look up at him.

"Can you do this? This case could be a big deal. I need to know you're going to bring your A game, no matter how much you hate me, or just hate men in general."

I want to argue that I don't hate *all* men, but I don't think I could swear to it under oath. I hate more men than I don't, I suppose.

"I always bring my A game. But I'm not telling this woman what she wants to hear, or talking her into a garbage settlement just so *you* can count it as a win."

His nostrils flare. "And you think I would?"

I thought I could insult Ben in almost any way, but this, apparently, is his Achilles' heel. "I've seen you in court. As I recall, you justify doing a whole lot simply to say you won."

"And you go just as far," he replies, his jaw tight. "The only difference is I'm able to admit it." His eyes lock unhappily with mine for a moment before he shakes his head and climbs to his feet.

When he walks out, broad shoulders tense, I sense I've disappointed him. He's acted irked by me before, but never disappointed.

I expected it to feel slightly better than it does.

4

The first time I ever set foot in a court house was for my parents' custody hearing.

The smooth, modern walls of the LA County Courthouse are a world apart from that first one, but I still think of it every time I'm here.

When Lisa Miller, my client, goes on the stand, I think of my mother, with the shitty lawyer she could barely afford, the one who phoned in the entire case and didn't ask her a single pertinent question. When Lisa looks at me, I give her the same smile I wish someone had given my mom while she sat there pale and terrified. It's a smile that says: *we've got this, you're in good hands.*

Her husband, Lee, hired Paul Sheffield, who's made a reputation for himself by being exactly the kind of attorney my father hired—the kind who's willing to destroy anyone and worry about the damage later. Today, though, he is evenly matched because I'm that kind of attorney too.

Someone has to be, to make sure women like my mother aren't absolutely screwed by men who promise not to turn on them, and do it anyway.

I ask Lisa to describe what it was like, raising children with Lee. She talks about the kids' soccer games he never attended and the time he left them at a party when they were toddlers to go sleep with a woman he'd met there. She talks about the cruel things he said to her, both privately and in public. When opposing counsel brings up her antidepressant use, the night she had too much wine with friends, I complain until I'm hoarse.

It's what my mother's lawyer *should* have done. Instead, he sat there and let her get torn apart, and he never objected to any of it.

I glance over at Lee Miller's sagging shoulders as the case goes on, and feel a mean little spike of something in my blood. It's not quite happiness, but it'll have to do.

When the trial concludes, I walk outside with Lisa and discover she's blinking back tears.

"What's wrong?" I ask, placing a hand on her shoulder. She seemed happy a minute before. I got her everything she'd asked for.

"I'm pleased," she says. "I am. It's just so...final. You know he used to write me poems?"

She trails off, staring blankly at the pavement in front of her, as if this past version of them is displayed there like a puzzle. It's inexplicable to her that the shapes could create another picture entirely.

I think of Kyle, then, walking down the hall at Stadler—broad-shouldered and square-jawed and so utterly confident—smiling that secret smile at me and me alone. For a long time, I could only see one way we'd turn out.

"One day it will all make sense," I tell her, though I'm not sure that's true.

Kyle was over six years ago, and I still can't make the puzzle pieces fit.

I GO STRAIGHT from court to the Beverly Wilshire, where Ben and I are meeting Margaret Lawson for the first time. When I step through the large glass doors, Ben is the first thing I see, leaning against a column while he waits. He runs a finger inside his collar when he spots me, as if the mere idea of spending the next hour together makes him feel suffocated, and then his gaze drops to my heels.

I've noticed he looks at my heels a lot. *You wear a size 13, Ben. They won't fit.* I've thought it a hundred times, but I've never said it, as it would mean admitting I know his shoe size. I know far more about Ben than I should.

"You're early," I tell him, not slowing my stride as I pass.

"Only you would try to make that sound like a flaw," he mutters. "What a fun night out you must be."

"You know what's fun about the women you date?" I ask. "The way they all just seem to disappear after you've been out with them once. Someone should check into that."

"You know what's fun about the men you date?" he replies. "The way they don't exist in the first place."

I catch his smirk in my peripheral vision and pretend I haven't seen it, wishing I could make him invisible instead. There's nothing like the sight of his shoulders straining against his jacket to take my brain in the wrong direction.

We arrive at the restaurant to find Margaret waiting. My first impression, from a distance, is promising: she's professionally dressed, and there's no whiff of *crazy* about her—no frizzy hair, no weird pins, no cat-hair covered scarf or briefcase obscured by bumper stickers. It matters because the jury won't be asking themselves *Was this fair?* They'll be asking *Would I promote this woman?*

"She's perfect," I say under my breath as we head toward the table.

"Slow your roll, there, Castrator," he replies. "You haven't heard her speak."

"Don't need to, *Undertaker*. Mark my words: we're taking this case."

Margaret rises when we reach the table. Ben introduces us and holds out a chair for me as I take my seat, an irritating bit of fake chivalry on his part. If she weren't watching, he'd pull the chair out from under me and laugh at my fractured tailbone.

Ben makes small talk with Margaret until the waiter is gone, and then, with a glance at me, he begins. "What would be helpful," he tells Margaret, "is if you could start by walking us through what happened during your time at Fiducia, because it sounds like it began pretty well before it went downhill."

I like the way he asks the question. I don't hear any doubt or suspicion in his voice, and he hasn't asked her how she *perceived* their behavior, as if there's another side of the story that is, perhaps, more valid.

Margaret describes the years she spent watching male managers get promoted, the way her annual reviews turned sour after she asked why *she* wasn't promoted, and finally, the discovery that men just out of college were earning more than she was. Except she's simply reciting facts we already know, and I'm eager to get to the things we *don't*. My foot is tapping with impatience beneath the table...until Ben's hand lands on my knee. For a moment, all I register is the heat and size of his palm, which feels large enough to wrap clear round my thigh if he wanted. It's a little too easy to picture how his hand might slide farther, if we were two different people—the kind who don't despise each other—but he should certainly know better than to place his hand on the knee of a woman known as *The Castrator* without her consent, even if he's merely doing it to tell me to chill.

The waiter refills Margaret's water, and I take the break in conversation to give Ben a quick glare, which says *get your hand off my fucking knee.*

His mouth twitches in response, and he gives my leg one final, infuriatingly firm squeeze before he releases me, as if to say *Patience, Castrator. Let her tell this the way she wants.*

My thigh feels cold in his hand's absence. And while Ben gently reminds Margaret where she was in her story, his voice betraying absolutely none of my impatience, I cross my legs, trying to somehow grind away the memory of his palm on my skin.

Soon she's offering us more detail, the things we didn't already know, and I'm aggravated that Ben's been proven right as I begin to take copious notes.

"You're aware they're going to throw every word you've ever said in your face?" Ben asks as lunch concludes and he's signed the check. I'm glad he's leveling with her because it's an ugly process being deposed as a plaintiff and—if it comes to it—going on the stand. "Every misstep, every moment of anger or sick day is going to be broadcast. Are you ready for it?"

Margaret turns to him. She's been admirably calm while discussing the case, which is a good thing—a jury will label a distressed female as *shrill* or *hysterical* for the exact same behaviors they'd term *righteous indignation* in a man. She swallows now, continuing to hold herself in check. "I was a model employee. I only took three sick days in ten years of work. If that's their strategy, I wish them luck."

"There isn't enough luck in the world to help them win this case," he tells her. And for the first time today, she looks pleased.

I guess it's possible that there are worse things than sharing this case with him.

Not many, but some.

～

WE GET IN THE CAR, and I start making notes with a small smile on my face. I was absolutely right about Margaret, even if he won't admit it.

"Has no one ever told you," Ben says, "that it's unbecoming to gloat?"

He's already tapping away on his phone. Probably arranging his post-lunch sex with a struggling actress he keeps in a high-rise.

"This might come as a shock to you, Tate, but I don't give a shit if you or anyone else finds my behavior unbecoming."

"Based on your social life,"—He continues to type—"or lack thereof...no, that does not come as a shock."

I roll my eyes. As far as I can tell, Ben's social life only requires the female be pretty and have a pulse, and I'm not even sure about the pulse part. "How's that yoga Instagram girl you were seeing, by the way? Have you explained the difference between *your and you're* to her yet?"

He puts the phone down and looks at me, arching a brow. "I didn't realize you were following my social life so carefully. You almost sound...jealous."

This is one of those moments. The kind where I know what I *should* do—ignore him—but the devil is leaping in my chest, suggesting all the wrong things. We're nearly back to the office, thank God. Perhaps that will keep the damage to a minimum.

"That must be it," I deadpan. "If I wanted my vaginal penetration with a side order of disease, you'd definitely be the first person I'd seek out."

"Vaginal penetration?" he repeats. My nipples tighten, as if he just placed his hand inside my bra. "I doubt it would work anyway. Lot of cobwebs there. Too many to bust through, I imagine." His mouth curves upward, as if he's still considering the possibility.

"Well, your parts certainly wouldn't be up to the job. Or *any* job, if we're being honest."

"You bring up my dick an awful lot." His eyes fall to my mouth, and that traitorous devil inside me likes it. "I wonder if that means something."

For a moment I'm picturing him and *it*—together, obviously—and I'm so winded by the idea it takes a solid two seconds for my mean mouth to make a recovery.

"I *have* always had a soft spot for the small and the weak," I reply.

The car stops at the curb and he climbs out, but before I can exit, he ducks his head back inside, so our faces are level and far too close. Close enough to smell the soap on his skin, the starch in his shirt. "Gemma," he says, eyes glittering dangerously, "I promise there's nothing *small* or weak about me." He walks away, and it takes me a full second to recover from my shock. And another full second to catch my breath.

Gemma, I promise there's nothing small or weak about me.

I squeeze my eyes shut, trying to drive the memory from my head, but I can still feel it exactly where I did—between my legs, fluttering like a hummingbird.

I can't believe we just had a conversation about his dick.

And I really can't believe *I* started it.

THAT NIGHT, driving home, I go left when I should go right. Ben, I happen to know, lives in Santa Monica, though I can't imagine why: he works just as much as I do, so it's not like he's ever hanging out at the beach. I wonder if he takes the route I'm taking now. If so, he's an idiot. Even at nine o'clock, there are an irritating number of stops and starts.

I've never driven down his street, but if I take Alta I can see his house to the left. There's still a dumpster in front and a building permit posted in the yard. Whatever he's doing has been going on for two years straight. His neighbors must hate him as much as I do.

I do a U-turn a few streets later, take one final look, and then drive home, trying to forget this little moment of weakness, even when I know it won't be the last.

5

Somehow, I'm still a romantic at heart. I weep copiously during seasonal commercials in which racial divisions are bridged or a child and an old person bond. I have my dream home all mapped out on Pinterest, and have also choreographed the way my future husband will propose in Iceland (I won't expect it; a children's choir I never even noticed will begin to sing "All You Need is Love", and then *whoosh*...the Northern Lights appear).

I blame this on the fact that, together, my mother and I have watched pretty much every Hallmark movie ever made. Though ninety percent of them have nearly identical, misogynistic plots—career-minded woman from the big city is saved from herself by a hot guy in a small town, where she will eventually adopt a more traditionally feminine profession (baking, motherhood or inn-keeping)—I inhale them when I'm home.

"Which one are you watching tonight?" I ask when my mom picks up the phone. It's eight o'clock on a Thursday and I'm on my way to meet a potential client; it's eleven for her and she's recovering from her second shift of the day. Neither of us have a Hallmark-worthy life at the moment.

"He's the owner of a bed and breakfast and she—"

"Is stuck there because her car broke down?" I suggest, pulling out of the parking garage. Whoever writes these movies clearly believes it's impossible to leave the city without automotive trouble or a deer darting into the road.

"No, actually, she's there to buy him out."

"Ah, of course. So, she represents a heartless conglomerate that plans to destroy the town's charm by making it a tourist destination, and he's going to prove her wrong and help heal her wounded heart."

She laughs. "That does appear to be the direction this is heading, and speaking of heartless lawyers, how's it going with The Client-Stealer?" She, like myself, is not *#TeamBen*, but all her info comes from me, so it's unlikely she would be.

I groan quietly, turning off Fairfax onto Sunset and honking at some idiotic kids standing in the middle of the road. "He hasn't done anything wrong yet. But we only met the client last week. Give him time."

"If this was a movie, he'd threaten to fire you if you don't work Christmas, and you'd wind up in a quaint ski resort with a handsome client."

The *threatening to fire me if I don't work Christmas* part is entirely likely, but the partners keep all the fun destination travel for themselves. "Speaking of holidays," I venture, "what do you want to do about Thanksgiving?"

My mom can't afford many things on her own, which makes discussions like this tricky. I used to think that once I'd paid off my student loans, I'd be able to help her, but she's consistently refused to accept anything significant. When I bought her a car, she wept and they were not good tears. She said she'd never be able to look at that car without thinking her own daughter believed she was pathetic and desperate. Eventually I gave in and returned it, and I've had to proceed carefully ever since. I now know she will accept a hardback book, but not a first edition; a wool sweater but not a Canada Goose coat. If I claim to have bought her something on a trip, or bought something for us *both*, she will generally not object. She still believes I got us each a pair of high-end snow boots while skiing with friends, when in reality I found them online and bought them only for her. Ditto the baby-soft cashmere throw, the shearling lined moccasins, the ridiculously expensive face cream.

But there's no way to lie about airline tickets. I have more money than time—it's easier for me if she comes here, but I always defer to her.

"I can get you a ticket to LA or I can go there," I tell her. "My kitchen sucks, but there are some amazing places here that do Thanksgiving dinner. We could even eat outside."

"Oh, honey. I'm so sorry. Working retail now...I can't possibly get that whole weekend off, and I took a shift at the bar on Thanksgiving. I just assumed between work and all your friends there, I wouldn't see you."

I run a finger inside the neck of my blouse. It's possible I oversold how busy I am, but that's not what bothers me. It's that once upon a time, my mother oversaw an epic dinner for twenty every Thanksgiving, and now she won't even be celebrating. She was the perfect wife, and look where it got her: stuck in a shitty apartment alone, working two jobs.

"I'll come home for Christmas, then. Just let me know your schedule."

"You could always visit your father, you know," she says tentatively. "I'm sure he'd love to see you."

I wince. I'm not sure how my mother is so big-hearted, but it's a quality I did not inherit...and I'm glad. Seeing the best in people and forgiving the worst has never gotten a female anywhere, as far as I can tell. "I'll think about it, Mom," I reply, which is a polite *over my dead body, and his as well,* and she knows it.

When we hang up, I find a parking spot and brace myself

for the last event of the day and by far the worst: meeting a potential client, at Fields' request.

I hate doing it under the best of circumstances and am even less optimistic about tonight. West Forest Media could bring us a lot of work, but my impression of them and their CEO is that they are—*what's the legal term?*—douchey. I'm young, female, reasonably attractive. It's a combination that seems to embolden even the most average of men to act like complete dicks, and these guys *already* seem like complete dicks.

I walk into the bar where West Forest's senior staff has been holding a post-retreat happy hour. When the CEO, Tim Webber, gives me a once-over as I introduce myself, I know this evening will go just as poorly as I expected.

"Now I see why Fields insisted I'd like you," he says.

There are times when all you can do is ignore the innuendo. I take his extended hand, but my shake is firmer than it would have been.

"You look like that actress, the one with the—Hey, Jones!" he shouts to a guy near the bar. "Who does she look like?"

"Wonder Woman," says Jones, and I stifle a sigh.

"That's it," says Webber. "Wonder Woman. Gail something or other. You must hear that all the time."

I force a smile. "She's a lot nicer than I am."

He laughs, as if this was a joke when it was, in fact, a warning. "I bet that's not true." He turns to the guy beside him. "We're going to the restaurant. Just bill the whole thing to me."

His employees watch us move across the room, as if Webber's leading me upstairs to take my virginity, and when we reach the top floor, I understand why—the restaurant is posh, quiet, and *romantic.* I'm decidedly uncomfortable when he holds my chair for me then orders us a bottle of red without even asking me if I'd like a drink. He's the type of guy who's experienced a bit of success and let it go to his head. I guarantee he cheats at everything—marriage, taxes, corporate expenditures—and rationalizes all of it. I know men like this well. I was raised by one, after all.

I try to turn the conversation to his company's legal needs, and he waves me off. "We'll get to all that. Are you hungry? Let's order some food."

"I've eaten, thank you," I say crisply. It's a lie, but I'm not willing to be stuck with this man for ninety minutes over a steak dinner, especially not when he's clearly a *let's mix business with pleasure* kind of guy.

The waiter pours him a taste of the wine, and he swirls it in his glass, sniffs it, then swishes it in his mouth. He nods his approval without making eye contact, as if he's royalty.

It's obnoxious. I bet Ben Tate does the same fucking thing.

"So, tell me what you do when you're not at work," he says once the waiter is gone.

"I work seven days a week," I reply. "I rep—"

"We need to change that," he cuts in. "You're way too pretty to spend all your free time working."

Ugh.

I begin again. "As I was saying, I represented—"

"Have you ever been on a yacht?" he asks, and I give up. This guy does not give two shits what kind of work I've done. He probably doesn't even care that I went to law school. I'm simply here to be his pretty audience for the night, and nothing more.

I patiently listen as he tells me about his yacht, namedrops every celebrity he's ever met and every model he's ever dated, and then shares a somewhat pointless story about partying with "Demi" at Art Basel. What he does not do, no matter how many times I broach the topic, is discuss West Forest's legal needs.

Gemma Charles, FMG's first female partner, I repeat in my head.

I heave a sigh of relief when he pours the last of the wine in our glasses and throws his credit card on the table.

"Have you ever gone sailing around Coronado?" he asks. "We should go sometime."

"Like I said, I work seven days a week, so that would be a stretch. And speaking of work—"

He winks at me. "You come with me to Coronado, I'm happy to tell your boss we were working."

My jaw has begun to ache with the effort of faking my polite smiles. "I prefer work to yachting, I'm afraid."

"I can see you're going to be a challenge. That's okay. I like a challenge."

I'm not interested in being a challenge; I'm interested in drumming up business, and we haven't spoken about work at all. How much longer do I have to pretend to care about this man's dumb hobbies and social life?

"Let's discuss what your firm can do for us," he says when we get downstairs. He walks outside and I follow, wondering why the hell he's only bringing this up now. "My place is right around the corner, and I have a very nice Veuve Clicquot in the fridge."

Oh, my fucking God. I don't need anyone's business so much that I'll spend an hour in his apartment fending him off to get it.

"I've got to be in early tomorrow." I extend my hand. "But it was nice to meet you."

He grabs my wrist and pulls me against him. "I liked meeting *you*," he says, standing way too close. "A lot."

And then he presses my hand to his crotch.

I gasp, and he grins, as if this is all playfully charming. I try to pull my hand back but he holds my wrist tight, and places my closed fist against his erection.

"Let go of my hand," I snap.

His grip tightens. "Come on, Gemma. I think this could work for us both."

It's not the first time I've been hit on by a client, but it's by far the most egregious. "Let go of my wrist right *now*."

He moves my fist over his length instead. "You've had me hard all through dinner. You seem like fun."

I open my palm, then grab him and squeeze as hard as I possibly can. "How *fun* do I seem now, asshole?" I demand.

He releases my wrist at last, gasping in pain.

"You fucking bitch," he hisses as I walk to my car.

I flip him off, but my hands are shaking as I fumble with my keys.

In a different sort of world, I'd be going straight to the police to file charges, or straight to the media to tell them what an utter douche the CEO of West Forest is. In the real world, I'm on the cusp of getting the promotion I've always wanted, and the last thing I need right now is to get pegged as a *hysterical female* and have the partners suggesting I invited what Webber just did.

I want the world to be a different place for the women who come after me. And the only way to make that happen is to ignore the fact that it isn't different yet.

But I'm so goddamned tired of staying silent just to get the things I deserve.

6

The following afternoon, Ben asks me to meet him to discuss Lawson. Fiducia wants to settle, apparently, now that Margaret has switched to our firm.

I feel a weird sort of disappointment. I guess I was just looking forward to the fight.

We're both working out of the municipal courthouse all afternoon, so he suggests lunch at a restaurant nearby. It would be strange, having lunch with Ben alone, but I'm so distracted by what happened last night I barely notice.

I pick at my salad while he tells me things I already know. He wants to keep opposing counsel from getting too comfortable by behaving as if we're still going to trial. As I'd fully planned to do.

"We'll ask for copies of the managers' files," Ben says, "as well as Margaret's."

"I've already written the request," I tell him dully. "It's in your inbox." My fingers encircle my wrist, just beneath the sleeve of my jacket—it's bruised. And the reminder feels like a sort of condemnation, as if I've done the wrong thing, letting Webber get away with it. But am I really supposed to risk my career to right the scales of justice? Can't I just leave that to someone else?

Ben's eyes meet mine for a long moment. "You're quiet today."

"I'm always quiet."

"What did you do to your wrist?" he asks, brow furrowed.

"Nothing." I jerk my hand away while all the blood drains from my face, hating there's even a hint of emotion in my voice. Why the fuck am I sitting here feeling guilty about last night? Why does this stupid bruise bother me so much? If I'd complained, I'd be made to feel like shit by Webber and every man I work with. So I said nothing, yet I feel like shit about that too.

I guarantee Tim Webber hasn't given it a second thought.

We walk outside. "I've called an Uber," I tell Ben, looking past the sedan pulling up in front of us. "I can't walk back in these heels."

His gaze drifts to my shoes, a light flush grazing his cheek-bones. "Maybe you should wear normal shoes like everyone else."

"Maybe you should attempt to be good at your job instead of—" My words fall away entirely as a familiar face emerges from the sedan.

I've only seen Meg Lawrence once in six years, and the last time she pretended not to know who I was. That's the outcome I'm *hoping* for, at present. She had her chance to try to make things right, and it's long since passed.

"Gemma," she says, blinking in surprise. *Dammit.*

"Meg," I reply briskly, unsmiling.

Her gaze darts to Ben, then back to me. "It's been ages."

"Not long enough." I walk past her to our car, which has just pulled up, thank God. I regret making this a thing in front of Ben, but it's better than having her spill a story for him I'd rather no one knows.

"That wasn't especially friendly," he says, sliding in beside me.

"We're not friends." I look out the window to avoid the questions I know are coming. No way will he let this go.

"Are you going to tell me what she did, or should I run back over and ask her?"

My stomach tightens. I open my phone. "Go ask her," I say, as if distracted. "I'll wait." I'm banking on the fact that even Ben isn't *that* shameless. I hope I'm right.

"Gemma," he says with a sigh. "Come on."

"We worked together at Stadler Helms," I tell him. *And she was, once upon a time, my closest friend.*

He blinks in surprise. "When were you at Stadler? I thought you came to FMG straight out of law school."

I cross my legs then tap one dangling heel impatiently. His eyes dart to my foot then away.

"I was a summer associate," I reply, though summers only represent a fraction of the time I spent there. "If you're done asking about my personal life, I'd like to review my notes."

"They didn't make you an offer?" he asks, and my God I regret I ever told him anything. Because that's the red flag, isn't it? No one with my work history at Stadler isn't made an offer without having done something very wrong.

And no one gets their offer *rescinded* without having done something even worse.

"I have no idea how you made partner," I reply, opening my notes, and he gives up at last.

Attacking, as always, is the best defense.

I've been using it to keep Ben away now for two years straight.

7

M eg had been an associate at Stadler for a few years by the time Kyle arrived, and I'd been there nearly as long, working part-time during law school. She was technically my boss, but no one would have guessed this based on our conversations, which were mostly about parties, clothes, and boys. Lately they'd been focused on one boy, Kyle Cabrera, though referring to a thirty-five-year-old partner at our law firm as a *boy* seemed a little ridiculous.

He was only working out of the LA office temporarily. Needless to say, we hoped he'd make it permanent. *"He looks more like a Navy SEAL in a good suit than an attorney," Meg whispered when we first saw him walking down the hall.* She was not wrong.

For two weeks, he'd been the sole focus of my group chat with her and another associate. Every tiny bit of info gleaned was collected secretively and mulled over, as if we were members of an underground resistance movement.

> He works out at Equinox every night, apparently. On a scale of 1-10, how stalkerish would it be to purchase a gym membership I can't afford and *happen* to show up there?

MEG

As you have no intent to do harm (I assume), I think you're okay. Send photos.

> Hell, no. Get your own gym membership for that. Besides, I know what YOU'D want pics of and I'm not sneaking into the men's changing room for you.

KIRSTEN

I bet it's HUGE. You wouldn't even need a long-range lens.

> This conversation is so wrong. We still don't even know if he's married.

We'd checked into it, of course. He didn't wear a ring, and his bio said he was a father of two but didn't mention a spouse.

"There's no way," Kirsten said. "No wife is letting that guy go across the country for months at a time unsupervised."

"And he's got pictures of his kids on his desk, but there's not a single one of her," Meg added.

Under normal circumstances I'd have been the first to assume the worst—after all, I'd watched my father cheat on my mom, as if it was his job—but there was an honesty to Kyle, an inherent decency. He treated people well—he found work for Tom, an associate on the cusp of getting fired; he was on a first-name basis with the homeless guy who sat outside the building; he was just as nice to the janitor as he was to the managing partner.

He kept it all close to the vest, until the night I walked into his office and heard the tail end of an argument.

"It's my weekend with them," he said to someone on the other line. "That's what the agreement is for."

I began stepping back outside when he shook his head, waving me in as he hung up the phone.

I winced. "Sorry. Your door was open and—"

He gave me a reluctant smile. "It's okay. My ex and I are... things are a little tense right now."

"Well, that answers the office's biggest mystery," I replied. "Everyone has been wondering if you're single."

He laughed then shook his head again. "It's not common knowledge. We're trying to keep it quiet until the divorce is finalized."

"I won't say anything," I told him.

His eyes held mine. "I know you won't."

It killed me, but I somehow kept it to myself. I still texted and gossiped with Meg and Kirsten. I still played the *do you think he's married?* game with them, as if I knew nothing. I didn't tell them a single thing he'd said.

I guess that was my first mistake.

8

"You have not updated your Pinterest board in ages," Keeley informs me before she's even said *hello*. Based on her tone, failing to update Pinterest is the moral equivalent of failing to pay taxes.

"I don't have time," I reply, though it's not entirely true. Years ago, I was addicted to Pinterest. I had a house page, a fashion page, a travel page, a books-to-read page. It was my own version of a vision board: *here's what my house will look like when I'm different, these are the trips I will take and the books I will read.* I've given up on most of them. I'm too busy to read or travel. I've lost the desire for a cute cottage near the ocean with an herb garden out front—God knows where I'd find the time to take care of it. I still add to the fashion page, but these days it's mostly just clothes for work. I suppose this means I've given up on most of that future Gemma. Keeley and my mom are the only ones who refuse to give up with me.

"Is that why you're calling me on a Saturday afternoon?" I ask. "My Pinterest page?"

She scoffs. "Of course not. I'm calling because someone is covering my shift tonight, so you and I are going out."

"I've got to go to Miami tomorrow, Keels. And I'll be out of the office all day Monday. I really need to work."

Twenty-four hours with Ben Tate. I picture his slightly broken nose, his crooked smile. Him saying, *"Gemma, I promise there's nothing small or weak about me."*

Every time I remember it, it gets a little filthier.

"Are you seriously telling me you have to work on a Saturday night because you also have to work on a *Sunday* night?" she demands, proving why she's my only remaining friend in LA—because she refuses to take no for an answer. "You've got to make yourself leave on occasion. And you'll never meet anyone if you don't try something new once in a while."

I suppose she has a point, and exclusively seeking out Hallmark men has not panned out for me so far. LA is not rich in farmers, small-town veterinarians or widowed bar owners. Besides, the firm's retreat is in early November, and I'll need a date. Someone smarter than Ben, preferably, and taller than Ben. Though Ben's really tall and relatively intelligent, which narrows the field substantially.

I leave the office at 7:30, painfully early for me, even on a Saturday. I'm not at all surprised to find Keeley is already at the bar when I arrive and already surrounded. She's like a tiny bottle of champagne someone shook up. Every man who meets her wants to pop the cork.

She charges across the room when she sees me. "Thank God you're here. I couldn't get away from those two."

I raise a brow. "You didn't look all that troubled. If I'd shown up five minutes later, you'd probably be inviting them over."

She shakes her head. "Never. They're lawyers, therefore too boring to be serious about, no offense."

I shrug. "None taken. You know my stance."

"Ah, right." She hands me her drink. "You only want a guy who lives in a small town and wears winter clothing year-round."

"The winter clothing isn't a demand. More of a preference."

"My friend Mark wears like fifteen layers." She's referring to the homeless guy who lives outside her building, the one she brings her *Wall Street Journal* to every morning and from whom she often seeks financial advice. "I'll make an introduction."

"I'm going to respectfully pass," I tell her, but she's already on to the next thing, dragging me back to the bar and winking at some athlete in the corner before she smiles brightly at the bartender and holds up two fingers. He smiles back like he's won the lottery. He will now make two of every drink he knows in order to please the pretty blond.

"Speaking of FMG," she says, turning to me, "what happened with Fields' announcement? Did they make you partner? You never said."

My laugh is a trifle bitter. "They made an announcement to tell us they'll be announcing it later."

She rolls her eyes. She's been on me to leave for a while now. Like, ever since we met. "And what happens if they don't give it to you?"

My heart sinks. If they don't give it to me, it would be such a slap in the face I couldn't possibly remain. Yet, I've staked every single ambition on making it at FMG—at taking their obnoxious old-boys network and turning it on its head. I refuse to contemplate any other possibility. "They've got to give it to me."

"They're assholes, Gemma," she chides softly. "They've always been assholes. I'm not sure anything is a given over there."

I could tell her about Margaret Lawson's case, the way it will probably seal the deal for me. But that would involve mentioning Ben Tate, and I'm reluctant to do so. She's heard plenty about Ben over the past two years, and he's no less awful than he ever was. But there's this piece of me remembering the wrong things about him at the moment: the concern on his face when he asked about my wrist, his decency to Margaret, his mouth, shaping the words *there's nothing small or weak about me.* I know Keeley—she'll read those conflicted emotions before I've even sorted them out myself.

I guess that's why, when I discuss the Miami trip, I leave out the fact that I'm not going alone.

9

I arrive at LAX on Sunday afternoon, flustered and cranky. We could probably have handled the settlement conference over Zoom, but Fiducia's headquarters is in Miami where another disgruntled former employee resides, so it made sense to talk to her in person before we meet opposing counsel.

It made sense at the *time*, anyway. Now the former employee has canceled and I'm stuck with Ben for the next twenty-four hours, a prospect I'm unreasonably nervous about.

I've traveled with other colleagues before, but not him. And though I'd like to believe I will discover something I can use against him later on, something to damage his impeccable reputation, I'm not especially optimistic. The odds that he'll turn out to be the guy who gets drunk on free airplane booze are slim.

He's waiting for me near security, wearing jeans, a t-shirt... and an unbuttoned flannel shirt, with the sleeves pushed up.

We're about to spend six hours on a plane and won't meet opposing counsel until tomorrow, so it's not as if he needed to wear a three-piece suit. But I've never seen him in casual clothes before, and Ben in jeans and a t-shirt is brain-scrambling: flat stomach, trim hips, nice forearms.

Internally, I search for my ever-present chant of *we hate him, we hate him*, but it's feeling a little forced today. My steps falter as I get closer, taking in his unshaved jaw and cocky smile.

"See something you like?" he asks.

I feel pinned by his gaze. "No." I clear my throat. "I just expected more scales and open sores."

"We'll save that reveal for the pool," he says with a smirk, waving me in front of him.

The pool. Ben, half naked. I get a sudden image of nicely chiseled abs, trunks hanging low, a happy trail. *The penis that's apparently neither small nor weak, though based on my knowledge of the law I'd suggest he shouldn't be revealing it in public.*

Thank God we won't be staying that long.

I ignore him all the way to the plane. I definitely do *not* stop to watch him threading his belt through his jeans with agile, practiced fingers after we get through security. *Nor* do I notice the way he blocks people from shoving us in line with his broad shoulders, *or* how he moves me in front of him as our boarding passes are scanned, his hand on the small of my back, as if I'm someone who needs protection.

My phone rings and I answer gratefully when I see Keeley's name. Ben's currently lifting my carry-on into the overhead bin as if it's nothing—a toy car, a paper plate. I could use a distraction.

"I'm at Saks," she says. "Looking at those shoes you wanted. Will you be mad if I buy them for myself?"

I reach down to fish my laptop from my purse. "The yellow ones? Of course not. I'm probably not buying them anyway. What am I—or you—going to wear with yellow shoes?"

"Easy – the yellow wardrobe I'll buy to go with them," she says. "You, of course, will wear them with a boring black suit."

I laugh. "Good plan. This is why I love you. It's also why you've got so much credit card debt."

Ben has settled into his seat, clearly listening in, and he's not even trying to hide it. I stare hard at him. The universal signal for *mind your own business.*

Instead of respectfully opening a magazine or looking away, his mouth tilts into a shadow of a smug smile.

"If time is dragging while you eavesdrop, Tate," I hiss, "maybe you should find some other way to occupy yourself." I return to my phone call. "Sorry, Keeley."

"Did you just say *Tate*? As in, the terrible *Ben* Tate?"

I sigh. "I did."

"How curious," she says, sounding far too amused, "that you never mentioned your trip to Miami was with the terrible Ben Tate. And he *must* be hot if I've never heard you malign him physically even once, because you know you would."

"I'm not that bad," I mutter. It's difficult to defend myself with Ben listening.

"You ended a date early because you didn't like the way a guy's hair looked *from behind*."

I turn toward the window, away from Ben, so I can almost pretend this conversation is private.

"It was bizarre!" I reply. "It was like he had hair going halfway down his neck. Not long, but like...*coming out of his neck.*"

"And what about the guy with the weird knuckles?"

"What about him? Imagine what his hands will look like when he's seventy."

Ben laughs under his breath, and my head jerks toward him. "Don't you have a single mother you can evict somewhere?"

"I would," he replies, "but I think they're about to make us turn off our phones."

I sigh once more. "I'd better let you go, Keels. The Prince of

Darkness here has sensed I might be enjoying myself and is determined to bring it to an end."

"Bye, babe," Keeley says. "Tell me how the sex was when he leaves your room."

I hang up, and Ben turns to me. "So who's the lucky sixty-nine-year-old?"

I roll my eyes. "Your dad."

He smirks. "My dad is dead."

"That," I reply, "would explain why he's been so pleasantly quiet in bed."

He looks absolutely staggered for a moment. And then he starts to laugh. I'm not sure I've really heard him laugh before, at least not in a completely sinister way. I wouldn't have expected it to sound so...male, so pleased, all at once. I have to swallow my desire to smile in response.

After takeoff, I load up a movie while Ben makes himself comfortable, spreading his long legs wider, his knee almost brushing mine in the cramped space. He links his fingers over his very toned stomach—again, not that I notice—and closes his eyes. If his even breathing is to be trusted, he's fallen asleep. I have this inexplicable urge to look over at him, but we're halfway across the country before I finally give into it. My gaze brushes over his long lashes, his irritatingly imperfect-yet-perfect nose. I wonder how he broke it and why it's so goddamn hot to me, that small flaw. It's like an arrow pointing directly toward his generous mouth.

"Are you staring at me?" he asks.

His eyes are closed. I have no idea how he even knew. Must be some skill he gained via his last pact with Satan.

"Like I don't see enough of you already," I reply and force my eyes forward.

"What are you watching?"

I pause the movie and remove one headphone. "*Suite*

Française. You wouldn't like it. Subtitles, big words, no explosions."

"It does sound extremely unappealing," he agrees. "Let me guess: it's all about a woman's journey to tackle her inner demons and survive by acknowledging the hidden parts of herself?"

It's irritating, how freaking often he's right.

"Isn't it just the worst when movies show women growing and succeeding on their own?"

"I prefer *realistic* films," he says, his arm brushing mine, his muscular thighs spreading wider.

I don't know if I want to laugh or punch him, but that devil is in my chest, baiting me again, and it's never been harder to ignore him than it is right now.

10

The hotel lobby is full of older women wearing purple hats, though eleven p.m. seems like an unusual hour for a horde of senior citizens to be mingling in identical attire. Based on the amount of grumbling I hear while standing in the world's longest check-in line, the hotel is overbooked.

Thanks to both books and Hallmark movies, I fully expect the clerk to tell me there's been a mix-up when I finally reach the front desk. *You and Mr. Tate will have to share a room,* she'll say. *It has a twin bed, is only lit by romantic candlelight, and there's nothing else available in the entire state. You'll be sleeping in his t-shirt, and he will be completely nude.*

Instead, she simply tells me my room is ready. I will, apparently, *not* need to share a bed or somehow accidentally brush up against his erection. It feels a little anti-climactic if I'm being honest.

His room is beside mine, so we head upstairs together, fighting for space in the crowded elevator. Neither of us has mentioned dinner or drinks, which is probably for the best, given the hour. I've had more than enough of his quiet laugh and his knee brushing mine for one night anyway.

He fumbles with his keycard while I fumble with mine. *We'll be sleeping feet apart.* This shouldn't be a big deal, and it's not a big deal, but I'm suddenly picturing thin walls, the sound of a stifled groan coming from his side. "'Night," I croak, flushing. I push the door open with unnecessary force.

And despite my best intentions, I listen more carefully than I should once I've climbed into bed. There's the slide of the closet door, the creak of a headboard as he leans against it, a news anchor's low, even drone.

I don't hear him groan even once, but *God* I can imagine it. I can so fucking imagine it.

I ARRIVE in the lobby the next morning to discover Ben waiting. He's fresh from the shower, his hair still damp, his suit perfectly cut. He's clean-shaven but you can already tell it won't last. He looks like a model in an ad for expensive watches or men's cologne.

"You'd probably move faster if you'd wear relatively normal shoes," he says, with a click of his tongue, glancing from my favorite black heels to his watch. His odious personality has come to the rescue again, squashing any transient feelings of lust I might otherwise have had.

"I don't need to move faster," I snap, "because I was early. And what's wrong with my shoes?"

He holds the door of the car and climbs in beside me. "Your outfit screams *accidentally sexy librarian*, but those shoes belong on a dominatrix."

I blink. Did he just imply I was sexy? It's hard to tell, given how pissed off he sounds about it.

"These are Louboutins," I reply as the driver pulls onto Ocean Drive. "No dominatrix could afford them."

"I think you'd be surprised," he says casually.

"What's not surprising," I mutter, "is that you're so familiar with what they charge."

He gives an unwilling laugh. "That's not my kink."

Which suggests he *has* a kink. I picture him handcuffing wrists to a headboard. My eyes flick to his hands, and that deeply troubling ache thrums between my legs again. I shift in my seat, trying to will it away.

"Let me do the talking today," he says.

Ah, there's the dose of cold water I needed. "But of course, *sir,*" I snap in response, and I swear to God his nostrils flare, as if he liked it. Which lines right up with the handcuff fantasy.

The air in the car is suddenly too warm. I fiddle with the front of my jacket, undoing the buttons. Ben's eyes dart to my chest then veer away just as fast.

We arrive at the offices of opposing counsel and are shown to a conference room, where five attorneys wait—three partners and two associates, which is absolute overkill and leaves me feeling giddily optimistic for Margaret—if they've got three partners in here for this, they know it's serious.

It's all very civil, at first. It always is. There is the standard bullshit about the weather. They ask where we are staying and if we had a chance to go to dinner last night. One of them says we need to go to La Mar the next time we're here. And then Aronson, the lead attorney, folds his hands on the table and shakes his head, signaling it's time to get down to business. "Look, Miss Lawson does not have a leg to stand on."

Right. That's why you've got three partners in here.

Ben leans back in his seat, steepling his hands on his flat stomach. He's so long that this movement should make him look gangly and awkward. Instead, he just looks *more* powerful, *more* confident. "I'm not sure how you arrived at that conclusion."

"She had several negative reviews in a row and received countless warnings about her behavior," Aronson says.

My foot begins to tap furiously under the table, and Ben gives me a warning glance.

Aronson sips his coffee before he concludes. "My client had no choice but to move her out of a management position."

"It's curious, isn't it, that she didn't have a single negative review until she asked for a promotion?" I ask. I've already ignored Ben's request, but his request was stupid. "And that men in junior positions were earning more than her?"

Aronson glances at the guy beside him, who then slides a folder across the table. "This is what we're prepared to offer: Fiducia will give her an additional six months of severance in addition to the amount in her contract, along with a letter of reference."

It's the most insulting offer I've ever heard. I'm gripping my pen like it's a neck I'm trying to wring.

"Do you seriously think," Ben replies, "that after a decade of employment discrimination and a wealth of hostile workplace complaints lodged against Fiducia, I'm going to advise my client to walk away with *six* extra months of severance? That's less than the cost of this meeting."

I'm glad he said it. If he hadn't, it would have burst from my lips before I could stop myself.

"This is probably the best we can do," Aronson replies. "We might be able to go up to a year, but that's it."

Ben rises. "My associate and I flew across the country for this bullshit? See you in court."

Aronson looks at his colleagues and back to us. "Tate, be reasonable. You don't have a case. She'll get shredded on the stand."

"We wouldn't have taken it if we didn't have a case," Ben

says, "and now that you've pissed me off, I'm going to devote every available resource to making sure you regret what's occurred today. When I'm through with Fiducia, they'll be groveling to the press and restructuring their entire company."

It's exactly the kind of threat my future husband, owner of a small-town bar or struggling ski lodge, won't make. He'll be the kind of guy who is philosophical in the face of adversity, rather than the sort—like Ben—who clearly wants to punch adversity in the face.

But I can't help it. When we get out of the building, I'm smiling. I turn to look at him and I'm *still* smiling, even though I really wish I could stop.

He blinks at me for a moment, and then something in his face softens. "Liked that, did you?"

"Of course not," I reply, climbing into the car.

"Sure you didn't." The corner of his mouth lifts just a bit.

"So...every available resource?" I ask, slightly too eager.

"I want every goddamn employee review they've ever written. And every single expense report. I can't believe they pulled this shit, but I guaran-fucking-tee they won't do it again."

I'm sweating under my jacket and now need to change my shirt. Watching Ben get vindictive has my muscles tight, my breath coming too short. It's just the kind of weirdness I'll have to squash once I move to a small town and become someone who enjoys long walks at sunset and casual conversation with strangers.

"My secretary got us on an earlier flight," says Ben, as we pull up to the hotel. "Can you be ready to go in thirty?"

"The sooner the better," I reply, climbing out of the car and walking ahead. His vindictiveness has left me such an oversexed mess that I can barely walk a straight line, and I can't walk one anyway, thanks to the lobby now stuffed full of women in purple hats. I'm not sure what's up with the hats, but their tendency to block public spaces is something their leadership should address.

The elevator doors open. We climb in and are followed by approximately a hundred of the purple-hat brigade, talking so loudly I can barely hear myself think. They continue to pile in, surpassing the elevator's maximum capacity, as I'm forced farther and farther back.

Their noise level and good cheer makes the fact I'm currently turned on that much worse, that much stranger. Also not helping matters: my back is pressed to Ben's unusually firm chest, and I can't stop imagining where this might go if we were two different people who didn't hate each other and weren't surrounded by old women in purple hats.

"Stacey! Fiona!" someone shouts. "We'll make room for you!" Suddenly they are pushing us backward once more. Maybe the purple hats signify their inability to maintain reasonable personal space.

"For fuck's sake," groans Ben, as my ass presses into his thighs.

"It's fun for me too," I hiss. "We'd be farther apart if we were having sex."

I meant it as a complaint, but I flush as soon as the words exit my mouth. It sounds like it's something I've pictured repeatedly and am perhaps picturing now: Ben sliding my skirt up in this crowded elevator, pushing my panties aside.

Gross. I shudder. *Stop.*

And then...something registers. Pressure against the curve of my back.

His—apparently ample—penis is wedged there. And hard.

"Oh my God. Is that what I think it is?" I ask in a not-so-quiet voice, but there is no way the purple hats are going to hear me over their shouts to each other.

He gives the slightest sigh, as if disappointed in me for

asking when he should actually be disappointed in his penis for acting like it's thirteen.

"Don't get too flattered," he says under his breath. "There are a lot of women in here. It could be for any of them."

I feel my mouth curving upward and promptly turn it back down. "Mommy issues. I should have known."

I hear something that sounds suspiciously like laughter. "Don't judge. My mother is a very attractive woman."

I choke on a laugh of my own and try to disguise it as a cough, which only presses me closer to him.

God.

We arrive at our floor and maneuver out the elevator doors, Ben holding me against him the whole way, probably to make sure his penis doesn't send anyone into cardiac arrest.

From the feel of it, that's entirely possible.

When he finally releases me, I let my eyes drift back to him then *down*, but he's now holding his briefcase in front of him.

"I knew you'd look," he says. He's flushed, but also the tiniest bit...pleased.

"I thought it might be best to get a visual," I reply, fumbling with the keycard, "as it will be giving me nightmares for the next few weeks."

After stumbling into my room, I let the door fall closed behind me then grab my phone and open Tinder. Maybe no one in LA is straight out of a Hallmark movie, but I can no longer deny I'm deeply in lust with Ben Tate, and no one knows better than I do that's a recipe for disaster.

Nothing about Kyle and I worked, on paper. He was getting out of a ten-year marriage after his wife went back to her high school boyfriend. I was twenty-two, and had been scraping by to survive ever since I left for college at sixteen.

But we did work, and it was perfect and thrilling and terrifying all at once. I went to my job and school, but everything else in my life fell to the wayside for him. I just wished we didn't have to keep it a secret.

We should have reported it to HR, but I was scared I might mess up my job offer from Stadler, and he was worried Josie, his ex, would use it to slow down the divorce...which she would. Increasingly, the things she said and did implied she wasn't sure she wanted to let him go.

The decision was as much mine as it was Kyle's, but I hated that it meant I couldn't tell Meg and Kirsten. When I was with them, every word out of my mouth felt like a lie. I told them I was busy with school at night when I was actually with him. When they'd text about Kyle, I'd text back, as if I knew nothing, as if I wasn't basically living out of his apartment. I'd laugh along as they whispered about him: *someone forgot to shave*, Meg would say as he walked into the office. *Wonder who he was busy doing this morning?*

I wanted to shout about him from the rooftops. I wanted to tell someone about the flowers he sent to my apartment, the sweet things he said, the way he'd tuck a blanket around me when we watched TV at night. Sometimes I thought I'd burst with the desire to share just how *good* it was.

"I hate keeping this a secret," I told Kyle one afternoon, watching the dying sun land across his bare chest in stripes of muted gold.

His arm slid beneath my pillow as he pulled me closer, pressing a sweet kiss to my forehead.

"Next summer it will all be behind us," he said. "I'll be divorced, you'll be full-time, and no one will ever be able to imply you slept your way into a job."

The funny thing is I never got the job and they wound up saying it anyway.

12

By the time Ben and I leave to catch our flight, I have a date lined up with a chef named Thomas. I picture him bringing me breakfast in bed, garnished with fresh herbs he's grown himself. I don't actually eat breakfast, nor do I lay around in the morning, but I see myself becoming someone who does both, eventually.

Thomas will probably need to teach me to slow down and enjoy my life before he starts up with all the cooking.

Ben is strangely tense on the way to the airport and agitated as we go through security. I lean over to remove my shoes and he makes an irritated noise, probably because he had pre-check and I did not.

"Sorry for the extra two seconds this is taking," I say, with my fakest smile, going more slowly than is necessary. "I did tell you to go through the pre-check line, though."

"Take all the time you want," he replies. "There might be one man left here who hasn't looked down your shirt at this point."

"I just hope the one man was you."

"Unfortunately for us both, it was not." His voice is an irritated growl, but I spy a hint of a flush along his cheekbones. "I could see straight down your shirt half the ride here."

I glance down the front of my blouse. My bra is La Perla—pale peach, indecently sheer. I'm not sure why the idea of him glimpsing it is more titillating than embarrassing. Maybe I just like how much it seems to bother him.

Our flight boards late, and once we're in our seats they announce the plane is grounded until the storm overhead has passed.

"Shit," says Ben, looking at his watch.

"Not going to make it back before your girlfriend's curfew?" I ask.

He raises a brow. "You're pretty mouthy for someone who appears to never date."

"I date," I reply nonchalantly. "In fact, I have one tonight."

"With *who*?" he asks, as if what I've said is too incredible to be believed.

My patience starts to fray. His penis didn't seem to find me undatable a few hours ago, and the air has grown warm and way too humid in the stuffy plane. Anyone's patience would fray.

"Is it really so implausible that someone might want to take me out?" I demand.

"I never said it was implausible. I just wondered if it was, you know, a fully functioning individual. A *human* individual."

I pinch my eyes shut and take a few quick breaths through my nose. My second shirt of the day is now sticking to me and I'm officially miserable. If I respond, it's likely to be in a way that alarms the staff and gets me kicked off this flight.

"So," he says after a moment, when he realizes I'm ignoring him, "it's not someone from work?"

I roll my eyes. "The last thing in the world I want is to date another lawyer. I want the opposite."

"Wouldn't the opposite be a criminal?"

"Hardly." I attempt to peel off my jacket. I don't know why the hell they had us all get on board if they knew we weren't going to leave.

"Fine," he says. "What's the opposite of a lawyer?"

"A guy in a Hallmark movie," I reply, one arm now half trapped in my jacket sleeve. "Someone with an honest job. Someone rigorously ethical."

He laughs. "Ah, rigorously ethical like you?"

"I'm ethical *enough*." Yes, I'm aware that by qualifying how ethical I am, I may have proven his point.

He sighs, helping me pull the jacket off before handing it to me. "So what does this guy do? Your date tonight?"

I glance over at him. I imagine he's hoping to ridicule Thomas somehow. In this one instance, I'm glad the guy does not own a Christmas tree farm. "He's a chef."

"Guess you'll be paying for dinner. Good thing you're so liberated."

Heat, fatigue, frustration...they're rapidly eroding my ability to put up with this situation, and even more rapidly eroding my ability to be around Ben. "Lots of chefs do really well, and I don't care how much he earns anyway."

"Spoken like someone who's never had a broke day in her life."

"Right," I reply. "I forgot you're from the mean streets of *Newport*."

He raises a brow, and his mouth curves upward, as if to say, *Gemma, how do you know so much about me?* It's a question I should probably be asking of myself.

"So tell me about this guy," he continues, turning his head my way. "I mean, aside from the things I can already deduce: that he shares a two-bedroom with four other men, and still drives his mom's 2005 Honda."

"You've clearly never watched a Hallmark movie. Chefs live

in cute cottages, either on the beach or in the mountains, with a small herb garden in front. Everyone knows this."

He rises from his seat and moves into the aisle. "I'm gonna go out on a limb and say you don't know a lot of real-life chefs." He reaches up, pulls off his tie, and then begins unbuttoning his shirt.

That's when any shred of restraint inside me...evaporates.

"What the hell are you doing?" I demand. "This isn't your weekend Chippendales' show."

"Gemma, it's three hundred degrees in here. I've got a t-shirt on under this. You'll live."

He peels off the shirt, and I divert my eyes away from his very, very nice biceps, his smooth and surprisingly tan forearms...and they fall to his belt.

Then they fall lower, which is when I think about the elevator.

I *felt* it. He's large. *Too* large. It would be irritating, having to deal with that thing nestled up against me every morning and night.

"If our positions were reversed, I'd be complaining to HR right now," he says.

Shit.

"I have no idea what you're talking about," I reply, quickly looking away.

He closes the overhead bin and takes the seat beside me again. "I practically watched your thoughts scroll across your face and they were surprisingly filthy. I'm not sure I could even say them aloud."

I press my thighs together, feeling breathless. It's probably the heat. "Considering most of the women you date don't read yet, I figured you'd be better at talking."

"Really?" he asks, his mouth twitching. He closes his eyes, pressing his fingers to his temples like he's a psychic. "So, I see you in a room, and...wow, you really want me to put my tongue *there*? I mean, I don't know. I've never done that before."

I roll my eyes. "You do seem like the type who wouldn't have done much with his tongue."

"I've done plenty, Gemma," he says, his gaze on my mouth, his voice so gravelly that I have to swallow to get the air moving through my throat. He sits back in his seat and closes his eyes again. "Anyway, I didn't say no to that really surprising—and some might say unsanitary—thing you want me to do. I'm just saying it's a big step this early on. I normally start with the regular stuff first."

"Do you even *get* to the regular stuff, or can you not wait that long before you dismember the body?"

His mouth twitches. "Now you're *trying* to get me worked up."

I laugh, hating myself for it. On the intercom, the airline attendant announces we've been cleared for takeoff, and that's probably for the best. I don't need any more time spent considering whether I could be friends—or *more*—with Ben Tate. I shut the window shade and close my eyes, quietly praying that Thomas the chef sweeps me off my feet so I never have to consider this question again.

I MEET THOMAS—WHO apparently goes by *Tad*—at a bar in North Hollywood.

His hair was short in the photo but is longer in real life, pulled back in a small ponytail. I'm fine with this, but he does not exude the calm authority I'd hoped for. He's one of those twitchy guys whose free hand drums on the table constantly, as if he's nervous or bored or fresh out of cocaine.

I tell him I'm a lawyer, hoping he will then ask if I'm *fulfilled*. Maybe he'll get me talking about some secret interest of mine and suggest a change in careers. If I was someone who liked to bake, for instance, he'd encourage me to open a cupcake shop in his quaint little home town. If I was an artist, he'd convince me to start selling my work and he'd have a studio on his property that I was free to use. But I can't paint, and baking seems like a waste of time, so I'm counting on Tad to come up with something better.

"I bet you make bank," he says instead. Not quite what I was hoping for.

We talk about our interests. Mine include long walks at sunset, which is something I plan to like in the future, and work. His include fantasy football, "dank memes" and Xbox.

Our love was written in the stars.

I offer to pay the bill and he enthusiastically accepts. This also does not happen in Hallmark movies, where the men are old-fashioned and insist on holding doors and paying tabs, ignoring the heroine's weak feminist protest.

As we leave, he asks if I want to *hang out*, which I assume is a euphemism for something more naked. "Your place is probably better," he adds. "All my roommates are home."

For a moment, despite how consistently disappointing Tad is, I consider it. My libido has been like a furnace at peak temperature for a full day now at least. But I can only picture overeager fumbling and awkwardness, a sweaty pale torso covered in idiotic tattoos—a Tasmanian Devil waving a rebel flag or a cartoon character peeing on a car—so I tell him I've got to get to bed.

I arrive home and discover the one plant I own is extremely dead. Keeley bought it when I was discussing getting a cat to prove I could not take care of a cat—I guess it's a good thing we ran this experiment first. I sigh, "Sorry, my little plant friend, it wasn't meant to be." I throw it in the trash and the apartment seems emptier than before, which is an accomplishment because it's been empty since I moved in.

I bet Ben's house is gross. I picture a leather sofa covered in bodily fluids, a dartboard and artwork of the "Dogs Playing Poker" or "James Dean sitting in a 50s cafe" variety.

And I would definitely look down on him for all of this, but when he stepped into me, when his hands ran from my back to my ass and he started moving me toward the bedroom...it would not matter all that much. The next morning, I would, indeed, be appalled I just slept with someone who owns "Dogs Playing Poker" but for the hours preceding it—Ben's weight pushing me into the bed—I bet I'd be able to look past it.

13

Y ou can make anyone seem like a monster if you know enough about him: if you put him on the stand and ask about the time he drank too much at a party, told an off-color joke, got into an ugly argument in public, was late for school pick-up. The trick is to *know* about all these things.

Dennis Roberts, a college basketball coach in the process of divorcing my client, has practically done my job for me.

"Oh, Dennis," I say aloud, going through his social media accounts, "I deeply appreciate your lack of discretion."

I hear a laugh and look up at Ben standing just inside my door. He's smiling...and he has *dimples*. I don't know why that makes my heart give one overly loud *thump*. "What did he do?" he asks.

I've learned, after what happened at Stadler, that no one you work with is truly your friend, but I've missed being able to share a victory with the few people who will truly understand it. "Sent a picture of his dick to a temp," I reply, unable to hold in a grin. "And then tried to pay her off."

His smile, for a moment, is almost affectionate. "Only you

would be so excited about potential harassment of an employee."

"You'd find it exciting, too, if you weren't hoping to get away with it yourself. Did you need something?"

He blinks, as if I've caught him at something. "Did you finish the records request?"

I sigh. "I did it this morning. If you'd checked your inbox, you'd know that already. Also, I'm not an idiot, so don't treat me like a first year."

He shoves his hands in his pockets as he comes a step closer. "I don't need to check my inbox when I can just ask. And you're not partner yet, so it's not like I'm going to assume you're *competent*."

That devil on my shoulder starts whispering suggestions again. She's full of bad ideas, and I lack the restraint to ignore her today. "Someone's in a bad mood. Did your girlfriend not ask you to the winter formal?"

"I'm sure she will, once she's in high school."

My traitorous mouth twitches. "You're disgusting."

"Speaking of things that don't impress you," he says, a flicker of unease in his gaze, "how did it go with the *chef*?"

"Great," I reply briskly. "Really fun." Though I'm not sure listening to Tad talk about how "turnt" he got the night before and then paying for the opportunity was as superb as I'm making it sound.

"And how was his cottage?" His face says *I know for a fact that asshole did not have a cottage.*

"Amazing. Six-burner Wolff range. Subzero refrigerator. He made me popovers this morning and served them to me in bed."

He freezes, and for a moment he looks sort of...pissed off. "Are you serious?"

I roll my eyes. "No, because it was a *first* date. Visiting his cottage and having him make me a gourmet breakfast is more of a third-date scenario."

His eyes are still narrowed. "Your expectations might be a bit high."

I pull out a pen. "*Lower expectations...*" I repeat, scribbling the words on my desk calendar. "That's great life advice, Ben. Anything else?" I hold eye contact with him and bite the tip of my pen, as if waiting breathlessly for more.

"Yeah," he says, heading for the door, nostrils flaring. "No *chef* is ever going to make you happy. And you'd fucking hate breakfast in bed."

What's strange is that he seems angry about it.

What's even stranger is that I suspect he may be right.

I KNOCK ON VICTORIA JONES' door Saturday morning, and Lola, twelve, opens it and ushers me inside. The place is a mess, but if I was a single mom with rheumatoid arthritis and three kids, I'd probably be cutting some corners too.

I hand Lola *A Wrinkle in Time* because it was a book I loved at her age. She hugs me and I endure it, but in truth I want to walk away and not know this world here exists. Not caring is so much easier than caring.

There's a fallacy you tell yourself, sitting in an upholstered chair in a high-rise, looking at shoes online, and it's that people like Victoria are different from you in a fundamental way. That she and her children are okay with living on a disability payment and little more, and probably wouldn't actually want your life any more than you'd want theirs.

And then you meet a shy eight-year-old who only wants to sit in the corner and read, just the way you did at her age. You meet her little brother, Phillip, who wants to show you his diagram of the Earth's orbit around the sun and tells you he really wants sheets for his birthday. Fucking *sheets*, as if they're a luxury. And then you realize what bullshit it is, those distinctions you've made, and that the only person they were convenient for was you.

"This isn't getting you into trouble, right?" Victoria asks.

Yes. If not this time, then soon. Fields told me to stop taking pro bono cases two years ago, and it's a wonder I haven't been caught.

"No," I reply. "It's fine." And technically, I haven't taken on any *new* pro bono cases because I was *already* working with Victoria when Fields issued his edict. I doubt he'd agree though.

Travis, boisterous and cuddly, has spent my few minutes here running repeatedly into my legs, but now he scrambles onto the couch and climbs into my lap, pressing sticky hands to my dry-clean only suit.

A few minutes later, Victoria's friend, Rae, arrives with a battered face. I help her fill out the request for a restraining order and coach her on what kind of documentation she will need to bring. When we finish, Lola is looking at me with bright eyes, as if I'm a hero.

I want to tell her not to. Because Fields must be a monster to tell me not to help a woman like Rae, and the only way to defeat a monster is to become one yourself.

I sometimes wonder if I'm not already there.

AFTER THE HAPPY chaos of Victoria's apartment, the office feels unusually quiet. There are never a ton of people working on weekends, but I've grown accustomed to seeing Ben's smug face here, and the irritating way he'll raise a brow as he passes, as if to imply I'm doing something wrong.

If he isn't here, it means he has a date. Maybe he's taken her away for the weekend, probably to a place teenagers enjoy—Disney, perhaps, or Tijuana. He'll buy her a few drinks and a sombrero with her name stitched in hot-pink cursive and she'll think he's a prince among men.

I could have a date, too, if I wanted. Tad texted, but I've decided that perhaps *chef* is not the optimal career for a partner after all. I'm now thinking I'd like a very tall former Peace Corps volunteer, but only one who doesn't look like he'd wear ponchos and smell like weed, or a very tall doctoral candidate, but one who isn't going to bore the hell out of me discussing things that don't matter to real people, like whatever he's studying. Obviously, therefore, I've found no one.

Ben isn't as picky, however.

I wonder who he's with, and my hand slides toward my phone despite several oaths I've taken to stop stalking him online. Ben's Instagram feed is a lost cause—the only thing he's ever posted is a meme about the Lakers—but Drew Wilson, his most famous female friend, tags him constantly.

She's changed her last name to Bailey, I've noticed, which must be her husband's name. It's a rookie mistake. When I write a book about marriage, it will focus on making the whole thing easier to dissolve when it's done. I'll hand it out to the newly engaged and stop getting invited to weddings and showers. Win-win.

Drew has a new picture up of her hot husband hoisting a massive pumpkin on his shoulder. I scan the photo's background for Ben, but I don't see him. I can't really picture him at a pumpkin patch anyway, unless he's there to shut it down.

I scroll through the old photos until I get to the one I like best. It's from Drew's wedding, and Ben is walking her down the aisle. He's in a suit, just like he is every day, but there's something sort of sweet in his face, something hopeful.

If I didn't know better, I could be persuaded, when looking at this photo, that he isn't evil at all.

14

Ben and I are in a car, in an area of town I can't identify. The air is suffocating, and no matter how much I mess with the vent, nothing changes. I try to roll down the window but the button doesn't work. "This is ridiculous," I groan aloud. "Why is it so hot in here?"

Ben smiles. It's his filthiest smile, the one that chafes against me like no other. "Maybe you should take something off."

And suddenly, the heat is not my biggest problem. It's that devil on my shoulder, whispering now, saying, *Do it, Gemma. Call his bluff.* His voice is cool and seductive...a flicker of glee in my stomach, a frosty breath over my skin. I can't resist it today.

I smile back at Ben with *my* filthiest smile, like a witch about to unleash a curse. He's amused as I pull off my jacket, but I see something in him, a quiet eagerness, and it flares to life when I reach for the top button of my blouse. He watches it opening, as if it's a bomb being defused, as if nothing could induce him to look away.

I reach for the next button and notice the ungodly bulge in his pants, straining the zipper. I lick my lips and my smile widens. "You're enjoying this a little too much."

"I'm about to enjoy it more," he replies, pushing me flat onto the seat, pinning me there, while his free hand slides inside my skirt. And just before his hand arrives where I want it most...I wake.

I'm in bed, panting, my t-shirt flung across the room. I can't even pretend to be disgusted. Right now, I'm simply furious that I woke up before he could get the job done.

How completely like Ben Tate to be disappointing, even in dreams.

I WEAR a fuchsia skirt to the Monday morning staff meeting because Keeley says I wear too much black. It's paired with the same heels Ben suggested a dominatrix would wear. I do not, even once, wonder if my outfit screams *sexy librarian*.

I stride into the conference room with the devil a delicious flame in my chest, ignoring Ben as I take my seat and chat with Terri about her weekend. I feel his gaze and can't stop myself from meeting it.

"How was your weekend, Gemma?" he asks, his tone sickly-sweet, baiting, but for some reason the sight of my name falling off his lips makes that flame in my chest double in size.

"Just lovely, Ben. And yours?"

There's a flicker of delight in his dark eyes. "Ecstatic," he says. *Ecstatic* implies sex, some dumb InstaModel slavishly serving his every whim while posting grammatically incorrect captions on social media.

"Ecstatic for one of you, anyway," I reply. I mean for the words to trill lightly, ambivalently, but they emerge sharp instead. That thing in my chest, that childish glee, has suddenly gone sour. It was champagne, freshly poured—now it's a glass of milk set on a sunny stoop all day.

"Did you have a few popovers this weekend?" he asks, and he's smiling but there's an edge to his voice too.

"*Loads.* So many popovers."

"What the hell is a popover?" asks stupid Craig, entirely missing the point of this conversation.

"Yes, Gemma," Ben says, nostrils flaring, "tell us all about the popovers."

My mouth opens to reply, which is when I realize I've only *read* about popovers, and in my head they were much like turnovers but fancier, more like cream puffs, and I'm not sure that's true. For all I know they're another word for pancakes, a food which, inexplicably, has ten thousand synonyms.

I shrug. "You'd have to try them to understand."

His responding smile is irritatingly victorious. I would like to grab him by his tie, yank his face down and sink my teeth into his jaw until he begged for mercy. I'd like to dig my nails into his skin until he...

I clench my fists to stop my imagination in its tracks. I don't know what the hell is wrong with me, why I want him in a way I've never wanted anyone else.

I just know I need to make it stop.

EARLY IN THE EVENING, the office hallways are abuzz with laughter, empty chairs being slammed to desks, dinner plans shouted from one cubicle to the next.

It is, as always, the loneliest period of the whole day.

I was like them once, though it's getting harder to remember. Sometimes it feels like all my joy is treasure buried so deep and far that I have no clue where to start looking for it. At other times, it feels like a myth I've just convinced myself was once true.

The office is entirely cleared out when I call my mom. She's eating a "surprisingly good" Lean Cuisine and watching a Hall-mark movie about an advertising exec whose car breaks down in a rural village in upstate New York.

"Who's rescuing her?" I ask. "Widowed farmer or wise bar owner?"

"He's a veterinarian," she says, "but he *is* widowed."

We laugh, and then grow quiet. "I wish I was there."

"I wish you were, too, honey, but don't worry about me. I'm having a cozy night in and have no complaints." My mother has never complained once because she doesn't want me to worry or feel bad for her. She's created a fiction in which sitting alone in a shitty apartment watching a Hallmark movie is as good as it gets. "What about you? Are you going out tonight?"

"Not tonight," I reply. "I'm still at work."

"Oh, Gemma. This late? You should be out somewhere."

My mom wants a different sort of life for me and I want it for myself, but maybe it's time we both accept the situation for what it is. "I like what I do, Mom. This is more fun for me than going to some bar."

She's quiet for a moment. I sense a gentle lecture coming, which is the hardest kind for me to hear because I can't just ignore it. "I know you're driven," she finally says. "But is what you're doing going to make you happy in the long run?"

"It'll make me partner, which is better than being happy." I phrase it like a joke, but the truth is, if I were offered a choice between happiness and making partner...I'd probably choose the latter. "And I'm not sure happiness is really in my makeup."

"Of *course,* it is. You've forgotten the little girl who used to spin in the yard for the fun of it and jump in every puddle, but I haven't," she says.

I quietly crumple a Post-it note in my hand and leave it clenched in my fist. I haven't forgotten the kid she described either, but I think I may be too broken to get any of it back.

When the call ends, I rise and head to the break room. It's

late, and I should probably go home and eat a real meal, but I suspect the emptiness of my apartment would get to me tonight.

I take two steps inside and come to a sudden, graceless halt. Ben is there, reading on his phone while he waits for coffee to brew.

The coward in me would probably turn and walk out except I've already been seen. His gaze—startled, then predatory—starts at my face and finishes at my shoes, where it remains for a long, long moment.

I continue forward, doing my best to act like he's not here. If it weren't for ten straight years of dance training, I'd definitely be stumbling right now, however.

"I heard an interesting rumor about you, so I investigated," he says.

My stomach drops.

"Your mom's Etsy shop is endlessly fascinating."

It's not what I thought he was going to say, but it's a bad night to have anything involving my mother thrown in my face.

I give him my best dead-eyed look. The one that says *If you continue discussing this, I'll make sure they never find your body.* "Maybe you should be doing a little work on the Lawson case instead of online shopping."

He gives a genial shrug and opens up his phone. "We've got a few spare moments. Outfits for cats, right? I might need to contact her."

"Looking for a special bondage outfit for yours?" I ask, jerking a drawer open more roughly than is necessary. "My mom won't support your weird habits if that's what you're hoping."

He grins. "Wow, such interesting pictures." He holds up his phone.

Sadly, my mother still hasn't mastered her in-home photography skills. She's showing the cats curled up on the linoleum kitchen floor when I've told her a thousand times that she should at least use a white sheet.

"I love the way that shelf is hanging haphazardly off the wall," he continues. "It's kind of dark, like she wants you to fear for the cats' lives while admiring their outfits at the same time."

I feel a hard pinch, right in the center of my chest. I wonder if my father is laughing right now—just like Ben—while showing my mother's poor attempt at independence to his country club friends, his new wife giggling as she says, *"Oh, Adam, stop"*—as if she isn't enjoying it the most of them all.

"Don't make fun of my mother," I snap, but there's a lump in my throat that warns me I'm not going to be able to hold it together, whether he stops or not. I hate that he's won this round. I hate that he found this out, and I hate that there are things in my past I'm even more scared he'll discover. I turn on my heel, stiff as I walk from the room.

"Gemma?" he asks, but I just keep going, because if I try to utter a single word in response, I will absolutely lose it. My lungs feel like they're lined with shattered glass, so jagged I'm scared to take a full breath.

I go to my office and shut the door, hating that I'm falling apart here and now and with *him* of all people. I grab my bag and shove my laptop inside.

He knocks, tries the handle, and finds it locked. "Gemma, I—"

"We really don't need to discuss it," I announce, making my voice as sharp as possible. "It's fine."

I want him to just walk away, but he doesn't.

"I don't understand why it upset you so much," he says. "I was just kidding. You've said far worse to me."

Rage cures my sadness faster than time ever could. I jerk the door open, swinging the bag over my shoulder. "I make fun of the women you date, you make fun of me for not dating at all. That's fair. Making fun of someone's mother for being poor while you sit there with your fancy car and big house is not."

He blinks in surprise, and I see something an awful lot like shame pass over his face. "Gemma," he says, "I'm sorry. I honestly had no idea. None. You have that whole posh, East Coast, private-school vibe. I assumed you had wildly wealthy parents."

I did, and now I don't. Now I've got a mother who has to do everything for herself and won't let me help. That shelf in her kitchen will probably fall eventually. And her car will break down, or she'll slip on the ice outside her apartment again and I will be here, unable to make it stop.

"You can say what you want about me, but leave my mother out of it." My voice cracks at the end and I turn away from him, staring into my purse, as if searching for my keys when all I'm really trying to do is hold it together.

"You're right," he says, turning me toward him. "And I'm so fucking sorry."

I want to continue lashing out, but there's something so gentle and genuine in his gaze that I can't do it. His hand is on my hip. We are standing close enough for me to smell his soap, to make out the glints of gold in his eyes, to see up close just how much he needs to shave. I picture how that scruff would feel beneath my lips.

"It's okay," I say quietly. "It's just a sore spot."

His eyes travel over my face, land on my mouth. His breathing is shallow and so is mine.

I want him to kiss me. I want it more than I've ever wanted anything.

The realization hits all at once, shocking and terrifying, and I stumble away, heading straight for the elevator.

And he stands there, frozen, watching me go.

15

Kyle and I had begun dating in September. By October he'd decided to move to LA permanently. The hitch in our plan was Josie. His settlement offer had been more than generous—I'd reviewed it myself—but she kept coming back with new demands: all of his 401k instead of half, the vacation home that had been in his family for two generations in addition to their apartment in New York.

And every time he flew home, there was a part of me that worried he might not come back. If Josie realized what she'd lost, would he give her another chance for his kids' sake? I had to fight the desire to look her up online. Was she cuter? Sexier? More impressive? I knew it was a rabbit hole that would lead nowhere good, but it was a struggle, after the way my mother's life had been upended, not to worry mine would be too.

His work in LA ended in early December, and that was when things got harder. Josie was unreliable—drinking too much, failing to show up when it was her turn with the kids. Half our weekends together were canceled last minute because she'd somehow thrown a wrench in our plans.

And after one of those canceled weekends, crushed by disappointment, I asked him if he was even sure he wanted this.

"There must be a part of you," I said, "thinking it would be easier just to take Josie back. And I really need to know before this goes any further."

"Hon," he replied, "is this really about me, or is it about your dad?"

I had no idea how to answer. I thought my concerns were valid, but yes, there was a part of me that would never stop being stunned by how fast my mother had been abandoned. Three weeks before my dad left with Stephani, he'd taken my mom to the Bahamas for their anniversary, where he gave her a tennis bracelet equal to a year's tuition—one she sold a few months later to pay legal fees. People change their minds, and you don't even know until long after they've decided it. "I don't know," I admitted.

"Honey," he said, "I think you need to talk to a therapist, or this will never work. I don't want to fail at marriage twice."

"Marriage?"

He gave me an uncertain smile. "I thought it was heading there. Didn't you?"

I stared at his face on the phone. "I hadn't really thought about it," I replied after a moment. "I mean...you're still married. You're still based in New York."

"It's not going to be that much longer until it's over and then I'll be there. Unless I misunderstood." He frowned. "You're young and I know it's a lot, the fact that I have two kids."

I shook my head. "It's not that. I guess it just never occurred to me we were that serious."

"Gemma," he said with a quiet laugh, "we are absolutely that serious."

Over the course of one conversation, he'd taken me from worried to obscenely hopeful. But I guess I can't fault him for that: I'm the one who should have known better.

16

For the rest of the week, I barely see Ben. He's busy preparing for a big trial in Charlotte, and spends more time out of the office than in. It's for the best. I don't know what that was between us, when I thought he might kiss me—temporary insanity, I suppose—but I need some distance from it still.

The office has mostly cleared out the following Friday when a delivery guy comes down the hall, his hand truck stacked high with boxes. "I have a delivery for Gemma Charles?"

I direct him to the conference room, then dig into the first box from Fiducia while he goes back to his truck for the next batch. You'd think he was bringing me a dozen roses, as excited as I am.

The files are not alphabetized, nor are they divided by division or location or employment date. It's going to take forever, and is the sort of job I should farm out, but I'm looking for tiny slivers of information, easily missed, and I don't trust anyone but myself to find them.

It's tedious, time-consuming work, but finding those little slivers is like finding clues in a mystery. The thrill keeps me going, chasing the truth even harder. I don't register the *ding* of the elevator or the steps in the hall until Ben's imposing form fills the doorway. His gaze lands on the heels I kicked off, as if they're the first piece of evidence at a crime scene. "Don't you have somewhere to be?" he asks. "It's Friday night."

I shrug. "The files just arrived. And I could point out that you *also* are at work."

"I had a client dinner. I just came back to get my laptop." His brow furrows. "Can't it wait? Get the first years in on it Monday."

I could admit I have nothing better to do tonight, but I refuse to give him the satisfaction.

"I'd rather do it myself," I tell him. "That way I know nothing's been missed."

"What are you looking for, exactly?" He sets his bag down and walks toward the table.

My skin seems to tingle at his approach. "Anyone who was written up but not punished during their review," I reply. He perches on the arm of a chair. The jacket is already off, but when he reaches up to loosen his tie, I have to struggle to maintain focus. "When Lawson asked for a promotion, they started calling her all these gendered words—*shrill, abrasive.* I'm looking for all the men worse than her who still got ahead."

His tongue goes to his cheek. "That seems like a needle in a haystack."

I smile, because I've already *found* the first of several needles. "And I suppose *your* suggestion would be to just give up and hope they offer to settle again?"

"No. But it seems like the kind of thing you could trust someone else with." He unbuttons a shirt sleeve and starts to roll up the cuff.

My eyes narrow. I'm not sure why the fuck he's acting like he plans to stay, but I certainly don't want him here. I'm already painfully distracted and he's only been in the room for thirty goddamn seconds. He pulls out a chair and prepares to sit.

"What are you doing?" I demand.

"Helping you, obviously."

Ugh.

"On a Friday night in October? Isn't there a cheerleader waiting for you under the bleachers?"

He gives a tired laugh. "You make that joke so often I'm starting to wonder if you think it's true."

"You dated a nineteen-year-old, Ben."

"For fuck's sake," he says wearily, running a hand through his hair. "We went out *once*, she was twenty-one, and I had no fucking clue she was that young. She owned her own business —how was I supposed to know?"

I smile sweetly. "Most dates involve this thing where you learn about each other. Evidently, yours do not."

He leans over and examines the piles I've arranged. "I enjoy hearing about how dates are supposed to work from someone who has such limited experience with them."

I don't have a quick response because, of course, he's absolutely right.

I focus once more on the reports in front of me and hope he'll go away, but he takes a seat and grabs a file instead. I do my best to forget he's here, which is a lot harder than it sounds. Even his small movements—tugging at his tie, running a hand through his hair—throw me off my game. He taps a pen against his mouth, and my eyes fixate on that indentation in the center of his lower lip. I sometimes picture resting my thumb there, measuring the size of that divot.

It's a welcome distraction when my mother texts to tell me the couple bought a Christmas tree farm together at the movie's end. I'm smiling as I reply, and Ben's gaze darts to the phone with a sneer. I swear to God if he criticizes me for two seconds of personal time this late in the day, I will literally explode.

I cross the room to grab another box of files and catch his gaze on the seam of my stockings, traveling up to the hem of my skirt. His jaw shifts, and he throws down his pen in disgust, looking away.

Maybe I'm not the only one who's distracted.

"You okay?" I ask. "You look like you're having a stroke."

"It's cute that you're worried about me," he says, even more irritated than before.

"It's cute that you think that was worry, not optimism."

I dump the box on the table and go to the other end of the room, mostly because I need space from him. I pop a coffee pod in the Nespresso, though I'm already so wired I half-expect small sparks to shoot from my fingertips momentarily.

"How are things with Thomas?" he asks.

I turn, squinting in confusion. "*Who?*"

"Your *chef*, with his romantic cottage on the shore."

"You continually utter the word *chef* as if it's a euphemism," I reply. "It's a real job."

"And you say *chef* as if he's Gordon Ramsay, when he's probably just the guy in charge of the deep fryer at Bennigan's."

The devil on my shoulder is suddenly there, goading me louder than he ever has before, manipulating me like I'm his fucking marionette. *I've* led an extremely careful life. It's that thing inside me that wants to overthrow the system. That wants to take my career and my future and my carefully honed image and set them on fire. "Someone like that will get a lot further with me than you ever will," I say.

He's gone instantly alert, an animal about to pounce. Suddenly all his focus is on me, and it makes my breath catch in my throat with its intensity.

"Oh, is that right?" he asks, the muscles in his forearm tensing as he tightens the grip on his pen. His eyes sweep down my body, and I swear I can feel his gaze like it's a physical touch. "And why is that?"

There's a tension to his voice, a challenge. Goose bumps crawl over my skin. My nipples tighten until they're visible beneath the thin fabric of my blouse, and his eyes dart immediately to my chest.

I touch my neck. "You wouldn't know what to do with me."

I am throwing down a gauntlet I know he can't pick up.

His gaze sharpens. And then he rises from his chair. "What did you just say?"

My breath skitters over my lips while I contemplate repeating it, but I've done this before, and it didn't end well for me. "Nothing."

His steps glide over the carpeted floor—slowly, purposefully—until he is directly in front of me. My pulse triples.

"No, I want you to say it again."

His eyes dip to my mouth, and I find words emerging from my throat, words I don't approve of.

"Fine. You. Wouldn't. Know. What. To—"

His hands slide through my hair, gripping it tight, and then his mouth is on mine.

His lovely, full mouth. I shiver at the perfection of it. Kissing him is like sinking into a warm bath when you're freezing cold. His lips open, his tongue teases, and everything about him is suddenly soft and warm and hungry. His hands, holding my face, are firm and rough, possessive and gentle all at once. The voice in my head screaming, *"but we hate Ben!"* is overridden by every ounce of blood in my body, which is straining toward him.

He pulls away only long enough to breathe, and then he's back, even harder now, more determined. His hands slide down my back and grab my ass firmly, as if it's the award he's wanted to snatch for years. The hard bulge of him, pressing into my abdomen, makes that devil crow with delight.

I already know how he'd be in bed—the way he'd be so fucking focused until the end, pinning me with his gaze until he started to fall apart. There's nothing I want more right now than to watch Ben Tate wind tighter and tighter until he explodes.

My fingers dig into his hair, desperate for that moment; it can't come soon enough.

He pulls away though. His eyes are hazy, intense—but there's a hint of a smirk on his mouth, which suggests maybe this wasn't about me at all. Maybe he just wanted to fucking *win*.

I push him away, missing the heat of him even as I do it. His smile doesn't fade at all, smug fucking asshole that he is. If he thinks he's won something, he's gravely mistaken.

"Was kissing me without my consent supposed to prove something?" I ask, sounding more breathless than indignant.

He raises a brow, and his generous mouth quirks up at one corner. "Are you really going to pretend you didn't kiss me back?"

I kissed him back. I ran my hands into his hair, and I'm pretty sure I *gasped*. Denying it, at this point, is illogical.

"You took me by surprise."

"I should have fucked you then, too," he says, eyes flashing, "just to see how else surprise makes you yield."

My jaw falls open. A thousand responses come to mind, but instead of voicing them, I brush past him, snatching up my keys and phone as I rush to the elevator.

Because if I'm in here for even a second more, I don't know what that devil on my shoulder will make me do next.

17

"I think I'm sick," I tell Keeley.

"What are your symptoms?" she asks. I sometimes forget Keeley's a doctor. Probably because she mostly leads her life like a teenage heiress who's just arrived in LA with unlimited funds and a fake ID.

"I'm feverish."

I hear the sound of a vending machine in the background. Keeley has the worst eating habits of anyone I've ever met. Maybe that's why I keep forgetting she's a doctor.

"*Feverish* is not a thing," she informs me. "You either have a fever or do not. What's your temperature?"

I hold a palm to my forehead. My hand is cold, my face is hot, so who knows? They ought to invent a better way to assess this. "Are you asking because you're concerned or because you plan to make me go out tonight if I answer wrong?"

"Both," she says. "But mostly option two. Because if you're well enough to go to the office, you're well enough to go out."

"I'm not at the office," I reply...because I already raced there like a coward at six in the morning to get some files and am now working from home.

She gasps. "Not at the office on a Saturday afternoon? I'm calling you an ambulance. No, wait. A helicopter. Can a helicopter land on the roof of your building?"

I laugh. "Shut up. I'm just a little off."

It isn't a lie. I spent the entire night tangled in my sheets, sweating and miserable, and I still feel overheated and raw.

I think Ben might have given me a virus. That kiss went on for a while.

I should have fucked you then, too, just to see how else surprise makes you yield.

There was something so shockingly filthy in the way he said it, as if he hadn't ruled the possibility out. As if he knew I hadn't either. Maybe he did it to win and maybe he didn't, but I remember that bulge of his pressing insistently against me, so it wasn't *only* to win.

I close my eyes, and it's almost as if he's here. Almost as if his mouth is brushing mine and his hands are fisted in my hair. It leaves me feeling like I'm all nerve endings, as if even the slight breeze of my door shutting behind me is sexual in a way.

I imagine that's just the virus too.

I PREPARE for the staff meeting Monday as if it's some bizarre battle with rules only I'm aware of: my favorite V-neck blouse, my best lingerie and, of course, my precious baby-blue, suede slingbacks. Though I'm not sure what, precisely, I'm hoping the lucky shoes will bring me.

Maybe just the return of my sanity.

I don't feel any better now than I did Saturday. No matter how hard I try not to think about that kiss, I can't seem to stop, and I suspect the only cure might involve getting him to do it again. Getting him to do *more*. And since I refuse, I guess this situation is permanent.

I take the seat across from his in the conference room. Our gazes lock. He doesn't smile, nor do I. We are definitely at war now, though I don't know what *he's* got to be pissed about. Neither of us speak, and the meeting ends unusually fast, which leads me to think our bickering might have been wasting more of the staff's time than I realized.

When he walks out without a word to anyone, I tell myself I'm relieved. It's strange, sometimes, the way relief feels a bit like disappointment.

I spend the day trying to ignore the lingering effects of the virus he gave me—the repeated clench of a muscle low in my abdomen, the warmth and occasional breathlessness. I almost feel normal again by the time I meet my favorite client for dinner. Walter is in his early sixties and is possibly the one person capable of restoring my faith in men: he adores his wife and kids and he cares deeply about the well-being of his employees. That he specifically requested *me* when he came to the firm—right on the heels of Ben stealing my biggest client— was nothing short of a miracle, and since that time he's sent me more work than the rest of my clients put together.

We meet at his favorite steakhouse, and briefly discuss some litigation I'm handling for him before he sets down his fork and knife and looks at me.

"So, when are they going to give you a piece of the pie over there, at that law firm of yours?" he asks. "You've certainly earned it by now."

I force a smile. "If it's up to them, never."

"You can always come to us. You told me yourself I needed in-house counsel."

"You do. You're paying FMG twice what you would otherwise." I don't understand why he's still going through me.

"Then work for us. Think how much shorter your days would be. These are the best years of your life. You're letting them pass you by."

If FMG doesn't make me a partner this winter, I'll have to consider it—it could be another five years before the opportunity comes again—but the mere possibility fills me with dread.

"This isn't the time to let my foot off the gas," I tell him. "I'll think about having a life once I've made partner."

"You could still find time to date," he argues. He's said it before. I used to worry he was going to try to set me up with one of his umpteen children, but fortunately he has not. "I bet there's some nice young man in your office, working the same hours you do."

All I see in my head for a moment is Ben. Ben, who beats me to work most mornings always looking like a million bucks in his perfect fucking suits, that smug smile permanently fixed on his face. Ben, who lives to torture me, who tortured me all weekend in my apartment when he wasn't even there.

"We're lawyers, Walter," I say with a smile. "None of us are nice."

He laughs and shakes his head. "Forget I said anything."

I go back to the office after dinner. The halls are empty, but there's a light on in the conference room and, somehow, I know it's him. *I can't avoid him forever*, I tell myself, but I'm walking awfully fast for someone who is theoretically reluctant.

His face is deadly serious as he watches me walk in, his gaze almost palpable. A shiver ghosts over my skin, and my thighs press tight as I try to will away the effect he has on me.

I take a chair and his mouth quirks, as if he just thumbed through every filthy thought I've had over the past seventy-two hours and their sheer depravity has left him embarrassed for me.

"How are you?" he asks.

I kick off my heels, placing them on a chair beside me. "What are you doing right now?"

"It's called conversation, Gemma. You tell me you're fine, then you ask how I am."

He needs to shave—I bet it would feel like fine-grit sand-paper between my thighs.

"Do I have to pretend I care about your answer? Because that sounds like a lot of work."

He holds my gaze. "Fine, then tell me something...have you thought about it? I'll admit it if you will."

"You just admitted it already."

His laughter is low, over-confident, already certain how I'd answer if I was *willing* to answer. "I'm wondering which part you thought about," he begins, stretching back in his seat, palms behind his neck, as if he's lounging at the pool.

Next, he'll mention my hands in his hair, which hardly implies unwillingness. Or my intake of breath, the way I arched against him seeking more.

I rise to my feet, buoyed by seventy-two hours of pent-up frustration and rage. "Stop."

"Quitting so soon?" he challenges. "Typical female. Mouthy until the going gets tough. With the way you were—"

I was reaching for my shoes already, but it's as if my brain has mixed up my intent. I grab only one...and I whip it at him, as hard as I can, realizing after it's airborne that if that spiky heel hits the wrong thing he could wind up in the hospital—or worse, the heel could snap.

But he catches it, and his eyes gleam—an evil look if I've ever seen one. "Thanks," he says, rising to his feet. "I've always wanted one of your shoes."

And then he turns and walks out of the room.

I stand frozen, astonished by the whole thing. And then it hits me: He has one half of my *lucky* heels, my irreplaceable seven-hundred-dollar Manolos. *What the hell?* Why couldn't I have thrown a book or a stapler, or a microwave like a normal person?

He might break it. He *will* break it, intentionally. "*Ha-ha,*" he'll say, laughing maniacally like the villain he is, *"she'll have to go home barefoot."*

I *need* that shoe.

Panicked, I grab the other Manolo and run around the table to chase after him. "Wait!"

He goes into his office and shuts the door. "Ben! Please! I'm sorry! Don't destroy it!"

There is no response, so I grab my phone and text.

> Please. I'm sorry. Please don't hurt my shoe.

I hear the low hum of his laughter from the other side of the door and the distinct sound of scissors. Then there are three dots beneath my text, and then...

> Beg.

Rage spikes in my chest, but for once in my life common sense overrides it. Those shoes are irreplaceable.

> I'm begging. Please give me back my shoe.

> In person.

I try his door, which is now unlocked. He's sitting behind his desk with a broad grin on his face. He holds my shoe aloft in his left hand, the scissors in his right. "Hello, Miss Shoe," he says. "Have you met my friend, Mr. Scissors?"

"Don't," I plead. "I'm sorry I threw it, okay? I'm sorry."

He spins the slingback around on his index finger. I want to demand he stop because he might stretch out the delicate suede, but I somehow refrain. "You know what you have to do," he says.

I squeeze my eyes tight, breathe deeply, and pray for

patience. "Please give me my shoe back. I am very sorry I threw it at you."

"Did you think about our kiss?" he asks.

My jaw grinds. "Is a confession you extorted really the best you can do?"

"I'll take your refusal to answer as an answer." He rises and comes to my side of the desk, where he then kneels beside my foot and picks it up in his hand, his thumb sliding slowly over the arch.

Goose bumps break out across the surface of my skin. A small fever starts to spread through my blood.

He slips the shoe on before he takes the other from me and slips that on as well, his hand lingering on my ankle. "You aren't very good at begging, by the way," he says, his voice low and rough.

"Maybe you're not good at making women beg," I reply, my words husky and full of longing.

"What's that?" he asks. And then slowly, insistently, his hand slides up my leg. The soft trail of his palm over my skin and the rough purr to his voice make it hard to think. All concern about my shoe is abandoned and now there is only want, a wave of it so strong that I need to grip the desk to keep my bearings under it.

"I said—" I inhale as his palm slides above my knee "—maybe you're not good at making women beg."

His hand brushes against my inner thigh and I make no move to stop him.

"You know what I think?" he asks, climbing to his feet just as his hand reaches my thong. He's never watched my face more carefully than he is at this moment. "I think you get off on fighting with me."

This is crazy, Gemma. You need to make it stop.

"I think you talk too much," I whisper.

He holds my eye as his fingers slip under the seam of my

thong. "Jesus," he groans, "you're so wet." It's embarrassing, but before I can pull away, he steps closer, his free hand landing on my hip to hold me in place. "Don't even think about backing out now," he says against my ear, and there's both command and desperation in his voice.

His fingers begin to move—small, delicate circles that have me bracing against his desk, sucking in tiny sips of air. His eyes are on my face, his free hand still spread wide and unrelenting over my hip. It's almost too intense—the things he is doing to me, the way he watches. My gaze lowers to his clenched jaw, to his chest, rising and falling faster than normal.

I can't believe I'm letting him do this. I can't believe I basically *encouraged* him to do this and, oh my God—I'm already close. My eyelids lower, and he steps near enough for me to feel his breath on my face, to smell his soap and aftershave and the starch of his shirt.

Two fingers slide inside me, harder, more insistently than before. My muscles tense as he moves his index finger in exactly the right way, and I grip the desk.

"I've wanted to watch your face when you come for so fucking long," he says, gripping my hair, pulling my head back so all I can see is him. His jaw is locked tight, as if he's barely restraining himself. "Go ahead. I know you want to."

I've never seen what Ben looks like when he wants something desperately, until now. It's that, as much as anything, forcing me to give in at last. I let go with a small cry, my eyes closing, the world going black and blissful as his fingers maintain their pace.

"God, I love that," he rasps.

I reach for his belt, then flick the button of his pants before tugging down the zipper. I slide my hand inside his boxers and he gives a single, sharp inhale.

He is hot, hard as steel, long and *wide*. Air hisses between his teeth as I run my palm over him, once, twice. I can already imagine the feel of it along my tongue, the greedy way he'll watch.

His eyes fall shut for a moment before they open and he takes charge, pushing me back on his desk then wrenching my skirt up around my waist. He glances down at me, splayed out before him. "I knew it," he says, sounding almost angry as he tugs at my wisp of a thong, letting it snap back against my skin. The sting it leaves behind is pleasure and pain at once. "I fucking knew it was something like this under that skirt."

He reaches past me. I hear the telltale crinkle of foil, a reminder that this is common for him and that I'm undoubtedly not the first female who's been fucked on this desk. It will bother me later, but right now, it's washed away by a heavy fog of anticipation.

He grabs one knee and holds it aloft as he lines himself up. "You're sure, Gemma?" he asks, his voice low, desperate.

"You're still talking too much," I reply, and he thrusts. The fit is tight, exquisite and painful at once, and he's only halfway in.

"Fuck," he hisses. "You okay?" His voice is all gravel now.

"Yes," I groan, and then I grab his hips—a silent plea for more—and he pushes in the rest of the way.

He holds still for a moment, eyes squeezed tight, waiting for me to adjust to his size. It's only when I arch my hips that he begins to move, sliding slowly in and out. I never come twice in a row, but...I think I'm going to. The way he's focused on me, the fullness of it, even the hint of pain—somehow, they conspire to create something bigger and brighter and better than anything I've felt before. One handed, he unbuttons my blouse, still pushing inside me. His fingers slip into the cup of my bra, pinching my nipple. It hurts and threatens to topple me right off the edge at the same time. I cry out involuntarily, and he flinches, trying not to come. His brow is damp, his face strained.

"Beg," he commands. His thrusts come fast and then *stop*.

I'm seconds away.

"Oh, god." I arch against the desk. "Please."

"Please what?" His hands grip my hips hard enough to bruise.

"Fuck me harder. I'm so close."

He does. He gives me everything, and then he leans over and finds my mouth, kissing me with the same degree of force, and I meet him—kissing, biting his skin in my desperation.

"I'm going to—" is all I get out before it's on me again, rolling over me while he thrusts jerkily once, twice, groaning, against my ear.

His weight falls atop mine, and we are as close as we could possibly be, both of us gasping for breath. I turn my nose toward his neck and breathe him in, the smell of his soap mingling with his sweat.

I wish we could stay like this forever.

It's a bizarre thing to think, clearly the product of oxytocin, a hormone known to cause stupidity, but I feel lost when he finally pulls away.

He ties off the condom and puts it in the trash while I push my skirt down and rebutton my blouse.

I have no idea how to gracefully extricate myself from this situation. I want to leave and I want to stay, and I wish I could press pause on this moment just long enough to figure out which of those things is the right response.

He meets my eye, a small grin on his face. "Told you you'd beg."

I stiffen. It's not like I expected him to write me a love poem now, but I wasn't ready for *this*. I wasn't ready for him to act like it was all a fucking game, and why I ever expected anything more of Ben is beyond me. It's a lesson I've had hammered home more than anyone alive.

It shouldn't hurt, but it does.

I walk straight out of his office, grabbing my purse from the conference room and heading for the elevator. I can't imagine why I'm so bitterly disappointed. I can't imagine why I feel so beaten and bereft. I haven't actually *lost* anything.

The elevator doors slide open and I step inside.

"Gemma," he calls after me, zipping up his pants. "Fuck. Gemma, *wait*. It was a joke."

The elevator doors shut and I let my weight sag against them. *My God, I will never fucking learn.*

ON MY LAST day at Stadler, I was escorted out by a security guard, as if I was a criminal. A group of male partners sat inside a glass-walled conference room watching—men with all the power, who thought nothing of destroying a young female if it made their lives a little easier.

Meg and Kirsten watched too. Impassively, without an ounce of guilt.

I was ashamed and I was horrified, but most of all, I was angry. *Fuck all of you*, I thought, *every last one of you.*

And, really, I never stopped thinking it. About them. About everyone.

It was a good strategy.

18

I wake in the morning to find my pajamas missing and the sheets stuck to me. The entire night was basically one long, pornographic dream about Ben. A dream he kept ruining by saying, *"I told you you'd beg"* at the end.

In my head, he's now said it a thousand times, and that smirk of his gets a little more smug and evil in each iteration.

He's texted several times. *It was a joke. A stupid, poorly timed one,* he said. And then: *Fuck. Will you please say something?*

Forget about it, I replied. *I already have.*

Even if it isn't true, it should be, and that's the best I can do for now.

I take extra care getting ready for work. I wear my Louboutins with a skirt that shows slightly more leg than normal. "This is not for him," I tell my reflection as I apply mascara.

It's solely for me, so I can exude confidence. And if it happens to make him *extra* regret the way he behaved, that's okay too.

I call Keeley on the way to work. "I think I sold my soul to the devil last night."

"You're a lawyer. You did that a long time ago."

She may have a point. "Fine. So, I sold him my soul and then I had sex with him on his desk."

Her gasp is pure drama. "Ben? You *didn't*."

I pinch the bridge of my nose. "I did."

"But how?" she demands. "You hate each other!"

"I know!" I cry, letting my head fall back against the seat. "But I threw a shoe at him and..."

She laughs. "Are you seriously going to tell me *throwing a shoe at him* led to sex?"

Someone behind me honks though the light *just* changed, so I give him the finger. "Well, no. He told me I had to beg to get it back and then he put it on my foot and..."

"Why was he putting it on your foot, Cinderella? Why didn't you make him hand it to you like a normal person?"

"I don't know," I tell her, because I'm too embarrassed to admit the truth: I wanted to see what would happen. I wanted to see how far he would go, and—apparently—I was hoping he'd take it just as far as he did. And it was so fucking good, until he opened his big mouth.

"How did you leave things?" she asks.

I hiccup a sad laugh made of misery and self-loathing. "He said 'I told you you'd beg.'"

Her inhale tells me all I need to know. I didn't overreact at all. "What. A. Dick."

"He tried to say it was a joke, but..."

"Fuck that guy," she says. "Freeze him out."

"I know," I reply. It's the only thing I can do, under the circumstances.

After arriving at work, I stride into the office with purpose, a polite smile plastered on my face as I greet everyone. Because absolutely nothing is wrong.

There are roses on my desk. For a regrettable half-second I soften, before common sense prevails and I'm enraged by those too. If I hadn't gotten in so early, half the office might have seen them in here and would have spent the day discussing it.

I put them into the trash, which I hide on my side of the desk, and am shredding the card without reading it just as Terri walks in and shuts the door behind her. "What's wrong?" she demands.

I smile, folding my hands before me, as if this is the opening summit of the model UN. "Why would anything be wrong?"

She points at my face. "*That.* That is the weirdest, fakest smile I've ever seen. You look like you were possessed by an alien attempting to inhabit human form for the first time. One who's not sure how the smiling thing works."

My lips purse. "I'm just trying to be a model employee. Making partner and all that."

"Oh-kay, boss," she says. There's a knock on my door, and when she sees Ben standing there, his ever-present smirk absent, she laughs out loud. "You're telling me later," she whispers.

He waits until she's through the door before he walks in. He's in a fresh suit, but he's forgotten to shave, and his hair is even more fucked-up than normal. I hate how *good* guilt makes him look.

"I'm sorry," he says.

I drag my eyes to his face. "It's fine."

"If it was fine," he replies, carefully enunciating each word, "you wouldn't be pissed."

"I'm not pissed. Pissed would involve caring and I don't. It's forgotten."

He takes a single step toward my desk and leans over it, his face two feet from mine. His eyes have gone black as night. "You are full of shit."

He pushes away and walks out of the office, leaving me with

my mouth ajar. What the hell was that? *He's* mad? I'm the one who gets to be pissed, not him.

I didn't expect anything from yesterday and I certainly didn't expect him to act like it meant something—so why is he?

And why is my heart thumping, as if I wanted it to mean something too?

I MANAGE to make it through the morning behaving like a reasonable human being and not, as Terri suggested, an alien inhabiting human form. The effort leaves me feeling like I want to sleep for a thousand years, like I'm incapable of faking even one more polite smile for as long as I live. And then the reminder pops up on my computer screen: *partner/senior associates meeting*, and my stomach drops. *God, why today?*

Terri's mouth twitches when I exit my office. "Don't think just because you buried me in work this morning that I've forgotten what I'm going to ask."

I frown at her. "Why bother asking? You've clearly figured it out."

"Yes," she says with a wide grin. "But it's the difference between reading *Fifty Shades* and having someone tell you 'they had sex'. I need all the dirty details."

I grimace. "I assure you, you won't be getting anything close to *Fifty Shades* from me. It would be one shade that was thirty seconds long, and no one's buying that book."

It was way more than thirty seconds and a whole rainbow of shades, but this is the story I'm trying to tell myself.

I make a point of facing Fields' position at the table's head, but when Ben enters the room, the right side of my body tingles, as if his gaze is a physical thing. I turn and my eyes lock with his.

They always lock with his, though, don't they? Every time

I've ever sat at this table with him, every time for two freaking years, Ben's been looking at me whenever I turned, and I've been looking right back. Every single time there's been this same clench of want in my stomach, this same half second in which it's impossible to look away.

I think of the hunger in his face as he watched mine last night, the strain. Him saying, *"I've wanted to watch you come for so fucking long."* I swallow hard and turn my chair away from him, facing the front of the room, where Fields has already begun to drone on.

He talks about billables and the retreat, and then he asks us to each give him a quick status on our clients.

When he gets to my nemesis, Ben glances at me before he speaks. "The Lawson suit against Fiducia is coming along. We've found plenty in the personnel files. Now we're looking at expense reports." He's just summed up my work, and the only substantial thing I had to report. "We're ready for the class-action in Charlotte, and I'm meeting with Brewer Campbell later. They're sending a lot of work our way, so it's going to be all-hands-on-deck soon."

The point of my pencil snaps. Brewer Campbell is the client he *stole* from me, and now he's bragging about it. And he didn't say a thing about the cases he's assigned to boring Craig, which means *I'm* the only one at the meeting left with nothing to report.

"Gemma?" Fields asks. "Anything?"

I grind my teeth. Having to follow up Ben's coup with absolutely nothing fills me with loathing for him all over again. "I've been pretty buried with the Lawson case," I tell him, sounding like a goddamned intern. "And Roberts was supposed to go to mediation but they postponed."

Have you brought more work to the firm, Gemma? No.

Have you spearheaded something on your own? No.

Did you just let the worst person here fuck you on his desk? Yes. Yes, I did.

I wouldn't make me partner either.

I march out of the meeting as fast as I can and head straight for the elevator with Ben at my heels.

My finger stabs at the button to go downstairs. "Are you following me?"

"Are you running out of here early because you're scared of my devastating sexual appeal?"

I roll my eyes. "You've now fucked me twice. Once last night and once at today's meeting. That seems like enough."

His nostrils flare. "Lawson's the biggest case either of us have. Of course, I was going to discuss it. You'd have done the same thing."

He's right. If I'd gone first, I'd have discussed Lawson, as if I'd done all the work on my own too. I'd have *delighted* in it.

I step into the elevator and he follows. I walk clear to the other side and hold my bag to my chest, as if to ward him off.

He glances over at me and his nostrils flare once more. "You're impossible."

I laugh. "Oh, is this the part where you act like a dick and make it out to be my fault? We've managed to move through all the stages of a relationship without actually having one. Impressive."

His jaw is locked tight. "I made a mistake. I admitted it. I've apologized until I'm blue in the face. But you are hell bent on seeing the worst in me no matter what."

The elevator doors open, and I walk out, grateful to escape his clean, testosterone-scented air. "No, because I don't see anything in you at all," I reply. "Go play your games with someone else. Or better yet, don't. Grow the fuck up and stop treating women like pawns."

19

For the next week, Ben and I avoid each other like the plague. We converse only via email, which is absent even the barest hints of cordiality. No *thanks*, no *let me know if you need anything*, no *regards* in the signature line.

To: **Ben Tate**
   From: **Gemma Charles**
   We need to file the motion by Wednesday.

To: **Gemma Charles**
   From: **Ben Tate**
   Send to me for review before submission.

To: **Ben Tate**
   From: **Gemma Charles**
   Motion attached.

. . .

To: **Gemma Charles**
From: **Ben Tate**
Send it.

I FLY into a silent rage at each of those emails, at the way he's treating me, as if I need his fucking supervision. *I'm* the only one of us who's ever even handled a gender discrimination suit. Our whole strategy was *my* idea.

But underneath it all, I just feel lost. I was fueled by viciousness and vengeance before, yes, but also hope: hope that my life could eventually be something that makes me happy. Without that, it all feels wrong. When I listen to a client rant about making her husband pay, when I sneak out of the office pretending to go to lunch so I can coach another one of Victoria's friends before she goes into court, when I walk into my empty apartment at night...I sense that things have gone drastically off-course and I'm not sure they can be set right.

And I have no idea why I'm taking it all so hard. Ben was never what I wanted. He was a shameful mistake I made, but I've bounced back from shameful mistakes before. My mom can tell something's wrong, but I'm not sure how to explain it to her when I can't even explain it to myself, so I simply go out of my way to avoid that conversation.

"So what are you watching?" I ask when I call her.

"He's a neurosurgeon and so is she," my mother replies. "But they won't admit they like each other."

"And they both hate their jobs," I continue, "but he actually has inherited an old farm the two of them are going to refurbish after she realizes she no longer wants the big-city life?"

My mom laughs. "No, actually, she really likes her job. So does he."

I frown. "Well, I don't see how that could possibly work out well. That doesn't even sound like a Hallmark movie."

"It's *Grey's Anatomy*. I'm on the fifth episode."

"I tried to get you to watch that for years and you refused!"

It takes her a moment too long to answer. "I used to only want to watch things about happy people," she says quietly. "Now I'm wondering if I did you a disservice."

My scalp prickles. "What do you mean?"

"You were so angry at your father over the divorce. You seemed so broken by how far he took things. I thought I needed to give you examples of these perfect romances, and I liked them, but I worry now...that I've set you up to want something that might not exist."

The words *"might not exist"* kill me. And it's less for me than it is for her. I know how badly she has wanted someone to come along, someone so wonderful that everything she suffered at my father's hands would finally make sense. She wants to be able to say, *"I went through hell, but I wound up in a better place"* and I want it for her just as much.

"Mom," I say, "sure it exists. You're going to find someone."

She *has* to find someone. I have to believe the world is a decent enough place that she won't end up empty-handed after everything she's been through.

"I don't know about that, Gemma," she says softly. "But the thing is, I have other pleasures in life. I have you, and I have all my memories of your childhood. I just wish I'd done a better job. I wish you were happier."

"I'm really happy, Mom," I tell her, but then I ruin it when my voice breaks.

I've been telling her I'm happy for years now. I've been telling myself that too. But this is the first time I've realized that neither of us believe it.

20

Fields catches me just as I step off the elevator. He tells me the judge on a case I just won said I was *singularly vicious*.

It's not an insult, at least not in Fields' eyes.

"I did what I had to," I tell him.

A better person might argue that Chip Reardon, my client's ex, made mistakes, but also clearly loved his kids. A better person would argue that even our heroes, even Martin Luther King and Gandhi, would look a bit flawed under a microscope and that messing up and being a jerk to your wife doesn't necessarily make you an unfit parent. But why should I have to be a better person when no one else is? Why should I be a better person when Reardon's piece-of-shit lawyer wouldn't have been?

"I'd like you to represent me at a gala we're co-sponsoring on Thursday," he says.

I blink. Fields doesn't do much legal work these days but he sure likes to hit all the parties and take all the credit. Asking an associate to represent him is a huge honor.

"Of course," I reply. "I'd be happy to."

"The company car will be here to take you at seven. Everyone who's anyone will be there. Might be a good chance for you both to drum up some business."

"*Both?*" I repeat.

"Tate's going too," he says.

A party with Ben, at night. Him in a tux.

My breath leaves me in an audible rush, and Gemma Charles, good girl, quakes in fear. The devil on my shoulder, though? His crowing, in this moment, nearly deafens me.

~

"MY GOD, GEMMA," Keeley says, entering my apartment. "It looks like you just moved in. Are you *never* going to decorate?"

She says this every time she comes here, which is, admittedly, not often. Even when she lived next door, we always hung out at her place, and now that she has a lusciously equipped two-bedroom fully stocked with junk food and alcohol, it's a given.

"I have a couch and a TV," I tell her. "What more do I need?"

"Some sign that you're human, or female?" She places a garment bag over the back of a chair, then looks around at my bare walls, as if it's her first time seeing them. "I've stayed in executive hotel rooms that are homier than this."

I wave a hand at her. "I'm too busy. I'll worry about it once I've made partner."

"Yeah, *then* you'll be on easy street," she scoffs. "*Partners* do no work at all, right?"

I open a bottle of wine. "I'll worry about your very valid point once I've made partner. What did you bring me?"

"A selection of four dresses that are going to make Ben Tate weep," she replies with a triumphant smile. My eye roll has zero effect on her enthusiasm.

This makeover, of sorts, was Keeley's idea when she heard Ben was attending this thing. I initially refused, but she said, *"promise you're not wearing that funeral dress"*—by which she meant the one and only cocktail dress I own—and I conceded because, yes, that was what I intended to wear.

"I'm not dressing like a hooker," I warn, handing her a glass of wine while I peek in the bag. "No sequins, nothing that barely covers my ass or has the midriff cut out."

She stares at me balefully. "I'll try very hard not to take offense at that statement, Gemma. And it will be nearly impossible."

I notice, however, that she did indeed bring both a sequined dress and one with the midriff cut out.

I take one of the remaining two and go to my room to put it on. It's purple, a gorgeous matte jersey with just the right amount of cling, but as I look down at the figure-hugging dress, I'm not sure.

"Maybe it's too bright?" I ask hesitantly, walking back into the living room.

"Dude, all you wear is black or navy blue. It's time to stand out a little."

I shuffle in place. "I don't want him to think I'm doing this for him."

"Look at yourself in the mirror," she replies, turning me to face the cheap mirror hanging on the back of my bedroom door. "He's going to be too busy kicking himself to think."

I look at my reflection...and I'm forced to agree. The dress is sleeveless, with a draping Grecian neck and tucked-in waist, and it makes me feel like a goddess.

Which is probably how I need to feel to survive an entire evening by Ben Tate's side.

∽

SHORTLY BEFORE IT'S time to leave Thursday night, I go into the bathroom at work and change into the dress before attempting day-to-night makeup, which I read about unnecessarily often as a teen, given how little I've needed to do it.

My eyeshadow is a bit smokier, and my lips go red. I'm not sure I needed an article to figure that much out.

I don the dress, slip into a pair of glittery Jimmy Choos, and I'm ready to go. "This isn't weird," I tell myself in the mirror as I slick one coat of gloss over my newly red lips. *It's not weird at all that you're going with him. It's just like any other event you'd attend with a colleague, as long as you'd allowed that colleague to fuck you on his desk first.*

At least it won't be weird for *him*. I'm sure it's not the first time he's been in this situation.

I ignore the quick pace of my heart as I walk toward the elevator, where he waits in a tux. I think of that wedding photo on Drew Bailey's Instagram, and the tender way he looked at her. I could almost believe there's something similar in the way he's gazing at me now, but that would be a really dangerous line of thought, under the circumstances. Refusing to forgive him feels like the only thing keeping me safe.

A muscle flickers in his temple. "You look nice."

"Thank you," I reply coolly.

If he's waiting for me to say it back to him, he'll be waiting a very long time.

I push the button to call the elevator since he apparently doesn't plan to do so, then walk in ahead of him. I draw in a calming breath but get the smell of his soap and aftershave, which is the opposite of calming. Before I can stop myself, my brain flashes back to that night on his desk, his mouth buried in my neck as he came. His smell, his sweat, how tightly he held onto me for a moment before he pulled away.

"Look," he says, shoving his hands in his pockets as we walk off the elevator, "can we just call a truce for tonight? There are going to be enough people there trying to stab us in the back without stabbing each other too."

Every childish bone in my body wants to refuse, but he's right, and admitting I'm still hurt by what he did would give him a power I don't care to hand over anyway. I'm going to put this behind me and act like the soon-to-be-partner I am. I haven't come this far to fuck it all by sleeping with colleagues, and I'm not going to fuck it up by playing games afterward either. It's done.

"Of course," I reply, my smile forced, but civil. I take a deep breath and drive the night in his office out of my head. From now on, I'm only focusing on work when he's around.

We climb into the car. I fold my hands in my lap and force myself to meet his eye. If we were colleagues, *only* colleagues, I'd probably discuss the case we have in common, so that's exactly what I'm going to do. "We just got the results of the financial inquiry of Fiducia," I tell him. "They spent a significant amount of money on corporate retreats."

"So we need to find out what they did and if any female managers were invited."

No shit, I'm about to say, and then I stop myself. The sex has to stop, obviously, but the bickering that leads to sex needs to stop too. "I've got someone checking," I say instead.

The driver weaves through LA, and I stare out the window. We pass Kyle's old apartment and then the Tiffany's where we chose a ring. It was princess cut, and we compromised on two carats though he wanted me to go bigger. *"When we get married,"* he'd said, *"I want everyone to know you're taken."*

For a single moment I can remember the girl I was back then. I wasn't the child jumping in puddles that my mother discusses, but I wasn't nearly so removed from her as I am now.

"Could we try something?" Ben asks, pulling me from my memories. "Could we just talk? Not about work."

I turn my head toward him. It seems like a bad idea—

boundaries are clearly not my strong suit when it comes to Ben, and maintaining a strictly professional relationship is easiest when our interaction remains work-related. "I'm not sure what else we'd talk about."

"You could tell me what the deal is with your parents," he suggests. "Why'd you get so upset that night I brought it up?"

I laugh. "Wow, Ben, you're so good at small talk. Why don't we talk about the worst thing you've ever been through instead?"

He runs a finger inside his collar. "My father's death. What would you like to know?"

My head whips toward him. Slowly, my body follows, twisting his way. "I thought you made that up to make me feel bad."

"You thought I'd lie about something like *that*?" he asks. "Especially when the odds of you experiencing guilt about anything seem shockingly low? Yes, he's really dead. He was in a car accident when I was ten."

I wince. "I'm sorry." Perhaps I'm capable of guilt after all, because I'm feeling something like it right now. "I spend a lot of time wishing my dad would die, so I guess I was a little insensitive."

He barks a startled laugh. "Are you serious?"

I wave my hand. "We're talking about you right now. Ten is really young."

His lips press together. "It was just a bad situation all around. My youngest brother, Colin, was only a week old at the time. It was...hard. For all of us."

I picture a woman like my mom, overwhelmed with a newborn, suddenly a widow, presumably still in love with her husband. It would be agonizing, but at least children would give you a reason to keep plowing forward, and that's what you need in life when the worst things happen: a reason to keep going.

My father and I were *all* my mother had, and he tried to remove us both from her life. I think that's what upset me most: the way you can, in theory, love someone and then just *stop*, without warning. I wonder if it bothers Ben that it can happen by accident too.

"She was lucky she had you and your brother, at least," I suggest. "To give her a purpose."

A muscle flickers, just beneath his cheekbone, as if he disagrees. For a moment, he seems very far away. "What happened with your parents?" he asks.

My trauma now seems small compared to his, barely worth discussing and certainly not worth hiding.

"My father left my mom when I was fifteen," I tell him. "He completely pulled the rug out from under her."

Ben's head turns. "Was he a lawyer?"

I give a small, bitter laugh. "Yes, so he knew exactly what to do and who to call. He hid assets, took the house, even repossessed her car. She found herself without a penny, with every credit card cut off. She was absolutely screwed."

His tongue taps his upper lip, as if he's learned something about me that he hasn't.

"Don't get that look on your face like you suddenly have some deep insight into my psyche," I warn with an irritated click of my tongue. "It's all very much on the surface. My father treated my mother terribly in their divorce, like tons of men before and after him, and I want to even the playing field. You all call me The Castrator. You know what I bet they call Paul Sheffield for doing the same fucking thing? *A really good attorney.*"

He's quiet for a moment and finally nods. "Yeah, you're probably right."

I blink in surprise. Males, especially male *lawyers*, love to tell you you're wrong about these things, then pontificate for hours on *how* you're wrong.

"I honestly have no idea what to say when you agree with me," I tell him, hiding a smile. "You just made it awkward."

He laughs. "How rude of me. I'll try to do better."

The car slows and I realize, to my surprise, that we've arrived at the Getty Center. Even more surprisingly, I sort of wish we hadn't.

Ben climbs out first and extends a hand to me. I accept, reluctantly, and try not to think about how much I like the feel of it—his large, firm hand swallowing mine. Staying close to my side, he moves me toward the red carpet, where a photographer stops and insists we pose. I'm on the cusp of saying, *"we're not together"* when Ben's arm eases around my back, as if we're a couple. It's bizarre, how natural it feels. There's no weird *"where should I put my hand?"* moment, no question of whether we're too close or too far apart—we just fit. But I'm not going to think about that right now. *Boundaries, Gemma.*

"Do I need to remind you not to hook up with a client's wife in the bathroom at regular intervals?" I ask with a grin while the photographer gets in place. "Or do you just, like, set an alarm on your phone to remind yourself?"

There's a flash. The photographer has just caught me smiling up at Ben like he's Prince Charming. *Super.* "I wasn't hooking up with her," Ben says, steering me toward the entrance. "That client's wife? He was taking money from their kids' college funds to go to Vegas, and she wanted me to tell her how she could stop him."

I still. Offering legal advice to someone opposing your client is a breach of ethics. She put him in a terrible position. "What did you do?"

He observes me for a moment. It's a risk, answering this question. I could get him in a lot of trouble if he messed up. "I gave her some advice and the name of an attorney who could help."

I stare at him, shocked that he's trusting me with this. I've been terrible to him. I've been terrible to him *about* this. "You let everyone think you were hooking up with her all this time to protect her."

He shrugs, as if it's meaningless. "And to protect myself. Fields wouldn't have approved, obviously."

"That—" I whisper, "was very decent of you."

His eyes hold mine, and I swear for a moment I see an apology there once more. "I'm capable of it on occasion."

I give him the smallest nod and look away. Something about this conversation leaves me feeling oddly fragile and defenseless. I hate this feeling. I hate the inclination to trust him.

"I see some guys I know over there," Ben says, nodding to the right. "Let's get a drink and I'll introduce you."

I follow his gaze and stiffen. A partner from Stadler is among that group he's indicating. I can still see him as he was on my last day, sitting behind that glass wall, condemning me with his eyes.

"You go ahead," I say, taking a sharp left. "I'm heading this way."

I don't give him a chance to object as I push my way forward, wishing fervently that I hadn't come. But that's always the risk, isn't it? You might run into something from your past, and discover the shame of it all hasn't improved in six fucking years.

For lack of anyone else to speak to, I find a group of female attorneys I know only vaguely and insert myself into the conversation. They're older than me, more secure in their fields. None of them were at Stadler, obviously, or I'd have to run from them too.

"How's the shark pit?" Emily Greenfield asks dryly.

I smile, and it's a relief to have it come naturally for once. "I think sharks are unfairly maligned."

"Tell me if you think that in a decade when they haven't

made you partner," she replies. "I was there, you know, when I was just starting out. My career went nowhere until I left."

My stomach tightens. I want to think I'm different somehow, but she's really good at what she does. "Things are changing. I'm not sure any firm can get away with only promoting men these days."

"FMG will," she says, and her certainty shakes me a little. Does she know something I don't? "Come talk to me when you get tired of the boys' club there."

I accept the card she hands me with a polite smile, though I have no intention of using it. I'm not interested in giving up on the boys' club—I want to sit at their table. When they're holding men to a different standard than they do women, I want to be the one who tells them *no*.

I walk away, wondering what the hell I'm going to do here for another two hours. From a distance I see Ben smiling his best glib, square-jawed smile at a woman who is probably the next Miss Universe or *Vogue* cover. He glances around him, his eyes finding mine for half a second before they return to hers. It shouldn't bother me as much as it does.

I head toward the bar because only a second glass of wine will persuade me to work any harder at this than I am, then find myself talking—reluctantly—to some wannabe rock star. I hear Keeley in my head saying, *"give him a chance"*, but that's because he's exactly what *Keeley* wants—hot, under-dressed and over-confident. If she were here, the two of them would already be making plans to escape. She'd know of a better party, or he'd suggest a spontaneous trip to Amsterdam, and she'd be saying, *"let me just grab my passport."*

"You want to get out of here?" he asks. "A friend of mine is having a thing at this club in West Hollywood."

That's when I see Ben, still across the room, but staring at me and Machine Gun Kelly or whoever this guy is, as if he's about to kick someone's ass.

"Sorry, I think I'm probably too boring for you," I tell him. "But you need to meet my friend Keeley."

I get his number for her and then cut through the crowd again...and discover I'm heading right toward Tim Webber.

I hate what he got away with. I hate even more that he's looking at me now with that self-satisfied smile, as if he *likes* what happened. As if he stole something from me that night. We are, perhaps, twenty feet apart. We are in a public space, but my pulse explodes anyway, as if he's just cornered me in a dark room. He's closed the distance between us before I can make my escape.

"Fields told me you'd be here," he says, which I guess explains why Fields *honored* me with the invite, because no matter how good I am at my job, Fields still thinks my vagina is my best asset. "I was hoping I'd run into you tonight."

"Funny," I reply, "I was hoping the opposite."

I turn, thinking *find Ben*, and Webber grabs my arm. His expression is mild, but that hand on my arm is just as unyielding as it was the last time he grabbed me. "Let's go talk somewhere. I think you'd be very interested in what I have to offer."

"Let go of me," I hiss.

"You could at least let me explain," he says, and then Ben is there, grabbing Webber by the lapels.

"Maybe *you* can explain why you're grabbing her like that first," he growls.

"Who the fuck are you?" Webber asks.

"I'm the guy you answer to when you grab my—" he stumbles over the last word. "—colleague."

"Colleague?" Webber repeats. "You're at FMG? Well, Fields and I go way back. He'll be very interested to hear how you treat a potential client. Security?" he calls, looking past Ben. "Can someone get security over here?"

Ben could probably talk his way out of this just fine, but I'm not sure he will. He's looking at Webber right now like he can't decide what to punch first.

"We were leaving," I announce, linking Ben's arm with mine and tugging him toward the exit.

He holds still. "*We* shouldn't be the ones leaving," he argues.

"Don't create problems with Webber," I snap. "Fields is angry enough with me for messing it up. No reason to make him angry at you too."

His jaw locks tight, and I'm certain he's going to continue arguing, but instead he ushers me out, calling the driver to pick us up as we walk.

We reach the curb and he turns to me, pinching the bridge of his nose. "He seemed pretty possessive for a guy you ostensibly met once."

My eyes drift to the pavement between us. "I met him, we had a difference of opinion about what I was there for, end of story."

He steps closer. "It was more than that. I heard what he said. About letting him explain. He must have done something."

I'm about to lie when he touches my arm. "Gemma," he says softly, waiting for me to look up at him. "Tell me what he did."

I swallow, and my eyes fall to his chest, which feels safer, more impersonal. "We met, in theory, to discuss what the firm could do for him. When we left he...he shoved my hand between his legs and refused to let go until I forced the issue."

I wait then, for the doubt and blame I expect to see on any man's face when an accusation like this is made. I wait for him to say, "*are you sure you didn't misunderstand? Are you sure you didn't encourage him? Explain it to me in detail so I can tell you where you went wrong.*"

But his eyes are black in the light, a muscle flickering in his cheek. "That lunch," he says, with rage in his voice, "when you kept rubbing your wrist."

I nod. The car pulls up, but for a moment he just stands there, frozen. "Why the fuck didn't you tell me?" It sounds like an accusation.

"Come on, Ben," I say, rolling my eyes, which means *We aren't friends. Why would I have told you?*

I climb in the car but he simply remains where he was, frozen in place.

"You're not coming back to the office?" I ask.

He shakes his head. "I've got some loose ends to handle real quick."

I hesitate. "Webber's not one of them, right?"

He shakes his head. "No. Just a few things I need to deal with."

There's a *plink* of disappointment in my chest. I imagine those *things* involve some woman he met inside, the potential Miss Universe who is probably texting him lewd propositions even as we speak. But it's not like I expected him to escort me home. This isn't a date. "Okay. Well...I'll see you tomorrow."

He merely nods, carefully shutting the door, remaining there as the car pulls away.

The driver meets my eye in the rearview mirror. "Back to FMG, ma'am?"

My shoulders sag. I'm tired and alone, and suddenly the idea of going back to the office doesn't appeal in the least. "Can you just take me home?"

We drive through those same suburban neighborhoods, past Stadler's building, past Tiffany & Co. It's only when we reach my apartment that I realize I didn't think about Kyle once.

21

I walk into the office with measured, precise steps, uncertain what I will find. I don't know if there will be any backlash from my argument with Webber, and I also don't know where things stand between Ben and me.

If I'm being honest, it was sort of Hallmark-worthy, the way he intervened when Webber grabbed me. It's the exact kind of toxic masculine bullshit I'm not supposed to like but thought about for hours last night anyway.

Ben's office is empty. He must have had a late night, and my heart sinks a little at the idea of *why* he'd have had a late night.

I ask his admin where he is, despite begging myself not to do this very thing, and she gives me a curious look. Dory is older than most of the staff, a grandmotherly sort who's always been surprisingly fond of Ben. Rumor has it he's actually nice to the people who work with him closely. "He'll be in late. He had a long night."

So I was right. I bet it was Miss Universe. She was all over him like a rash, though I can hardly blame her: he did look ridiculously good in that tux. A little twinge of jealousy twists in my gut, but I squash it down.

I'm in no way listening for the sound of the elevators, nor am I intentionally looking up each time they *ding* to see who's arrived. I just happen to see him when he steps in at eleven, freshly showered but looking slightly more ruffled than normal. I force my gaze back to my laptop, determined to put him out of my head, but only a few minutes later Terri walks into my office with wide eyes...and somehow, I know it's about him.

"Guess who was arrested last night?" she whispers. "*Ben.* He just met with Fields about it. Debbie told me."

I blink. "*Arrested?*" It has to be a mistake. Ben is too smart for that.

"He hit some guy at the party," she says, "and the guy is a friend of Fields'. He won't even explain why he did it. All hell is breaking loose."

I stare at her, speechless. Ben didn't go back into the event last night for Miss Universe at all. He went in to kick Webber's ass.

"I can't believe it," I whisper. "I can't believe he's not defending himself."

Except—that's a lie, because I can believe both those things. I might not like when he makes me look stupid in staff meetings, but it's mostly because he's beaten me to the punch.

Even the *told you you'd beg* moment...it's what we do. Someone other than me might argue he was simply continuing to play a game *I* set in motion. The banter, the insults, the constant passive-aggressive humor: I'm the one who started it after he arrived at FMG and stole my client. I tossed him a ball and he lobbed it back. It's been in the air ever since.

I sigh heavily and push away from my desk. The right thing to do, a thing even ruthless Ben would do in this situation, is come clean. I didn't need him to fight my battles, but he's not losing his job because he tried.

I knock on the door of Fields' office and then enter. Fields is on one side of the desk and McGovern is on the other, which shows how serious this must be, because McGovern almost never comes in anymore.

"We're in the middle of something, Gemma," Fields says, his voice sharp.

"I know," I reply. "That's why I'm here. Last night...Ben was defending me."

Fields grows utterly still, while McGovern finally deigns to turn toward me. "Defending you from what?"

My nails bite into my palms. Their faces are already *wary*, already inclined to disbelieve whatever I say next, though in my six years at this firm I've never complained about harassment of any kind once, and it's occurred plenty. I'd be pissed about it if there were time. "Webber assaulted me at that client dinner you had me go to. I kept it to myself because I didn't want to cause problems and maybe I shouldn't have. He grabbed me again last night and refused to let go."

Fields' expression flattens. "Assault is a serious accusation, Gemma," he says, as if I wouldn't fucking know this on my own. "I assume you thought carefully before making it."

Everything in his tone says, *"you should have thought more carefully before you made it because I'm certain you misunderstood."*

"Situations like this are often...up to interpretation," McGovern adds. "It's easy to misconstrue the intent. Did this alleged assault occur here?"

Alleged assault. *Misconstrue*. I've worked with him for six years, but he's sitting there creating Webber's defense for him.

And Webber, if asked, will tell them we flirted all night—that outside the bar, I stood close to him while we discussed going to his apartment, and one thing led to another. He'll imply I wasn't unwilling at all, but am simply someone who later had regrets, and they'll believe him, instantly, because they'll have stood in his shoes. Because at some point, every man *thinks* he's navigating the "mixed signals" a woman is sending out, even when they're not mixed at all.

I guess none of that matters now, however. What matters is getting Ben out of trouble, which requires a strategy.

Even if they think I'm full of shit, and they clearly do, they're both from that generation where men defended their womenfolk —probably from the Iroquois, or perhaps the British Army during the Revolutionary War—so they'll respect his decision to protect the *gentler sex*. "Ben saw Webber grab me and saw how upset I was," I tell them. "He risked his job to defend me. I'm sure you both can appreciate how difficult the decision must have been for him."

They nod. "He's a good man," says Fields approvingly. I'd be irritated by how easily they forgive their favorite partner if it wasn't the outcome I was hoping for.

"A stand-up guy," adds McGovern. "Good for him."

Jesus Christ.

I force a smile. "Great," I say. "I'll let you get back to it, then."

"I understand that you're upset, but it would help if you could make things right with Webber," says Fields. "Persuade him not to press charges."

I stiffen. They want *me* to call the guy who assaulted me and ask for a favor, for fuck's sake. Fields is as well-connected as anyone in LA and could handle all this with a few well-placed words, but he wants me to do it. He's punishing me because he sees this incident as a problem I created, what with my female tendency to *misconstrue* things.

"Absolutely," I reply through gritted teeth. "I'll call him right now."

I walk slowly back to my office. Webber won't be satisfied with an apology, if I'm even capable of one. He got beaten up in public and is probably humiliated and lashing out. The only thing that will stop him in his tracks, at this point, is fear.

I spend a few minutes at my desk, rehearsing what I will say, which will involve some creative storytelling on my part. Webber answers on the first ring, as if he was expecting me. "Your boyfriend attacked me," he says. "So this had better be worth my time."

"I went to the ER the night you grabbed my wrist," I reply. The trick, when lying, is to make yourself really believe it's true. Right now, I can almost remember the hospital, late at night, fluorescent lights overhead, the smell of bleach. "The bruising is documented. I discussed the incident with several people at the time—the doctor treating my injuries was very adamant about me reporting the attack to the police. Drop the charges against Ben or I file for assault."

"You think you can threaten me, you fucking bitch?" he demands. "You've got no proof."

"I'm pretty sure I just *told* you I have proof, and I guarantee there was a camera that caught what you did outside the bar. But if you want to go up against me in court, let's go. This kind of case is how I make my living. I will clear my goddamn schedule."

He hangs up, which is when I stare at my shaking hands and admit, for the first time, how much this matters to me. That I didn't go running to Fields' office because it was the right thing to do. I did it because I don't want to work here without Ben Tate.

I thought his presence at FMG was a glaring, obnoxious light.

But maybe it was simply the only bright spot in my day.

∽

By eight-thirty, I'm too edgy and amped-up to work. I know I need to thank Ben, but it's awkward, and my feelings at present are confused and chaotic, which leads me to avoid them entirely.

I'm running through a list of Ben's greatest hits, trying to continue disliking him, trying to justify the fact that I haven't said a word to him all day.

He stole my client.

He said "I told you you'd beg".

But none of it holds the sting it once did, and I'm not sure how to keep my boundaries in place without that. Finally, I spring from my chair and begin packing to leave. Maybe I'll go talk to him, but more likely I'll sneak away like a coward. He'll be in Charlotte next week...if I just avoid him entirely, perhaps things will be normal by the time he gets back.

I've slung the bag over my shoulder and am about to head out when Ben appears, looming in the frame of my door, looking at me without an ounce of his trademark certainty.

My stomach ties itself into a knot so tight it hurts. "Did Webber drop the charges?" I blurt out.

His mouth moves, a passing suggestion of pleasure. "He did." He walks into the office, closing the door behind him. The sound it makes seems to echo through the room. "I thought you might have had something to do with it."

I stare at my shoes before I look up to meet his eyes. "Thank you," I say quietly. "For what you did. You didn't need to, but... I'm glad."

He's moved closer since we began talking. "I'm so sorry that happened. I wish you'd told me."

I fidget, hoisting the bag farther onto my shoulder. "We don't tell each other things like that."

His brows draw together, as if he is considering his next words. "Maybe we should start." He's close enough now for me to see the pale bruise under his eye. *He got into an actual fistfight on my behalf, in public.* I'm drawn to that small mark on his cheek, as if it has value, as if it means more to me than all my possessions combined.

"You got hit," I whisper.

He gives me the smallest possible shake of his head. "That was just security, not Webber," he says, as if that lessens the fact that he got hit on my behalf.

A thousand caustic responses come to mind. But what's overriding them all is a single thought: *I can't imagine being here without him.*

I close the distance between us and, on tiptoe, with my hands on his lapels, pull his mouth to mine.

For a moment he is still, shocked, and then—with a quiet grunt of surprise—his hands go to my hips and he pulls me closer. His mouth is soft but growing more determined by the second, and I've never wanted anything more. His low groan vibrates in his chest as he deepens the kiss, his hands sliding over my ass, tugging my body tight to his. The smell of his aftershave, his body hard and looming over mine, the heat of his palms gripping me—it's both too much and not nearly enough.

There's a dull *thud* as my back hits the wall. *No* part of him is reticent now, and I'm arching to get closer, to feel the press of him, hard as steel against my rib cage. I will contort myself into a thousand shapes to be the one that fits him best.

My hands are on his belt when I hear the *ding* of the elevator...and reality hits like a hammer. What the hell am I doing right now? I'm hooking up with a partner, putting everything I've worked for at risk, without a single guarantee.

I swear to God, I'll never learn.

He blinks at me, as if coming out of a trance, his eyes dark and drugged. I slide out from the wall and stumble backward. Jesus, I have no idea how to get out of this. "Okay, well then, um..." I say, snatching my bag off the desk and heading for the door. "Good day to you, sir. Don't beat anyone up in Charlotte."

I saunter away, as if nothing happened here at all, but I'm dying inside as I hurry toward the elevator. Did I really just say, *"good day to you, sir"* like we are gentlemen in Victorian-era Parliament? I'm going to convince myself I imagined that part.

But the rest of it...*God*, the rest of it. Ill-advised, yes, but I can't swear I'd take it back.

22

Ben isn't at the meeting on Monday because of the case in Charlotte. I knew this, but it's still oddly disappointing, not seeing him across from me. I arrive early for once, since I slapped on my makeup in the car and didn't bother flat-ironing my hair.

There's no devil on my shoulder today, goading me and making me feel overcaffeinated. In its absence, I can't seem to stop yawning. Debbie prattles on, at length, about next weekend's firm retreat. There will be seminars, followed by activities and a black-tie party. I could still attempt to bring someone, I suppose, but it no longer matters all that much. Ben's trial is expected to last weeks, and he's not flying to California Saturday just to fly back Sunday. I wouldn't bring someone anyway—the drive to prove him wrong or show him up is now completely lacking.

"Don't forget to sign up for your activities," Terri reminds me as we leave.

"Activities?"

"For the retreat," she says with a mildly exasperated laugh.

"All the good stuff is getting full. Hurry or you'll be stuck with golf. And you need a dress for the black-tie thing."

I've shown up like a good little associate for every single event this firm has ever held, and now—at the biggest event of the year, with my promotion on the line—I'm wondering if I can lie my way out of it entirely.

I make a weak attempt at doing my job, but I'm distracted, and bored. For the first time in ages, I go online to my mostly abandoned Pinterest page, looking at all the things I chose for my future home—the kitchen island painted navy, a beaded chandelier in the palest blue, the bleached heart of pine floors. When did I stop caring? Why didn't I ever consider buying my own place? I've got the money. I still want those things.

Maybe I just gave up hope of being anything more than I am. But today, with Ben absent, I realize I absolutely don't want to stay this way, either.

On Saturday morning, I drive up to Ojai for the retreat. Most of the associates arrived last night to be here bright and early today, but I chose not to, as I'm not interested in being here at all. I go straight to the first of several windowless rooms to sit through the first of several dull talks—*Maximizing Profitability Realization Rates*, followed by *Due Diligence Checklists* and *Record Keeping Management*.

If Ben was here, I'd text him when a reference is made to inappropriate client relationships and say *I hope you're taking notes*. And he'd write me back something like *you're so obsessed with that. Next time I'll let you watch.*

Fields mentions the retirement of Springer and Cleary, which would be exciting, except Ben's not here to say, *"I can't wait until Craig makes partner. I'll ask him to throw you some work."*

I miss his bullshit. I told myself he annoyed me, but I'm now wondering if what annoyed me was the way it made me want to respond, to laugh, to keep the ball in play.

I fake a work call to get out of the afternoon "fun" and avoid everyone until the last possible minute. When I venture downstairs for the evening—my dress slinky and low-cut, more Keeley's style than mine—I look better than I ever have, and it feels entirely meaningless. I'm not five minutes in and I'm already wondering if I can feign illness to get out of it.

I make polite conversation during the seated dinner, but otherwise say very little. I've tried the routine where you become best friends with your colleagues and know how meaningless those friendships are in the end. If I make a single mistake at FMG, my supposed friends will shun me the same way my friends at Stadler did, so why would I bother?

Afterward, I get some face time with each of the partners, just enough that no one can doubt I showed up, but by ten I am entirely over this whole experience. I'm about to leave when Nicole corners me.

"Do you know what Ben's deal is?" she asks.

"Ben?" I ask, brow furrowed. "Ben Tate?"

I'm trying a little too hard. There's only one Ben at our firm.

"Yeah," she says. "Like...is he seeing anyone? I haven't heard any gossip about him in a while."

The idea of Ben seeing someone makes me freeze inside. "Why would I know anything about Ben?" I ask.

"Well, I mean...you're always together," she says. "And you're the only person he talks to."

I stare at her. "That's not true. Ben talks to everyone."

"About *work*, sure," she says, rolling her eyes. "You're the only one he...you know, seems to chat with."

I hardly think Ben implying my vagina has teeth is the same thing as *chatting*, but what a strange way for her to perceive us.

"Oh," she says. "Speak of the devil."

I follow her gaze to the door, and my whole body goes loose and tight in the same moment.

Ben is here, tugging on his black tie as he scans the room. It's only when he sees me that he stops looking. And for a single moment, locked in his gaze, I feel absolutely complete.

People approach, slap him on the back, shake his hand, and he's still keeping me in his line of sight.

"I can't believe he flew all the way back for this," says Nicole.

I can't either. It's at least a five-hour flight, and a ninety-minute drive, and then he'll have to do it all over again tomorrow when he returns.

"It's a waste of resources," I reply. And yet...and yet...I have the stupidest, most pathetic desire to smile.

He's already surrounded, of course. Ben is, for better or worse, the star of our firm. The partners all think he will put us in the headlines. The associates think he's their ticket to bigger and better cases. And I know I should stop watching him but I can't seem to make myself do it.

"He keeps looking over here," Nicole says. "Is my lipstick okay? I'm going to say hi."

Her lips are chapped and her lipstick is mostly smudged off aside from the bright red ring of her lipliner. It looks terrible. "Yes," I reply, "it's great." Not exactly my finest moment of supporting a fellow sister, but no one's a champion 24/7.

She saunters toward him, hips swaying, and a small fire starts in my chest. I consider following her except...what happens now, if I'm one of the pathetic associates who sidles up beside him? He might reference our kiss or—worse—not acknowledge it at all. Maybe he'll forget about it, in the mad rush of adulation from our colleagues. Maybe he'd have forgotten either way.

And I just...can't. I can't live through that right now.

I cut through the crowd toward the exit, escaping into the

empty hallway. *Pinterest Gemma*, the girl who wanted to see the world and decorate a home one day, would not approve, but Pinterest Gemma is someone who made tons of bad decisions and wound up with a broken heart.

When I reach my room, I strip off my dress and get in the shower, scrubbing the makeup from my face and telling myself I've done the right thing. The responsible thing.

I put on sleep shorts and a tank then grab my phone to plug it in...which is when I see the text, sent by Ben minutes ago, just as I was getting into the shower.

BEN

> I flew across the country and drove over an hour, only to see you. I'm heading to my room. #312. The door is unlocked.

I sink onto the bed. Is it true? Did he really come all the way here for me? And am I actually considering this? I picture him somewhere down the hall, stretched out, a tangle of sheets and bare skin, waiting for me. I picture what might happen if I did go—his weight above me, the sounds he might make.

No.

The absolute last thing I'm doing at this retreat is sleeping with a partner. Maybe he'll be disappointed, but it's for the best because he's not what I want, and I'm not what he wants, and this could never, ever end up being something I was glad I did.

I reach to turn off the light, and then it hits me: this chance might not come again. How many times, exactly, will he put himself out there before he just stops trying? And that thought is all it takes: I'm out of bed again, grabbing a robe before I slip into the hallway. I hesitate outside his door for only a moment before I turn the handle and walk inside, padding toward him in bare feet. Moonlight filters through the curtains, provides just enough light to see him there in bed, shirtless. I stop in my tracks.

This is a terrible idea.

"Gemma," he growls. "Come here."

It's a demand, not a request. It should hasten my exit from his room, but instead my feet are moving toward him. When I reach his side, he pulls me down to the bed, on top of him, as if he can't wait the extra few seconds it would have taken me to get there on my own.

I stare at him in shock, and his gaze locks with mine as he winds his fingers through my hair. I expect him to smirk, to look irritatingly victorious, but instead...he's *relieved*.

As ridiculously overconfident as he appears, he flew across the country and drove to Ojai for *this*, for *me*, with no idea at all if it would work. And he wanted it to work—from the feel of him, hard as steel beneath me—he *really* wanted it to work.

I lean down and press my lips to his—the lightest brush. He groans, as if he's been waiting a very long time for me to do it, and his hands press to my scalp, bringing my mouth back to his before I can pull away.

He's still kissing me as he rolls me to my back, as his hands graze my rib cage, my breasts, before gripping the hem of my tank. "Take this off," he demands, pulling it overhead. We are both naked from the waist up now. It's decadent, how good it feels to be like this with him, skin to skin. I think of that night on his desk, and the memory has me clenching, as if he's already inside me.

His hand slides up to cup my breast, to run the pad of his thumb over my nipple, making it ache before he takes it between his teeth. He pulls at it hard, suddenly, with a force that is pleasure and pain at once. I want more, but his lips press softly to the underside of my breast instead. My hips buck, impatient, and he laughs. "You liked that before, didn't you?"

"*Yes*." The word is carried on a gasp as his index finger slides inside my shorts. I'm so wet that I can *hear* it as his fingers glide between my legs.

Air hisses between his teeth. "God. I love that."

His thumb goes to my clit as he leans down again, sucking my nipple into his mouth, using his teeth in a way that...pierces me. Something in that pleasure with just a hint of pain has me raw and swollen and desperate for more. My nails dig into his back.

"I want you inside me," I tell him.

"Fuck," he groans against my skin. "*Yes.* But this will be over in seconds if we do it your way." He pushes my shorts off and slides farther down the bed before he spreads my thighs. The first hit of his tongue has me arching off the mattress.

"You don't need to do that," I gasp.

I feel his breath against my skin as he laughs. "Gemma, I'm doing exactly what I've wanted to do for two fucking years."

Holy shit.

His perfect tongue continues to flick and my breath grows short. He's so good at this, so certain of what he wants, and he watches me the entire time, as if nothing matters more to him in the whole fucking world than my reaction. I twist in the sheets, and his fingers push inside me, keeping time with his tongue.

"This has me so hard it hurts," he says. His free hand slides down to grip himself and stays there. Squeezing, stroking through his boxers.

There's a tiny burst of sparks at the center of my spine, and I gasp. "I'm close."

He pushes those fingers inside me again as I unfurl, barely aware of him continuing to draw my orgasm out, barely aware of the way he groans, watching me.

My eyes open—slowly, languorously.

"Jesus," he grunts, and then he's reaching for a condom on the nightstand, ripping the packet and rolling it on.

He pushes inside me with a quiet gasp, his eyes closing for a half second before they open again to study my face. He's making sure I'm okay, that *this* is still okay, and God, it is. He thrusts harder the second time, his hands sliding up to cup my breasts, then beneath me to grab my ass. Every sound I make is like a trigger for him, his eyes closing, his jaw grinding, as if he's about to be pushed over the edge.

His mouth is against my ear. "Do you have any idea how many times the memory of you on my desk has made me come?"

I thrill at his words, spreading my legs wider to take more of him. My nails dig into his ass, and his inhale is sharp, surprised. His hips jerk forward and then he's leaning over me, moving faster. "Oh. *God.*"

There's no part of him that isn't too big for me—his cock, his size, his ego—yet I'm the one making *him* dissolve.

"Yes," I whisper, my pulse racing, my body arching off the bed. "Don't stop."

My mouth burrows into his neck and he releases another of those sharp gasps. His hands wrap around my wrists, pinning me, and there's something in that tiny hint of possession and control that makes me come undone.

I bury my mouth against his shoulder to muffle the sounds I make as I let go.

"Fuck," he says and then he thrusts hard, again and again, before coming with a quiet groan.

We are pressed tight, his chest moving fast against mine, his harsh breathing against my ear. When he pulls out at last, gripping himself to keep the condom in place, the room is silent, and I hear my own thoughts a little too well.

I don't ever want it to end.

He rises to get rid of the condom and returns, pulling me against him. His mouth brushes the top of my head, but it's different now...as if I'm someone he actually cares about, as if this mattered. I'm scared I might start to believe it. And he isn't what I want anyway. I want someone simple, someone who won't lie to me or eventually change his mind, and I'd be crazy to think that could be Ben.

I slide out of the bed and grab my clothes off the floor.

"What are you doing?" he asks.

"I have to go," I tell him. "But thanks."

He laughs but the sound is muted and unhappy. "I can't believe you just *thanked* me," he says, running a hand over his face. "Get back in bed."

But I'm already pulling up my shorts as I walk away. "I've really got to go," I tell him, practically running from the room.

23

H e's gone Sunday morning when I reach the buffet.
"What a great guy," says Nicole. "He flew all that way for one hour at a party."

I think of him watching my face as he fucked me, his eyes hazy, his jaw clenching as he got close.

"Well, it's not like he was saving orphans from a burning building," I reply.

I skip the post-brunch activities, claiming I have work, but the thought of the empty office is just too unappealing, so I go home instead—which isn't much better.

"Are you busy?" I ask Keeley when I return her call.

"Yes," she says. "I'm trying to decide if I want Oreos or barbeque potato chips from the vending machine."

"Are you certain you're a doctor?" I open my refrigerator, which is just as empty as I anticipated. I should have actually eaten at this morning's brunch. "Like, was it a real medical school, or was it a strip mall with a handwritten sign out front that just *said* medical school?"

"Fine, Miss Judgmental. I'll get the Sun Chips. I'm pretty

sure they're health food because I don't enjoy them. Anyway, how was sex with Ben?"

I blink. "What makes you think I had sex with Ben?"

"Are we really doing this dance right now? You obviously did. You sound intensely invested, which *always* means it's about Ben, but you sound a little horrified, which means you either slept with him or murdered him. I can't help you with removing the evidence if you murdered him, by the way, because I'm stuck at the hospital until tomorrow."

I shut the refrigerator door. Clearly, no food is going to materialize through continued staring. "Like I'd ask *you* to help me remove evidence. You'd leave a trail of Hot Tamales leading right to the burial site."

"If you think I'd drop Hot Tamales and not eat them straight off the ground, you don't know me very well," she says. "Anyway. The sex?"

"It wasn't a big deal."

She laughs. "*Shut* up."

"It *wasn't.*"

"Fine. I don't believe you but I'll play your game. So what happens now?"

"Nothing, obviously. It's not like I'd date him."

"I'm no one to throw stones, but it seems to me your bar for who you *sleep with* should be set higher than your bar for who you'd *date.*"

As loathe as I am to accept advice on this matter from a woman who once seduced a *monk* during a silent meditation retreat, she has a point. "It's not that he isn't good enough," I admit aloud for the first time ever. "It's that he's not what I want."

"Ah, yes," she says, with a quiet laugh. "You still want flannel boy—the wise, widowed but strangely youthful farmer. I mean, what would you even wear on a farm? Do you own a pair of boots?"

"Yes," I begin. "I have the Burberry—"

"Boots that aren't designer, or suede or high-heeled."

"Oh," I say with a sigh. "Shut up."

She laughs. "Just think about it, honey. Because repeatedly hooking up with a man you've talked about obsessively for two years straight...doesn't sound like hate to me."

I guess it doesn't sound like hate to me either.

ON TUESDAY, Ben's case concludes. No one in the office can shut up about it, because it's the highest award FMG has ever won. Even *I'm* impressed, though I will never, ever, admit it.

I wake the next morning and put on a red dress before I take it off again. Red is the color of sex and I don't need him thinking I want a repeat of Saturday night when I don't.

He might not even be in today, I tell myself, watching the elevator as if it's my job. *There will be loose ends to tie up, a hotel room he's reserved for a few more days. We probably won't see him until next week.*

And just because he made me come in about ten seconds flat doesn't make him a keeper. But I think of him looking at my face as he went down on me. Saying, *"I'm doing exactly what I've wanted for two fucking years"*, and my thighs clench in both memory and anticipation.

It's late that afternoon when I hear a tiny smattering of applause, signaling his arrival, because he's the only person in this office anyone would clap for. He must have rushed back. I refuse to believe that means something.

I return to reviewing a promissory note, then I call my mother and convince her that the adorable pajamas I'm sending her are from a "cute little shop in Ojai" as opposed to Nordstrom. I clean out my inbox and cut and paste boilerplate to craft a threatening email to the school board on Victoria's behalf.

But every five minutes I'm thinking of Ben's weight above me and the sounds he made, and by the time evening falls my productivity has decreased to almost nothing. I want a repeat of Saturday like I want my next breath, even if it means going against every warning voice in my head.

I rise and walk to the break room, my heels *clip-clip-clipping* against the hardwood floor, a modern-day mating call, my way of luring Ben from his lair.

I slide open a drawer in the kitchen, surveying its contents blindly, *willing* him to come to me.

A door hinge creaks, followed by male steps, and I can't seem to regulate my breathing.

I'd know that footfall anywhere, the sounds he makes as he approaches, surprisingly quiet for his size.

I turn, expecting him to say something, to make a joke or address the way I ran out of his room like a coward last weekend. But he says nothing. He doesn't even smile. He simply moves forward, and he doesn't stop until our bodies are flush. I gasp—some combination of surprise and pleasure—while his hands grip my hips, pulling me closer.

"The outfits you wear fucking destroy me," he says. There is something so certain in his voice, so determined... Maybe he— like me—has been pushed too far to wait any longer.

Only the faintest shred of common sense has me yanking him into the closet. He pulls the door shut. "Someone could walk in," I warn. "This needs to be fast."

He spins me toward the closed door and places my palms against it. "Fast is my middle name."

"That's a terrible middle name," I reply, but then his palm is on my inner thigh, moving upward, and his fingers slide beneath the elastic of my thong, and I can't even remember what we were discussing.

"Jesus," he says quietly, against my ear. "You're so fucking wet."

I want to tell him it's not for him. I want to tell him almost anything that won't give him the credit, but then two fingers push inside me and my head falls to the door. "Condom," I demand. I hear the tearing of foil almost instantly. "Naturally you have one."

"I'm happy to skip it," he suggests, rolling it on. "Since you're complaining."

I laugh. "Yeah, you wi—" The words are cut off as he pushes inside me. I brace against the door, unprepared for the fullness of it, for how complete it makes me feel when we are like this. He does it again, harder, his hands sliding up beneath my shirt, palming my breasts.

"You," he says, the words timed with his thrusts, "are so fucking mouthy."

"You love it," I gasp as he seats himself inside me again. And it's only after I've said the words that I realize how true they are. He *does* love it. No matter what I do to keep him at arm's length, he keeps coming back for me.

The sounds we make echo inside the pantry—my gasps and his filthy words against my ear, my body hitting the door with each wet thrust.

"Jesus," he gasps, "I'm so close, Gemma. Tell me what to do."

I pull one of his hands between my legs. "That."

He gives a low groan. "That just made it worse. I'm gonna come so fucking hard, baby."

I can't begin to explain why his words have the effect they do. Why I shiver, why my skin breaks out in goose bumps. Maybe it's the quiet desperation in his voice as he says them. Maybe some stupid part of me likes being called *baby*. "God, yes," I whisper. "Just like that."

"You're close?" he asks. "Oh. *God*. God."

The idea of him losing control like this is what puts me over the edge. "Cover my mouth," I beg, and he does, sinking his teeth into my shoulder to muffle his groan as we both fall apart.

For a single moment it's like I'm floating in space, released at last from everything. I have no idea why we haven't been doing exactly this, all along. I don't even remember why I hated him or why I've been pushing him away.

When my eyes open, my cheek is flat to the door, my fingers and legs spread wide. I can still feel the rise and fall of his chest against my back.

"Jesus," he whispers.

I want to stay like this. I want him to remain inside me, pressed to my back, still overcome by something that had even a little bit to do with me.

He slides out, still hard. I tuck my shirt in while he does God-knows-what with the condom.

"If you're leaving that for Debbie to find, make sure you label it so she knows it's yours."

"I'll borrow those Sharpies you ordered," he says with a quiet smile, one that almost seems...affectionate.

That smile leaves me feeling strangely weak and uncertain. It makes me want to believe he's not someone like my dad, that he won't eventually take some naïve woman's best years and destroy her when he's ready for fresher fields.

I swallow. "Are we good?"

He arches a brow, and then he presses me to the door. His kiss is soft, slow and very thorough. "Has anyone ever told you your post-coital charm could use some work?"

I laugh. "Why would I bother being charming now? I already got what I came here for."

He tips my chin up to face him. "So you're admitting you came to the break room *hoping* this would happen?"

Dammit.

"I'm admitting I came to the break room hoping to find something to eat and didn't *object* to this happening."

He studies my face, searching for something. "Why don't we go to dinner?" he says at last.

I bite my lip. Why the hell would we sit down together on purpose? I can't imagine what we will possibly have to say to each other over a meal once we're through discussing the case. "It's late," I reply.

His head tilts. "Tomorrow, then." I'm not sure if his persistence is cute or aggravating. But then his lips brush my temple, my cheek, as if I'm precious to him, and the ice in my heart melts a little.

"This isn't some elaborate attempt to poison me, is it?"

His mouth curves to the side. "Not an *elaborate* one, no."

I laugh. "Okay," I concede. Maybe he's not irritating. Maybe there's a rope stretched taut between us and he's doing his best to keep me from dropping my end and walking away. And maybe, possibly, he's a little uncertain too.

"I'll get us a table at Bavel," he says.

It's a restaurant I've always wanted to try, but this is weird, us agreeing with each other. "What if I hate Mediterranean food?" I challenge.

"Then it would be pretty bizarre that you go get it on the three days you eat lunch. Salad with feta and hummus and grilled chicken."

How the hell does he know what I eat three days a week? It's unsettling.

"I see your poisoning scheme has been in the works for some time," I finally say, because it's safer than wondering too hard about why he knows my lunch order.

He laughs to himself, as if he's participating in a different version of our story than I am, and kisses me before reaching for the doorknob. "Stay put. I'll knock if it's clear."

A moment later the knock comes, and I step into the light,

my teeth sinking into my lip. There are terrifying things inside me right now—gratitude, hope, fear. I don't want to let any of them grow.

"Thanks," I say quietly.

"Six fifteen tomorrow," he says. "I'll drive."

"You don't have to—"

"I'm not letting you chicken out of this, Gemma."

I'm about to argue that I wouldn't chicken out of anything, but that's entirely untrue.

I've been hiding under the covers for the two years since Ben arrived.

24

I meet Ben in the garage and agree to let him drive. Bavel is far enough from the office that we're unlikely to be seen together, but I've brought some files with me just in case.

"Are you okay?" he asks, giving me a sidelong glance as he pulls out.

No, because this feels like a terrible idea on every front imaginable. "I guess I just never foresaw eating dinner with you by choice after you stole Brewer Campbell from me. Past Gemma is highly disappointed in Present Gemma."

"But she didn't mind you sleeping with me repeatedly?" he asks with a grin, and I squirm in my seat.

"Those were spur-of-the-moment mistakes." Mistakes I clearly plan to repeat. "This is intentional."

He laughs, because he knows I'm full of shit. "Brewer Campbell was not my fault. I had no idea until you started giving me death stares at every meeting that the client Fields assigned me was supposed to go to you."

I sigh. Holding that grudge has made me feel safe from him, somehow, but I guess it was no longer working anyway. "You could have at least sent some of the Brewer Campbell work my way," I mutter.

"It would have been awkward with you giving me the finger and telling me to go fuck myself every time I approached," he replies, and I give in and laugh, because yeah...that sounds like me.

He hands his car keys to a valet then walks me inside the restaurant, which is intimate and romantic—white tablecloths and candlelight.

"Is this where you bring all your nineteen year olds?" I ask as we take our seats.

He sighs and laughs at once, as if I'm both amusing and tedious. "If only you had any dating history to speak of so I could ridicule you as well."

"I've dated."

"Who? Thomas?" he demands. "Tell me, Gemma, where exactly was he a chef?"

That's really not a topic I want to get into. "Let's keep the past in the past."

His triumphant smile isn't nearly as annoying as it should be.

He opens the menu. "Is Malbec okay?" he asks.

I nod, trying not to let on how much I like that he asked. A man who can't even make sure you like red wine before he orders isn't going to worry about your feelings when he starts wanting to fuck his secretary, either.

When the waiter departs, I half expect awkward silence to descend. I'm on the cusp of bringing up Lawson, just to fill the space, but somehow we end up talking about other things, and we just don't stop. We discuss whether the new justice will affect the makeup of the court, how California should be dealing with the drought, whether Becky in accounting is sleeping with the UPS guy. And sure, we spend a fair amount of that time arguing, but it's...fun. I can't remember the last time I wasn't counting the minutes until a date ended, but with Ben, it almost feels like it's going too fast. Dinner is served, and there's so much to say, so much to hear, that I have to remind myself to eat.

Until he asks about Iceland, that is.

"What's the deal with that?" he prods. "You've mentioned it to Terri. Something about a proposal?"

I never realized he was listening to my conversations quite so carefully. I could claim it was a joke, but this is probably a good time to make a few things between us crystal clear. "That's where my future boyfriend will eventually propose. I saw it in a movie once." I grin widely. "My *non-lawyer* boyfriend."

He nods. "Right, right. Because you only date chefs."

"Not just chefs," I reply. "I'm open to several occupations. Widowed veterinarian, owner of a Christmas tree farm, or proprietor of a bed and breakfast."

His mouth twitches. "And how exactly does this proposal unfold?"

"You're ridiculing me and I don't care. One day when I'm posting a video of my small but tasteful ring with the Northern Lights behind me and a children's choir performing, you'll see how wrong you were."

"Ah, so now the Northern Lights happen to be behind you? I didn't realize you'd even planned out the acts of God that will need to occur. Very thorough."

I bite down on a smile as I shrug. "Obviously, I'd understand if that part didn't happen. I'd be *disappointed*, but I'd understand."

"That's generous of you. What about the fact that you'd hate Iceland? You get cold when the office is set below seventy-two."

"I—"

"And no owner of a small bed-and-breakfast can just take off for a few weeks to go to Iceland."

I set down my fork. "Any other dreams you'd like to crush, Ben?"

"Well," he says, "you'd have to share them with me first."

I laugh, and then our eyes hold, and he's smiling, and lust hits me out of nowhere. Not the normal kind of lust, not even the normal kind of lust I feel for *Ben*, but the sort that makes me feel a little deranged, that has me wondering if he'd follow me to the bathroom if I suggested it. Maybe that *is* sort of the normal lust I feel for Ben. I want him to pin me to his desk, just like he did the first time.

"Let's get out of here," I say.

His gaze sharpens, grows predatory, in a second's time. I've never seen a man pay a check faster than he does ours.

His fingers twine with mine as we walk to the waiting car, and even that tiny bit of intimacy makes my breath catch. He climbs in beside me, and suddenly...we're alone. In a small, enclosed space. I cross my legs and his eyes go to my bare calves and then my heels. He swallows and I can barely stand *not* to lean over and press my lips to his neck.

We get back to the parking garage in record time. He reaches over the console toward me, pulling my mouth to his. "I've wanted to do that all night," he says.

"I want you to do a lot more than that."

"God, yes," he groans, resting his forehead against mine. "Your place?"

"Uh—" If he comes to my place, then I can't get him to leave. Suddenly he's staying the night, showering, leaving items behind. I pull back. "Let's just go upstairs. It's closer."

He studies my face. "You only live a few blocks away."

"Your office is twenty seconds away by elevator," I argue.

I see a tiny flicker of disappointment in his eyes. "We aren't having sex in the office again."

My jaw drops. "Why the hell not? What was the purpose of all this, then?"

His hand reaches out to cradle my face. "Maybe I just wanted to get to know you better," he says. "Or maybe I really wanted to poison you."

"I know which of those is more likely," I mutter, rolling my eyes, "so it looks like I'm heading to the ER. Thanks, *Ben*."

He laughs, and then he gives me the sweetest, most tender smile. Not unlike the look he has on his face in Drew's wedding photos. "I want to be someone you trust enough to invite home, Gemma. And I'm willing to wait for it."

There's a small squeeze in my chest, and I can't tell if it's pleasure or terror.

"I'm only falling for this whole *dinner* ruse once," I say, unbuckling my seat belt.

He grins. "I'll have to come up with something new the next time."

I climb out. "There won't be a next time."

He waits until I'm safely in my car and driving away before he texts:

BEN

Sure there won't.

I smile like a fool the rest of the way home.

25

"I can't believe he told me *no*," I complain to Keeley.

She laughs. "That's just the worst when a man expresses interest in who you are as a person. What a *dick*."

"I just don't get it. I mean, I know it's not going anywhere. He knows it's not going anywhere. The milk is very clearly free so no need to buy the cow. Why wouldn't he take the free milk?"

"Please stop talking about milk," she says. I hear the beep of the vending machine—it's seven in the morning and she's already buying junk food. "It makes me think of cervical mucus, or breast milk. Maybe he just couldn't perform again?"

"It'd been twenty-four hours, and he's thirty-six. That's not old enough for stuff to stop working, right?"

"He's only thirty-six?" she shouts. "You said he was *old*! No, that's not an age at which anything stops working."

Which leaves me back at the drawing board, wondering why the hell he's acting like this is more than it is.

I put on the red dress I discarded a few days ago and take it right back off. Nothing has changed in the two days since I decided red was the color of sex and I refuse to let Mr. *Maybe-I-Wanted-to-Get-to-Know-You* think I'm trying to seduce him. That ship has sailed.

I will take my free milk elsewhere. Fuck Ben. *No more free milk. I'm putting it back on the shelf, in the paid marketplace.*

I probably need to work on my analogies.

I get to the office and try to focus, but it's a struggle. Every two seconds I'm picturing him looking at me last night—saying, *"I want to be someone you trust enough to invite home."* And each time I think of it, I soften a little, but how long would those good intentions of his possibly last? I let him come over once, and then he *keeps* coming over, and the moment I decide to trust him is the moment he'll decide to move on to something else.

I put my head down and focus on the Lawson case. I've found ten different employee reviews now of managers who got promoted despite "incidents". It's probably enough to get Margaret a decent settlement, but I want better than *decent*. I want a number so high that it gets the press's attention and Fiducia is forced to publicly admit they fucked up. But how? Margaret said there were outings she hadn't been invited to. Maybe it was discriminatory, or maybe Margaret is the pain in the ass they've implied she is, and they just didn't want her along.

I call and she sounds excited to be hearing from me, which is unfortunate since I don't have any especially good news. "How's it going?" she asks.

Not as well as I'd like.

"Great," I say. "But we need more, so I've got a quick question for you. You said there were a bunch of trips and nights out for staff that you weren't invited to. Were other women invited? And do you know what they were doing?"

"Not as far as I know," she replies. "It sounds like it was

mostly drinking, but a girl in accounting told me they were always at strip clubs too."

My foot starts to tap furiously. "Strip clubs," I repeat. If someone in accounting knows about outings to strip clubs, that probably means they were submitted as an expense, yet there was no mention of them in the reports sent to us. "Would she talk to us?"

"I doubt it," Margaret says. "She's still there. She'd lose her job."

"No one has to know," I promise. "It would be completely, one hundred percent off the record."

One hour later I've got a meeting set up with Leona, the woman in accounting. Ben's out of the office, but I'm too excited not to tell him. I call, feeling the oddest tension inside me at the sound of his gravelly, *"hello"*—I don't know if it's fear or excitement.

"Are you busy?" I ask.

"I'm pretty busy," he replies.

I roll my eyes. "You're not that busy. You wouldn't have answered if you were." I quickly sum up the call with Leona and tell him she wants to meet at her house because she can't afford to be seen with me.

"That's amazing," he says. "I'm in court all day, but I'll be out of here by five."

Oh. So, he actually is busy. And he still took my call.

I wouldn't have taken his.

"You're not going to convince her to testify," I argue. "I'm capable of collecting facts on my own."

"Are we certain about that? Because only one of us has made partner so far."

I laugh. "You just love to throw that in my face."

I can hear the smile in his voice. "I do. Mostly because you laugh, every fucking time."

WHEN WE ARRIVE at the address in Beverly Hills, Leona is waiting by the side gate. She leads us into the pool house she's renting and takes the seat across from us. "I need you to promise this will never get out," she says. "I can't afford to lose my job right now, and they'd find a way to fire me, I assure you."

"Your name will never come up, unless you change your mind," Ben says.

His voice seems to soothe her. He comes across as trustworthy to strangers. He's even starting to seem trustworthy to me. I wish he wasn't.

She crosses the room to the kitchen counter and grabs a file. "I made copies of the expense reports. It's been going on for years."

I take it from her and open it on the coffee table so Ben and I can look at the same time.

The amounts spent are outrageous. Some are out of town, accompanied by massive hotel bills and greens fees, but most of them are in LA, at a club near their office.

"It's always pissed me off," she says. "We have employees who need to work a second job just to survive, and these assholes are blowing twenty grand on girls?"

She tells us most of the staff knows nothing about these outings until the guys come in talking about it the next day, with an expense report filed a few weeks later. Only one female, Lauren, was ever invited. "They said she could come but only if she got on stage," Leona scoffs. "As if she'd want to come anyway. What woman would feel comfortable in that situation?"

And that's precisely the problem: men in power keep the circle closed by making it uncomfortable for women to step inside, which leads to a conference room full of men in gray suits making more decisions that only benefit them.

"We need to make sure we go about this in a way that it can't be traced to her," I say, once we're in the car. "We'll have to work backward. Get proof from the strip clubs that those charges went on a company card. I know an investigator who can help us."

"And talk to Lauren, if we can find her," he adds.

I notice he's driving farther into Beverly Hills, rather than back toward the office. "Where are we going?"

"I've got to run by a friend's house," he says.

"A friend?" I ask. I sound wary, which I am, but inside I'm the tiniest bit pleased. Kyle and I were on different coasts and had separate lives. If I'm ever with someone again, I don't want to be on the outside.

"Don't worry," he says, "no one's home. But he lives around the corner and asked me to pick up his mail."

I'm equal parts relieved and disappointed.

A few minutes later, he pulls into the circular drive of a monstrously tacky mansion.

I laugh as I climb from the car. "You have friends who live *here*?"

"They *used* to live here. Tali hated it. It's on the market now, and they moved into a much nicer place off Mulholland Drive."

"It's the turrets," I say. "Were they worried the Romans would invade?"

"Hayes went through a very long, very strange phase before he met his wife. It seems to be over now."

He enters a code into the front door and crosses the hall to disable the alarm.

"You're sure we're not going to get arrested for trespassing?"

"I'm sure *I* won't be," he says with a grin, scooping the mail off the floor.

He leads me through the mostly empty house and we walk out to a large covered terrace and down a flight of stairs, where a long, rectangular pool glimmers in the moonlight. At its edge, he kicks off his shoes and rolls up his pants before taking a seat, letting his legs slide into the water. Warily, I kick off my shoes and sit beside him.

I look around. "So where are your friends, anyway? Why can't they get their own mail?"

"They're in Italy working on a second kid this week," he says.

"Only married people would refer to having sex repeatedly as *work*."

He laughs. "They'd change your thoughts on marriage. They're happy together."

I want to say, *"sure, until one of them gets bored"*, but a part of me is tired of being that person. A part of me wants to be a bit more like Ben, someone who still has faith in the concept of *forever*.

"You've done some family law," I say quietly. "How can you still be such an optimist?"

"There's a reason I no longer do it. Once you see bad marriages, you start looking for more of them. You start believing that fifty percent of couples split up, and the other fifty percent are fooling themselves. And I know that's not the truth. It isn't that way for my friends. It wasn't like that for my parents."

His eyes darken for a quick second. I've known other people who lost a parent young, and most of them seem to have accepted it, moved past it. I get the sense, somehow, that Ben hasn't.

"That must have been so hard on your mom," I venture. "She's lucky she had you and your brother."

"Actually, there are four of us. It's me, then Graham, then Simon, and then Colin."

I blink. His mother was widowed with four young sons, one of them a newborn. My heart gives a small twist. "God," I whisper, "she must have been so overwhelmed."

"She was," he says quietly. "It took a long time for her to come back from it."

I want to ask what he means, how long is a "long time", but it's clearly a topic he's not comfortable with. Seeing that repressed sadness in Ben makes something soften inside me. I have an almost overwhelming desire to touch him, to twine my fingers with his. I slide my hands beneath my thighs instead.

"What about you?" he asks. "No siblings?"

I shake my head. "No, thank God. My mom always wanted more but it didn't happen."

His brow furrows. "You wouldn't have wanted siblings?"

"Sure, if they were my *mother's* kids. My dad always implied it was *her* fault she didn't get pregnant again, but then nothing happened with his next wife either, and I'm glad it didn't." It would have crushed my mother to see him create an entirely new family when she'd wanted it for them so much. "Go ahead: tell me how wrong it is to gloat over a couple's infertility."

He laughs, leaning toward me. "I'd have expected nothing less." He kisses me then, his lips soft and certain on mine, as if to say, *"it's okay that you're like this, it's okay that you're petty, that you're vicious in court, that you push people away. I like you anyhow."*

He pulls back slowly, reluctantly, and helps me to my feet. I kind of wish we were staying. I wish he'd kissed me a little longer.

"If it weren't for the turrets," I suggest, "this would be a pretty nice place."

"It's okay." He grins. "Not as amazing as your mom's though, obviously, with that shelf of doom hanging over her cats."

I don't even think...I push him. He isn't expecting it, and I wasn't entirely expecting him to lose his balance—*hoping*, yes, but not expecting—and he goes right into the deep end. My laughter echoes over the pool deck, and I have not a moment's guilt until his head emerges...and he's flailing.

"Gemma," he gasps, "I can't swim."

"Oh my God, are you serious?" I demand, suddenly panicked. Who the fuck doesn't know how to swim in this day and age? His head goes under again, his hands above the water. It takes me one full second to unfreeze and jump wildly into the pool, where—the very moment my head breaks the surface —he starts laughing. He's treading water with a big fucking grin on his face.

Of course, he knew how to swim.

"You asshole!" I shout. "I thought you were drowning! Now I'm soaking wet."

He gives me a lopsided grin. "Is this a bad time to point out that you pushed me in the pool first?"

"You scared the shit out of me, though!" I cry, making my way to the edge. "It's entirely different."

"I completed an open water one-mile swim last year. I thought you knew."

"I did," I fume. Everyone in the office couldn't stop talking about *Ben's triathlon, Ben's triathlon*, like he'd won the Nobel Peace Prize. "I just panicked and forgot."

He pulls me against him, wrapping his arms around me. "It's cute you were panicked on my behalf."

"I was only panicking about my potential culpability if you died." My arms go around his shoulders, letting him keep us both afloat.

He pushes my skirt up and pulls me so my legs are wrapped around his waist.

"I'm not going to let you turn this bullshit into an excuse to have sex in your friend's pool," I inform him.

"Obviously not," he says, slipping his hand between my legs. "But I bet you let me get awfully close."

His thumb brushes back and forth outside my panties, the lightest, most delicate touch, strumming every nerve. I reach between us and palm him through his pants. He's so thick, so hard...My eyes fall closed. I will absolutely have sex in this pool.

He lifts me onto the edge before pushing me backward.

His mouth finds mine as he lowers himself on top of me. The adrenaline from only moments ago has shifted into something else, something desperate and reckless. His mouth descends to one tight nipple, and he sucks on it hard through the sheer fabric of my blouse. I wrap my legs around him until his erection is positioned exactly where I want it. If we could just get rid of all these fucking clothes it would take him two seconds to push inside me.

I reach for his belt, but he stays my hand. "Invite me over," he groans against my mouth.

"It's late," I reply. "We could be undressed in five seconds right here."

His lids close tight for a moment, and when they open, I see resignation there. "You know what I want," he says, lifting himself off me. "And I'm still going to fucking wait."

But...but...*goddammit.*

He reaches out a hand to help me up and I accept it reluctantly. Water pours from our clothes, from my hair. My mascara is undoubtedly proving to be less waterproof than promised. I want to blame him for how irritated I am right now, but I'm not sure I can.

We gather our things and walk through the side gate to his car, soaking wet. He drives me back to the parking garage and leans over to kiss me once we arrive.

"I'll see you Monday," he says as I climb out.

I assumed he'd be in this weekend. The fact that he won't makes me wish I'd given him a different answer in the pool. Maybe inviting him over *once* wouldn't have been the end of the world.

26

I wake thinking about Ben.

I think about him as I dress, as I drive, as I sit at my desk attempting to work.

Everything reminds me of sex: the seat beneath me, the breeze that gusts as I walk down the street, a male voice in the hallway.

I send emails without attachments, forget my own phone number at the grocery store. I call my mom Sunday and call her again an hour later, having completely forgotten we spoke. I'm halfway to my car Monday morning before I realize I'm wearing two different shoes. If Ben's trying to secure the partnership for Craig by making me stupid with lust, he's doing an excellent job.

We don't come face-to-face until Monday afternoon. I'm on my way back from a client lunch, running because it's starting to rain when he's suddenly in front of me, walking from the other direction.

His gaze falls to my wet button-down, now clinging to my curves. "Jesus," he says, holding the door.

"This can't be one of the outfits," I argue quietly.

He leans close as we wait to go through the metal detector. "They're *all* one of the outfits, Gemma."

I release a shaky breath, and my nipples tighten beneath my damp bra. His gaze flickers there, as if he knows.

We climb on to the elevator and move toward the back. I stand in front of him, the same way I did in Miami. Out of view, without making a sound, he pulls me against his semi-erect cock. I glance to our right but no one has noticed. I look over my shoulder at him and he simply holds my gaze, daring me to move.

I swallow loudly. The elevator stops and one person climbs out, two people climb in. In the resulting shuffle, he pulses once against me, very intentionally, and all my air leaves me in a rush. I try to keep my breathing even and my expression calm. If anyone from the office sees this, I'm screwed, but there is something incredibly erotic about the risk of it all.

He does it again on the next floor. I reach back and dig my hand into his thigh for balance.

The door opens again. "Let's go to your apartment," he says quietly.

My eyes fall closed. "The office is closer." We pass our floor but neither of us move, and when the last people climb off, he reaches past me, and hits the button for the parking garage.

"What are you doing?"

He laughs. "You live above Whole Foods. That's five minutes from here."

"But your office would be faster," I continue to argue, also wondering how he knows where I live. He pulls me tight against him.

"Nothing about tonight will go fast," he says against my ear.

~

I'M at my door and have just slid my key in the lock when I hear him approaching. My heart beats harder and faster. This is all I've thought about for a week straight, but I'm suddenly searching for a way to back out.

I turn, biting my lip as I glance up at him. His mouth curves to the left just a hint, and he presses me to the door, his body warm and solid against mine. He's so much taller I have to crane my neck to meet his gaze.

"No, Gemma, you don't get to cancel on me," he says.

My laughter is startled, but also relieved. I guess I'm more transparent than I thought.

"Okay," I whisper, sliding my hands up his neck as he leans down to kiss me.

Has it only been since Friday that we last kissed? It seems like so much longer. My palms slide into his hair, then to his jaw—rough, in need of a shave. He presses me harder to the door, his hand on my hip, pinning me there, and his mouth opens, demanding more. His erection is wedged right in the center of my rib cage. I reach between us and run my palm over him.

"Open the fucking door," he growls, and I can't even recall why I was resistant before. I turn the key in the lock, then he backs me inside the apartment. We don't stop until we're at the kitchen counter, where I grab his tie and pull his mouth back to mine. His hands, tight on my hips, slide back to grab my ass, to pull me tighter against him.

"Do you even live here," he murmurs against my mouth, glancing quickly at my bare apartment while I unknot his tie, "or is this just some rental you use for sex?"

The tie loosened, I begin to unbutton his shirt. His chest is firm and hot beneath my hands. There's so much of him to explore I can barely decide where to begin. "I've been too busy being a better lawyer than you to decorate."

"It's funny then," he says, pulling my blouse overhead, unzipping my skirt, "that you haven't made partner yet."

I laugh against my will.

He pushes my skirt to the floor and moves back just enough to let me step out of it, his eyes traveling over me—now in nothing but lingerie and Louboutins. I start to kick the shoes off and he stops me.

"Not yet," he says. "Those goddamn heels of yours have tortured me for two years straight."

I think maybe I knew this.

His hands are on his belt, tugging it free. His cock strains against his zipper. "Where first?" he asks.

"You're awfully certain there's going to be a second time."

"Gemma," he says, "I plan to fuck you on every surface of this apartment eventually."

He is smug and overconfident, and I should hate that...but I just don't. I *really* don't.

"Here." His surprised exhale is audible as I slide to my knees.

I pull his pants and boxers down at the same time. His cock springs free, heavy and stiff, a single bead of moisture at the tip.

"God, yes," he hisses as I take him in my mouth. His hand goes to my hair and he's watching, watching, his eyes dark and drugged, struggling to stay open.

His jaw locks tight as I find my rhythm. He moves my head with his hand, his encouragement guttural, barely intelligible. *So fucking good...the sight of your mouth around me...wanted this for so long.*

I take him farther, all the way to the back of my throat.

"Oh, God," he groans, his eyes squeezing tight. "Don't. You'll make me come."

The power I have over him right now is thrilling. I do it again, desperate to see him lose that last bit of control, and find myself lifted off the floor entirely. He grabs his wallet and carries me to my room, laying me under him on the bed. I arch, seeking friction, but he slides down instead, spreading my thighs wide. His tongue runs along the fine lace of my thong, which he then snaps hard enough to sting. Before I can complain, his tongue is there again, and he's pulling the thong aside, licking me, as if he's starved for this.

I could finish in seconds, but after nearly a full week of torment, I want more.

"Come up here," I beg, and his tongue swipes over me once more before he pushes my panties down my thighs and crawls above me.

He grabs a condom from the wallet he placed on the nightstand. I have an IUD and would probably let him go without, but say nothing as he rolls it on.

He grasps himself with one hand and slides inside me, watching my face as he does it.

I'd like to keep my eyes open but I can't. It's too *much*, too *good*. He already had me on the cusp of coming with his tongue, but now I can feel a different sort of orgasm building, one that has me clawing at him to get there. He moves my legs farther apart to watch as he pushes inside me. I'm spread wide for him, and in this new position, he's so deep that I feel him everywhere. The only thing better than the spot he is hitting is the way he watches it happen, entranced and heavy-lidded.

My nails dig into his back. "Faster," I demand, and he groans as he gives in, thrusting hard, his finger pressing to my clit, sweat dripping from his torso. The very second I shatter, he groans and lets go along with me.

"Jesus," he whispers against my neck. "I'm so impressed with myself right now."

I laugh, still trying to catch my breath. "Only *you* would claim to be impressed with yourself immediately after sex."

He ties off the condom, then pulls me against him. "I barely survived that thing you did with the back of your throat. Let's give credit where it's due."

I settle on his shoulder. It should be awkward, cuddling with Ben Tate, my enemy. Weirdly, it isn't.

He runs his palm over my bare hip. "So tell me something. How long have you been in this apartment?"

I narrow my eyes. I can already tell where this is going. "Three years."

"And in three years you haven't had a single spare weekend to—I don't know—hang a picture on the wall?"

"Oh, and because I'm female I'm supposed to care about things like that?"

"No, but you seem like the kind of person who'd have...I don't know, a Pinterest page devoted to decor?"

"You clearly don't know me very well."

His mouth curves into a half smile, as if he knows me better than I think.

I WAKE before my alarm in the morning. Ben is sound asleep beside me, dead to the world. I let my gaze drift over his lovely profile—the strong nose, the long lashes, the full mouth, serene in sleep. I consider waking him up the way he woke me in the middle of the night—pushing my thighs apart, his stubble against my softest skin, his tongue hot and warm and unhurried, saying, *"I couldn't wait anymore"*—but it's easier, less awkward, if I don't. I'll shower, leave him a note, ask him to lock up.

I'm being considerate, but Ben doesn't appear to think so when he walks into the bathroom a few minutes later.

"You weren't planning to shower and sneak off to work, were you?" he asks as he slides the glass door open. His eyes travel over me. I hold the loofah in the center of my chest, as if it's a shield. I have no idea how to play this now that he's shot my plan to shit.

"I was just trying to let you rest," I reply, which is a fucking lie and we both know it. I was avoiding him, plain and simple.

He decides not to argue with me as he steps into the shower. "You said my name in your sleep. I was going down on you, and you weren't even awake yet and you said, *'Ben',* all breathy."

"I probably would have said *'oh, Chris Hemsworth'* but it's such a mouthful," I reply, pouring body gel on the loofah.

"Is it so hard to admit you sort of like me?" He runs a hand over my hip, asking me to pay attention.

"Do you really need me to admit it when we just had sex repeatedly?"

"Yeah," he says softly. "I sort of do."

I can't entirely meet his eye. I've been here before, with someone asking me to open up, to be vulnerable. It was hard then, but it's harder now. Every time you gamble and lose, it gets a little scarier to try again.

He steps closer. Every bone in my body wants to make a joke right now, keep this light. But then maybe *I'll* be the one wounding him, and I don't want that either.

"On Mondays and Wednesdays, you go to the taco truck," I tell him, staring at the floor as I speak, divulging what feels like a shameful secret. "On Tuesdays and Thursdays, you get a wrap from the gym."

I can't tell him about driving past his house, or all the time I've spent on Drew Bailey's feed looking for photos of him. I feel exposed enough already. Too exposed. I swear to God if he makes fun of me for this it's over and I'll never speak to him again.

His hand comes up, curving around the corner of my jaw, pulling my gaze to his, our mouths inches apart. "You drink two cups of coffee every morning, always with milk, not cream, and a ridiculous amount of sugar. You'll eat an acai bowl at any hour of the day, and you're the only person alive who *prefers* strawberries to donuts, which is why I've been buying them for staff meetings for the past year."

I stare at him, asking myself how he knows all this, how long he's been watching me this carefully, and realizing the answer almost at the same time:

Always. He's always watched me, always documented my every move. I assumed it was for nefarious purposes, that he was looking for a crack in my armor or a moment of weakness, but maybe it wasn't. Maybe he watched me for the same reason I watched him.

Because he enjoyed it.

He leans forward and his hand curves around my neck as he presses his lips to mine.

It could be a really sweet moment, or it could be a story I later see was full of red flags.

The problem is you never really know for sure.

27

The therapist I began seeing at Kyle's urging—twice a month, three-hundred dollars a session, and dumped on a credit card I couldn't pay off—had a lot of good advice.

"It's okay to tell Kyle you're disappointed," she said, when I told her Josie had grown increasingly unreliable.

She'd helped me understand how scared I was of being destroyed the way my mother had been, and how scared I was that if I let Kyle see the mess in my head, he'd run the other way.

So, the next time our plans got ruined by Josie—drinking too much, as always—I told him I was tired of leading separate lives, of not knowing his colleagues, his friends, his family. That I was scared nothing was going to come of this and he'd end up staying with her.

"Fuck it, then," he said. "Let's just go public. I'm as tired of it as you are, and I want you to really know where things stand."

For a moment my heart leapt. I'd be able to come to him on the weekends Josie flaked out, I'd finally meet his kids and tell Meg and Kirsten the truth.

Except Kyle was no longer working out of the LA office, so it would probably be obvious to everyone that we'd been violating the firm's rules.

"You don't think Stadler would rescind my offer?" I asked. I needed the job. God knew with the amount I was putting on credit cards now and days of work I was missing, I really needed the job.

"Fuck," he sighed. "They might."

So we were back to keeping it to ourselves, but now it was my fault.

The next time he came to LA, though, he drove to Sherman Oaks—quiet and tree-lined—and asked which house I'd want. I pointed at one, then changed my mind and pointed to another. We passed a sale sign and suddenly he was calling the realtor, grinning at me as he did it: *My fiancée and I are interested in your listing.* It was his way of letting me know that the end of all the lying and hiding was coming, and when it did, he wanted everything with me. Fifteen minutes later she was showing us a house we couldn't dream of affording, not when he'd soon be giving Josie half his income.

But as Kyle started mentioning a nursery, his fingers slipping through mine, I decided to let myself believe him. The therapist had told me, after all, that I'd never love someone deeply if I couldn't let myself be vulnerable.

In retrospect, I wish she'd at least mentioned that sometimes you are scared for good reason.

28

I'm trying very hard to focus on Sophia Waterhouse and the numbers she's given me, but I'm only half here, the other half focused on that ache between my legs. It's so like Ben Tate to make my job difficult.

My cell is on silent, but Ben's name pops up when he texts, and that alone is enough to distract me. I turn the phone facedown and focus again on the task at hand—Sophia's monthly expenses.

People have no idea what they spend. They pay a credit card bill, or their husband pays it, and they look the other way. When I ask them to itemize it all—*how much did you spend on groceries? How much did you spend on your kids' after-school activities?*—they either go way too high or way too low.

Sophia has either gone too high, or she and her husband have been spending far beyond their 400k income.

"Is this correct?" I ask politely, trying to hide my incredulity. "You spend five hundred a month on manicures?"

"It's pedicures also," she says. "Gels, so it's more expensive."

"And doctors' visits—two thousand a month," I continue. "Can you tell me what that's about?"

It's probably wrong that I'm hoping she'll tell me she has a serious medical condition. In my defense, though, I have a better case if she does.

"I see an alternative practitioner for my food sensitivities, so that's about a hundred a week because I need these infrared colonics and supplements."

My optimism dies. No court is going to look at food sensitivities the way they might Parkinson's. "Okay, and the rest?"

"Well, facials and Botox and filler, mostly," she says. "It really adds up."

"Right, sure." So far, she's spending three grand a month just on her face, hair and nails, an additional eight hundred on personal training and a gym membership, and two grand a month on clothes. We haven't gotten to her mortgage, her car, insurance or her phone—we haven't even gotten to her *kids*—and she's already spending far more than I'll be able to get from her husband.

Sophia is telling me she needs acupuncture every week for some disorder few doctors believe is real, and my mind wanders back to Ben. Ben, moving over me in a dark room. Ben, cupping my face and kissing me like I matter to him. Admitting he's been bringing strawberries in, just for me.

Is this real, or is it just a castle of cards he's constructing, careless of the mess he'll make when it inevitably falls apart? My throat tightens the way it always does when the past creeps in.

"Don't get married," Sophia says. "At least not to an LA guy."

I blink, as if I've been caught at something. "I don't intend to," I reply.

～

BEN WALKS into my office at dinnertime, looking scruffy and slightly day-weary: tie loosened, some serious five o'clock shadow along his jaw.

I rise and walk around to the other side of my desk. I want to tell him I'm busy but I just can't. "Shut the door."

His eyes flicker over me, head to heels. His hand goes to his belt and his mouth opens slightly as he considers it, but then he winces, and his hand falls away. "Let's go, Gemma."

He's obviously going to be tedious about this. "I need to work."

"On what?"

"I—"

His tongue taps his upper lip, and I lose my train of thought. God, I love when he does that.

"Stuff," I conclude.

He gives a low laugh. "*Stuff*? Must be important. I'll be at your place in thirty minutes."

I have every intention of saying, "*that was a one-time thing*", but I'm already shutting down my laptop.

I'm at my apartment when he arrives with takeout in hand. I glance at it, wondering if this is the point where we start acting like boring grown-ups who eat dinner, watch TV, and fall asleep too fast.

He drops the bag on the floor and pushes me against the wall. So I guess we're not *that* boring.

"These outfits of yours are going to end me," he groans, tugging up my skirt as he kicks the door shut behind him.

My hand is already on his belt. I get his pants down, and he steps out of them while he moves me back toward the bedroom. We land on the bed together.

"Admit you're glad I came over," he says, as I roll him onto his back.

"Whatever."

He pushes inside me, and I gasp at the feel of it.

"I'm pretty sure that was a yes," he says.

An hour later, we're sitting at the little table in my breakfast area. He's only in boxers, and I'm wearing his t-shirt, which hangs to mid-thigh. It's bizarre that I'm sleeping with the terrible Ben Tate, but it's even more bizarre that we're sitting at my table together half naked, like an actual couple, and I'm completely comfortable with it.

My phone, sitting next to the rice, lights up with a Zillow notification. Having no respect for boundaries whatsoever, he lifts it to read. "Why are you hunting for houses in..." He squints, "Manassas, Virginia?"

I frown. "I'm not. It was for my mom."

"She's moving?"

I suppose this is where normal people open up, divulge a bit about themselves. I could tell him about the situation with my mother—about the shithole apartment complex she lives in and how I tried to convince her I wanted to buy a house there as an investment property, which all backfired on me when she said she wouldn't move—but the further you open yourself to someone, the harder it is to shut it off later, when it all goes to hell.

"No," I tell him. "She decided against it."

His gaze flickers to my face for a half-second. It's as if he's always assessing to see if I'm lying, and that's smart because a lot of the time I am. Whatever he concludes, he opts not to pry any further.

He places a dollop of wasabi on my plate. "Isn't this better than having sex on your desk?"

I lift my chopsticks. "If you think sushi is better than sex on my desk, I'm worse at it than I thought."

He frowns at me and I give in with a sigh. "Fine, it's better. But...just so we're clear, I've never wanted to date a lawyer and I'm not *planning* to date a lawyer. I have my future all set, and it doesn't look like this."

He raises a brow. "Two people fucking all night in a completely undecorated apartment? I can understand that."

I laugh. "No. It doesn't involve me with someone who's...just like me. I need one of us to be a decent person. Like a guy in a Hallmark movie."

There's something a little grim in his dark eyes. "What's the deal with that? The Hallmark thing?"

I wave my hand. "It's just a joke."

"Is it? Because you bring it up a lot."

I bite my lip. "It's a thing, with me and my mom," I tell him, pushing the food around on my plate. I'd like to leave it at that, but he's waiting for more. "We used to watch all these Hallmark movies together. I think they gave my mom a little hope after my dad left because Hallmark-movie men are never men like my father. They won't trade up when their wives get old, or betray someone's trust. They just want to do the right thing."

"That's your obsession with the chef," he says quietly. "You want a caretaker. Someone who will put you first."

He's probably right. I do want someone who will take care of me, someone who won't just leave, as if we never existed in the first place. "I guess. I can't even keep a plant alive. I'm not someone who's naturally going to make time for a relationship and do all the things you have to do. Neither are you. So how does that ever actually work?"

He pulls me onto his lap. "It kind of *seems* like it's working," he replies. And there's something so soft in his eyes, so genuine, that I have to look away.

29

I beat Ben into the Monday meeting for the first time ever and hide a smile as he walks in, though it's hard to feel too triumphant, given that he had to drive all the way to Santa Monica to get dressed when he left my apartment two hours ago.

If I were a better person, I'd offer to let him keep a few things at my place, but since he's never even invited me to his, I've chosen not to. Petty, yes, but no one would expect more of me.

His eyes meet mine across the table and my thighs tighten. I take one of the strawberries he's just brought in. I know exactly what he's thinking as I place it between my lips.

My phone chimes with a text.

BEN
Do that again.

I take another strawberry and make a show of putting it to my lips, just enough for him to notice but not obvious to anyone else at the table, reveling in the power I hold in this moment. His eyes flutter as it slides down my throat. It takes every bit of self-control I have not to laugh.

His next text is only one word.

> Lunch.

> > We'll see.

And he grins because he already knows this means *yes*.

If I'm going to let my foot off the gas, this is a good week for it. The office is entirely useless just before Thanksgiving, a holiday I couldn't care less about: the food isn't good, no gifts are exchanged, and women do all the work. In the future, once married to a small-town doctor/vet/Christmas-tree-farm owner, I plan to have his mother handle most of it, and I will bring the rolls and the wine.

Ben is going home, of course, followed by a trip to some vineyard with his posse because he has a rich family life, tons of friends, and typically some unchallenging arm candy by his side. He's a lawyer as seen on TV—flashy car, hot dates, glib smile, always winning—while I'm a *real-life* lawyer with a miserable backstory, one that suggests I should get accustomed to spending holidays alone.

The entire office empties on Wednesday afternoon, Ben among them. My apartment feels lonelier than it ever has that night, probably because Ben and I haven't slept apart once since I started letting him come over. Which leads me to think, *again*, that I shouldn't have been letting him come over in the first place.

HE CALLS ON THANKSGIVING. I told him I'm spending the holiday with Keeley, just in case he was pity-inclined to invite me to his home, so I claim to be getting ready to leave for her dad's house when I am, in fact, sitting at my desk—the sole person at FMG today.

There's shouting in the background, then someone tries to take his phone.

"Sorry," he says. "It's mayhem here. My brothers got in a fight over whether it's best to cook a turkey in the oven or a deep fryer. Needless to say, this means we've now got three turkeys being prepared, and my mom is yelling at us to get out of her way."

I laugh, trying to hide the part of me that feels a little wistful, imagining it. For all my grumbling about the holiday, I used to like Thanksgiving back when my mother invited people over. "How does your mom feel about you bringing teenage girls as guests, by the way? Does she make them sit at the kids' table?"

He laughs. "I've never brought a woman home for Thanksgiving. And you sound jealous."

"You wish."

"Yeah," he says, "I guess I do."

I don't know how to reply to that, so I tell him Keeley is waiting. The office feels even emptier after we hang up.

I work for several hours, enjoying a pathetic little Thanksgiving feast of coffee and cereal bars, and head home after dark. I'm climbing into my cold, lonely bed when my mother calls.

She's on her way home from the bar. Something dies inside me at the exhaustion in her voice.

"Did you have a good day?" she asks, struggling to sound cheerful.

"I'm so stuffed," I reply. The lie about going to Keeley's dad's house has worked out well for me this year. "They made two kinds of turkey. How was the bar?"

"Very festive. Lots of drinkers on Thanksgiving, it seems. And the owner brought in Thanksgiving dinner for all of us, and it was a thousand times better than cooking it myself."

She's trying so hard to convince me she's happy, and I'm

doing the same. I wonder what would happen if we just put that effort into making it *true*.

~

> Coming back early because I miss you. And I haven't slept since I left. Please tell me you're not going into the office.

I lean against the door of my apartment, which has just swung shut behind me because I was, indeed, going to the office. I read those words again: *Coming back early because I miss you*. They make me feel like a balloon is expanding in my lungs —I'm delighted, lighter than air, and terrified at the same time of the moment that balloon will pop.

I can't help it, though. Today, delight wins out. I unlock my door and kick off my shoes.

> I can be persuaded not to go in.

Oh, so casual, when my heart is beating like a drum.

I listen for his knock, and when it finally comes I want to leap over the couch to reach him faster.

I open the door, and he takes me in, wearing next to nothing before him. His eyes go from pleased to feral in a second flat.

"Undress," I command as the door shuts behind him.

"You first," he growls, closing the distance between us.

We don't make it out of the kitchen for the first round. The minute we're done I pull him to the bedroom and position him exactly how I want him.

"You're not done," I warn as he collapses on the pillow

beside me twenty minutes later. "So don't get any ideas about sleep."

His nose burrows into my neck, then his lips press a sweet kiss to my skin. "What's up with you today?"

"What do you mean?" I ask, already defensive.

He raises his head to look at me, mouth turned up in a quizzical smile. "You're...affectionate."

"Is that a euphemism for horny? Are we suddenly being delicate with each other? Because I've got your cum all over my chest, so it's a little late for delicacy."

He laughs. "No. I meant affectionate. It's almost like you missed me."

My eyes flicker to his and away. "I guess crazier things have happened."

t the next meeting of partners and senior associates,
Fields announces that Natalie Brenner and her
husband are dissolving both their marriage and
multimillion-dollar production company. She is looking for a
firm that can handle the divorce and financial proceedings, and
FMG is one of several she wants to interview.

My spine straightens, as if electrified. Representing a criti-
cally acclaimed actress in her divorce would make my career.
I'd need help with the dissolution of the production
company, but it's too much work for one lawyer anyway. My
first thought, to be honest, is Ben: he oversaw Drew's fight
with her managers and record company a while ago. He's got
a lot more experience than I do with the business side of
things.

Our gaze meets for a half second, and I can see he's
thinking what I am: we'd crush this, together. Fiducia will likely
settle once they see how much dirt we have on them—I'd like
to share another case with Ben when it's done.

"I'd be very interested in getting in on that," I tell Fields.

His gaze cuts to me without turning his head, as if I'm a

small child distracting him and the other grown-ups with my noise.

"Craig," he says, "I'd like you to meet with her."

It's a slap in the face. If Fields had yelled at me to shut the fuck up, it couldn't be more cutting than it is. Everyone looks away, aside from Ben, who turns toward Fields with narrowed eyes.

"With all due respect, Arvin," Ben says, his mouth a grim line, "Gemma's got more family law experience than the rest of us combined. It would help to have her in on this too."

"Gemma was given two shots at a very lucrative job, which has now gone to another firm," he says. "I'm sure she'll be happy to assist Craig if necessary."

There is no chance Natalie Brenner will hire Craig. None. Which means Fields figured she wasn't going to hire us anyway, and is simply doing this to humiliate me, to let me know I'm not forgiven for what happened with Webber.

What exactly did I do wrong, aside from refusing to sleep my way into a job? Nothing, but that's all it takes. Men will vilify you for enjoying sex, and they'll vilify you for using it to get ahead...but they'll punish you if you *don't* enjoy it, if you *don't* use it to get ahead.

There should be more choices left to me than either *slut* or *prude*. And I wonder if I'm going to have to leave this firm entirely to be allowed to choose one.

BEN IS angrier about the situation than I am.

"I don't understand why you stay," he says the minute he walks into my apartment that night. "This is hardly the first time he's been an asshole to you."

"I want to make partner," I say, dousing my pad Thai in siracha. "Nothing more, nothing less."

"Why do you want it so badly?" He looks around us. "You don't seem to spend much, aside from the shoes."

"Because of bullshit like today," I reply, my voice sharp as a new wave of anger rolls over me. "There was nothing you could have done, but there needs to be a woman in the room to keep this stuff from happening in the first place. If there'd been a single female partner at FMG, I'd probably have told her about the first incident with Webber. And I'm tired of having to listen to Fields when he tells me I can't do pro bono work or tries to whore me out to a client. I want a say, and nothing else can matter until I get it."

I see a glimmer of doubt in his eyes, as if he suspects there's more to the story—which there is, of course. I'm relieved he doesn't persist. "If we're going to keep doing this," he says instead, "we should probably go to HR."

Technically, we are supposed to sign a consensual relationship agreement, indemnifying FMG from any issues that arise because we, as colleagues, are dating.

Technically, the failure to do this is also why I lost my last job.

Except this thing with Ben is temporary. "Is that really necessary?" I ask.

His smile is half-hearted. "Ah, right. You want the widowed veteran instead."

He's only in boxers, so it takes me a second to remember I have no desire to end up with Ben Tate, that somewhere out in the world my future husband is still waiting for me to hit rock bottom and change everything about myself. For the first time, the idea of it makes me sad, rather than hopeful.

"*Veterinarian*, and he doesn't have to be widowed, just so we're clear." I hand him chopsticks. "I'd prefer he not be because people always glorify the dead, so he'd probably always secretly be like *my first wife was so much better*, and I'd have no clue he chose to be buried with her instead of me until he died. So, yeah, fuck that. No widowers. I guess I didn't think that through."

"You didn't think a lot of it through," he mutters. "And how is this guy supposed to *surprise* you with this Iceland proposal? It's not like it's a daytrip. And how's he supposed to get a children's choir there? Does he have relatives in Iceland who work at a school?"

"That's his problem," I reply, stirring the noodles with the end of my chopsticks. "I planned the proposal; if he can't even propose without me lining up the music, well—" I throw out my arms, as if to say, *"obviously it won't work."*

"Is this a good time to point out you'd hate living in a small town? Where will you get your açai bowl?"

"I didn't say a town off the side of a highway. I meant a *charming* town. There will be loads of açai places there."

He raises a brow, but what does he know about small towns? He grew up in fucking *Newport*. "And what will you do during your free time? Because I presume that, once married and living in this small town, you will no longer be working twelve-hour days?"

I'm not sure why he's persisting with this line of questioning. My future plans feel forced now, a little joyless, like New Year's resolutions I wish I hadn't made.

"We'll go on walks. We'll pick apples. We'll go to our favorite cafe, where a well-intentioned but nosy proprietor checks on us too frequently and tells us about her grandchildren."

"You hate hearing about people's grandchildren."

"Yes, people *here*, because their grandchildren are boring. Carol's will be mischievous scamps who call me Aunt Gemma and want to sit on my lap."

He leans back in his seat. "Who's Carol?"

"The proprietor of the cafe. Keep up, Ben."

He smiles, and this time it's less strained than it was. I'm weirdly pleased by that.

"Okay, so you and your veterinarian husband will pick apples, which are only in season for a matter of weeks." He refills my wine. "I think you're going to have to come up with a few more activities in that small town of yours or you'll die of boredom."

"That's where you're wrong." I push my bowl aside and slide my foot between his legs. "I'll be the kind of person who enjoys doing nothing at all by then."

He laughs quietly to himself, his hand wrapping around my ankle. "Sure you will, Gemma."

31

The Roberts case finally goes to trial, though it should not. I love a good fight, but the attorneys are the only ones coming out of this better off for it. Between the extra work we had to put in to get ready and the cost of the trial itself, they'll each be out a hundred grand by the time this is done.

That's how men win, because they're often the only ones with the money to keep going. My mother lost, and she was still paying off the credit card she used for her legal bills by the time I got out of law school.

I throw everything I have at Dennis Roberts: the employee he paid off, the affair, the family trip he no-showed for because of work. Melissa stayed home with the kids—she's a room parent, she manages the kids' soccer team—but Dennis doesn't even know who their pediatrician is. He isn't the one who took Jaden to the hospital when he broke his arm, he isn't the one who watched the baby while they were there. He wanted fifty percent custody, but as my questions continue, his shoulders sag, as if he already knows he's lost.

He gets the kids for two weekends a month, and a two-week

block during the summer. I congratulate Melissa, pack my bags, and go to the bathroom. When I walk out, Dennis Roberts is on his phone with someone, his shoulders hunched over.

"I don't know, Mom," he says. "I don't even get to see them for two weeks." His voice cracks on that last word, this big man with all his money and power. I watch as he covers his face with his hand, and his shoulders shake silently.

And I want to feel good about it, but instead, as I walk away, I'm sick. I hated those attorneys who attacked my mother when I was fifteen. I guess I should've known growing into one of them was never going to feel great.

BEN COMES OVER LATER than normal, following a client dinner. His mouth lands on mine with relief, as if I'm the one part of the day he looked forward to.

The bag he's got in his left hand presses to my thigh. I laugh against his mouth. "The dinner you've brought me feels excessively cold."

"You told me you ate already. This is dessert." He steps back and sets the bag on the counter. "You sounded unhappy on the phone, so I thought it might be an ice cream kind of night. I brought three kinds because I didn't know what you liked."

He sets the options on the counter and I point at one, fighting a smile. For a heartless lawyer, he's incredibly sweet sometimes.

He pours himself a glass of wine then leads me to the couch, where I curl up against him with my Cherry Garcia.

He sips his Malbec. "Tell me what happened. It was Roberts today, right? The basketball coach?"

"Yeah." I slide the spoon over the surface of the ice cream, looking for cherries. "I obliterated him."

He laughs. "That seems like the kind of thing you'd normally be happy about."

"I saw him," I whisper, "crying on the phone to his mom. And—I don't know. I thought I wanted to practice family law, but sometimes I wonder."

He presses his lips to the top of my head. "You want to fight for the underdog, Gemma, and divorce is rarely that cut and dry."

He's right. Even as terrible as my father was, he wouldn't have deserved to lose custody either. People are usually neither entirely bad or entirely good. There's a piece of me tired of pretending they are.

"You could always go to the public defender's office," he suggests, and I smile. He sounds a bit like a Hallmark hero right now. *Better* than a Hallmark hero, because he isn't trying to steer me toward motherhood or some form of homemaking in lieu of my current profession.

"I like shoes too much to live off a government employee's salary," I reply. "And I have to make partner. Men in upper management everywhere go out of their way to keep the circle closed, just like Fiducia has, hoping the women who want in will just give up. Fuck that."

"Then let's make sure you get it," he says, as if he wants it for me as much as I want it for myself.

I blink away tears. It's felt, for a long time, like I'm in this alone.

I'm scared to let myself think I no longer am.

On Sunday morning, he's in the process of getting dressed when I wake. "Sorry," he whispers.

"You're leaving?" I don't know why I care. I was going into the office anyway.

He nods. "Brunch at my mom's. It's kind of a tradition."

His gaze flickers to me. For a moment I think he's going to invite me, and I'll have to find a way to say no, but he just keeps getting dressed. We've been doing this for weeks now, and I've still never met anyone he cares about. I've still never even gone to his place—I've suggested the latter and he alludes to the construction or says it's too far. I can hardly argue that it's only twenty minutes away when I'm pretending I neither know nor care where he lives. If we were at all serious, though, it would probably bother me.

I sit up, holding the sheet to my chest. "Do all your brothers come?"

He hitches a shoulder. "Graham lives on the east coast, and Colin's doing his residency, so they're kind of hit or miss. Today it's just my mom and stepdad, and my brother Simon."

"I didn't know your mom got remarried," I tell him.

His tongue taps his lip, and he turns away to grab his shoes. "Yeah."

"You don't like him?" I ask.

He looks wary as he glances over his shoulder at me. "I do. He's a great guy. And things were pretty difficult until he came along."

I almost make a joke about what *difficult* means to a spoiled rich kid from Newport, but manage to stop myself. Someone could easily say the same thing to me—I was once a spoiled rich kid from DC too. "Difficult in what way?" I ask.

"My mom completely shut down after my dad died," he says, perching on the edge of the bed. "They figured out later that it was probably shock and post-partum depression, but it went on for a while, and I never stopped being scared she'd... leave us again."

"Shut down how?" I ask. My foot slides toward his thigh, suddenly needing contact.

He leans forward to tie his shoes. "She couldn't stop crying.

Couldn't even sit at the table through dinner, and it was often like...she'd forgotten we were there. I never once left for school without being scared shitless that Simon would walk off into traffic because she wasn't watching him, or that she'd forget to feed Colin."

I picture it all, and it hits me somewhere deep in the chest. He was only ten at the time. It hurt to watch my mom suffering, but it would be terrifying to be so little and feel responsible for three siblings. "I'm so sorry," I whisper. "How long did it last?"

"A while," he says, as if the specifics are too dark for him to delve into. "But it remained hard for a long time. Every time things went wrong...I was petrified she'd be pushed over the edge."

He must hope he'll find someone stable, someone who plans to stick around. Maybe he's not inviting me along today because he knows I'm neither of those things.

32

Two weeks before Christmas, Ben stops by my office. He's on his way out of town for a weekend in Palm Springs with his friends. I look away from those keys in his hand, the reminder he's leaving.

"So do you have plans?" he asks, in the manner of someone who very much hopes I'll say I have them.

"Keeley mentioned a party." This is not a lie, in that Keeley *did* mention a party, but *is* a lie, in that I have no intention of going.

The relief on his face is palpable, and if this were anything, if this was more than enemies-with-benefits, I'd probably be really hurt by that. I've seen enough of Drew's Instagram feed to know he's brought other women along in the past, and that they were idiots. Women he *should* have been ashamed of—but I'm the one he doesn't want to bring.

"So where *is* this party?" he asks.

My patience with him is fraying. "Certainly, you're not going away for your nebulous friends' weekend and thinking you get to grill me about what I'll do in your absence?" I ask tartly.

"*Nebulous?*" he repeats.

I hide a wince. I sounded more jealous than I intended. "My point is that you're going away for the entire weekend, *somewhere*, and with *some* people, and that's fine. So it's a little weird to have you grilling me about the small party I'll be at with Keeley for a few *hours*."

A muscle in his jaw contracts once, like the single beat of a heart. "Don't take a drink you didn't see being made," he says.

"Ben, I'm not eighteen, and this isn't my first rodeo," I reply, dismissing him, irritated by my disappointment.

Because I was really hoping he'd tell me not to go home with someone else. And I don't know why I wanted it, when I'd have refused to agree anyway.

I CHECK Instagram on Saturday morning. Drew hasn't posted a single thing yet. Maybe Ben's not with her. Maybe he's actually on a romantic weekend away, just him and a blond named Lotus who is extremely flexible and thinks 9-11 was a conspiracy because she wasn't born when it happened.

He texts but I'm not pleased, I'm resentful. How's it possible that I'm not as invite-worthy as a girl who doesn't know the difference between *your* and *you're*?

> BEN
>
> This place is spectacular. We should come here for the weekend.

We could have gone there THIS weekend if you'd fucking invited me.

> I don't see having any free weekends for a while.

I run to Victoria's apartment on my way into the office to meet a friend of hers. *"Paperwork issue"*, she was told, when her daughter wasn't released from juvenile detention as planned, *"things slow down because of the holidays"*, as if that's a valid excuse to keep a fourteen-year-old girl locked up. It's in no way my area of the law, but if you have a lawyer who can call on your behalf, casually throwing around phrases like *standard of care* and *civil penalties*, you tend to come out better than when you don't.

I tell her I'll make the call but promise nothing beyond that. I can't represent her formally without getting the firm's approval, and this is definitely not the time to get caught defying Fields. I shouldn't even be placing the call, but what am I supposed to do—force some teenage girl to remain locked up without reason because I'm scared of my boss?

We finish our meeting and I head to the front door. It's only as I reach for my purse that I notice the envelopes on the front table addressed to Santa.

Victoria has almost nothing left after she pays rent and buys groceries. I wonder how the hell she manages gifts too.

"They did it at church," she says, shaking her head. "I wish they'd stop encouraging my kids to expect more than they're gonna get."

"I can mail them for you," I offer.

She shrugs. "Won't make a difference. I think the post office just throws them out."

I grab the envelopes anyway, tucking them into my purse.

When I reach the car, I check Drew's social media again, though I really shouldn't, and find she's posted a photo from the night before. There are ten of them sitting at a long table in what appears to be a crowded bar: her and her husband, his friend Hayes and Hayes's wife, Tali, two men who seem to be a couple...and, at the very end, Ben, with his arm around Juliet Cantrell, a gorgeous singer I've seen in Drew's photos before. She's tucked into his side, her hand resting on his chest.

The caption reads *Three bottles of wine later...and @julescant-*

rell *was already having way too much fun* BEFORE *the wine arrived.*

My stomach starts to fall. He's never even mentioned her, but why would he? It's not like he owes me an explanation. We're not even a couple.

I start to scroll back through Drew's feed, driven by terror and also certainty: I don't know what I'm looking for, but I'll know when I find it.

And then I do. It's a picture from Drew's wedding—her and her husband slow dancing, and behind them, standing just as close, and looking into each other's eyes—Ben and Juliet.

With shaking hands, I turn the phone facedown on my lap, breathing through my nose. My eyes sting and I fight it, hands clenching into fists.

I knew this moment would come. I did. And I've dreaded its arrival every day since this thing with Ben began. As hard as it is, as sick as I feel right now, at least I get to stop waiting for it—the moment is here. Now I just have to put the pain—and him—into my past, where they belong.

I text Keeley and tell her I'm coming to the party after all.

THE RAIN HAS ENDED by the time I reach the mansion. The bass is thumping, a strobe light is flashing, and scantily clad girls are dancing by the pool and drinking something too blue to be natural.

"You made it!" Keeley cries, throwing her arms around me. I suspect she's had plenty of the blue drink, and that it's probably extremely strong.

One hour later, I've had two of them myself and Keeley is insisting I have a third. I showed her the pictures of him and Juliet—she was already inclined to think the worst of him, thanks to me, and that sealed his fate. She's now determined to get me laid, while I'm simply determined to become more numb than I am.

"Your phone is ringing," says a girl on the other end of the hot tub, grabbing it from the table behind her and handing it to me.

The phone is no longer ringing by the time I take it. The screen says I have two missed calls from Ben.

"Ignore him," says Keeley. "No, wait. *Don't* ignore him. Let's video call good ol' Ben." Her face stretches into an absolutely evil smile as she grabs the phone from me.

"What are you doing?" I demand. Talking to him is not a part of the plan. *Not* talking to him, actually, is my entire plan at present.

"Giving him a taste of his own medicine," she replies, handing me my phone just as Ben's face appears on screen. For a moment I'm struck by how much I miss him. How much it hurts that he didn't invite me on this trip, that he took someone else instead. I want to beg him to explain, but even drunk, I'm ashamed of the impulse. He owes me nothing, and even if he did...it would be pathetic.

He frowns, two matching furrows between his brows. "Where are you?" he demands, sounding a little pissed. Keeley just to my left, giggles.

"At a party," I reply, civil and nothing more. "Some gamer's mansion."

Keeley leans into the frame, resting her chin on my shoulder. "Commander Shane," she brags, as if he's going to be impressed by this or even know who the fuck *Commander Shane* is.

"I thought you said it was a *little get-together*." And now there's no mistaking how irate he is. "And why the fuck are you wearing a bikini?"

"Plans change, Ben!" Keeley shouts helpfully, before she slides away.

I take a sip of the blue drink someone's put in my hand. "It's a pool party, obviously."

"Did you just accept a drink from a complete stranger?" he asks, nostrils flaring. "And how are you getting home?"

I hitch a shoulder. "No idea. I'll figure it out." I want to keep him on the phone, suspended in this moment where an *us* still exists, but it's painful at the same time. Every second just reminds me more and more of how much I liked him. And I did. I really, really did.

A female calls to him from another room, and my stomach drops so hard and fast I feel sick from the sudden change. "It sounds like you need to go."

"They can wait," he growls. "So you're in the mansion of some gamer you don't even know, *drunk*, and you have no idea how you'll get home."

The female voice is approaching, insistent and possessive.

"You'd better go, Ben," I reply. "Before your date sees you talking to someone else."

And then I hang up the phone.

FOR THE NEXT two hours I continue to drink, but I can't numb myself enough to not be upset about the conversation.

All I really want to do is go curl up in the room Keeley's staying in here and weep, but I suspect she and the guy she's seeing already had sex in the bed, so I remain in place, perched on the edge of the hot tub while she persuades two guys to rub our shoulders and two other guys to rub our feet.

I guess I *am* drunk because there's literally no way I'd go along with this sober.

"I liked him," I whisper. It's possible I've said this several times since I ended that call.

Keeley leans her head on my shoulder for a half second. "I

know, babe. Pick someone here instead. Anyone. Sleep with Jason if you want. I really don't mind."

I laugh miserably. "I don't want to sleep with anyone. Not even Jason, but I appreciate the offer."

"More alcohol, then," she says, raising my empty glass and hers. "We need two more boys to fetch us fresh drinks!"

I laugh again and close my eyes, wishing I could just have this whole day behind me. And then Keeley says, "uh oh", and I open them again...to discover Ben standing on the other side of the hot tub. He's wearing jeans and an unbuttoned flannel shirt over a t-shirt, looking better than any man ever has...aside from the fact that he is very, very angry. Although that looks sort of good on him too.

The rubbing stops.

"Thought you were in Palm Springs," I call over the music, and for the first time I hear myself. It turns out I *am* drunk.

"Gemma," he says, eyes narrowed, "can I speak to you?"

I get the feeling he's not actually asking. I climb out—my feet no longer working as well as they did when I climbed in—and he pushes through the crowd to wrap a towel around me.

"What are you doing?" he asks.

"I'm celebrating Jesus's birth, obviously."

The DJ chooses this moment to put on "Talk Dirty to Me."

His nostrils flare. "You're drunk. Let's go."

I stiffen. *I'm not doing this again. I'm not letting someone else hold all the cards and dictate how I lead my life while refusing to invite me into his. I'm not letting someone convince me I'm the issue.*

"Fuck you," I reply, which is far less eloquent than I intended, but gets the job done. I turn and push through the crowd to get to Keeley's room on the second floor, but by the time I reach her door he's behind me again.

And it just makes me sad.

I hate that he's still being the Ben I'd begun to believe he might be, someone honest and *invested*, when I've already got proof he's not. "Go back to your date," I tell him, marching inside the room, looking for my stuff.

He follows me in, standing in the frame of the door with his hands shoved in his pockets and his eyes narrowed. "What the fuck is this about?" he demands. "I wasn't with anyone. I don't know what the hell you're talking about. And what was that downstairs? I leave you alone for one fucking day and find you getting massaged by two guys at once?"

"*I saw you*, asshole," I reply, and my throat tightens. *Fuck*. I refuse to cry in front of him. "You and Juliet Cantrell. Having 'way too much fun'. I'm not here to help you cheat on another girl."

He frowns. "Juliet? I'm not with Juliet."

I pull the towel tighter around me, suddenly freezing. I want him to get the fuck out so I can change. "Really?" I ask with an angry laugh. "Well, then you should tell your friend Drew, because she's saying something very different online."

He stares at me in shock. "You looked her up on Instagram," he says quietly. "You looked her up to see what I was doing this weekend." He sounds incredulous rather than angry, but it's an accusation nonetheless.

I point my finger at him. "Don't you dare make this about me and what I did. I'm not the problem here."

There's a quiet, pleased gleam in his eye. "Nor am I. Has it occurred to you yet that if I was with Juliet, I couldn't have left and driven two hours to come get *you*?"

He might have a point. But that doesn't explain everything, and I'm no longer willing to be someone who accepts half-answers and hopes for the best.

"Then what was that about Juliet having 'way too much fun'?" I demand. I'm showing all my cards, but it's not like I can backtrack at this point...he already knows what I did.

"I have no idea!" He pushes his hands through his hair, making it even more deliciously fucked up than it was. "We're just friends. We've *always* just been friends. Her boyfriend no-showed this weekend, so I imagine Drew was hoping to piss him off."

I pull the towel tighter. I suppose...that's exactly the kind of thing Keeley and I would do for each other if one of us was in Juliet's shoes. Hell, I wouldn't be surprised if Keeley *already* did something like that today.

"Now do you want to tell me why the hell I arrived to find you being manhandled in a hot tub, wearing next to nothing?"

"A bikini is actually standard attire for a—"

"You are *intentionally* missing the goddamn point."

"I don't know," I reply, too tired to be defensive, too tired to say, *"you have an excuse for everything, but you don't want me to meet your friends and it hurts."* "It was Keeley's idea. And now *you* sound jealous."

"Yeah," he replies, jaw grinding. "No shit."

We stare at each other for a moment, and then his shoulders drop and he closes the distance between us, pulling me to him. I go reluctantly. "Next time," he says, "just ask me."

"I'm asking you now," I reply, turning my face up to look at him and then dropping my gaze when it feels like I might cry. "I've seen the girls you take to these weekends away. They're all over your friend's feed. Yet you didn't bring me."

"And you wanted to go?" he asks.

"No." It's such a fucking lie. "I just want to know why."

"Did it ever occur to you that if pictures of the people I bring are all over Drew's feed, then *you'd* then be all over Drew's feed?" he demands, irritated anew. "Even if I asked her not to post, she can't go anywhere without getting photographed, and the rest of us get photographed too. And that would be a problem because *you* don't want to go to HR."

Oh. Right. *Shit.*

"Get your clothes," he says. "We're going home."

I want to agree. Even if I'm hurt, and he's the cause, he's still the only place I want to be. "You don't have to do that," I tell him instead. "I can Uber. Go back to your friends."

"Gemma," he whispers, pressing his lips to my temple and forehead in turn. "Do you really think for a second I wouldn't rather be with you?"

I let my eyes fall closed for a minute and rest my head against his chest.

I want to believe him. I want to stop being like this.

But I don't know how...and I'm still not certain I should.

33

Something shifts after the Palm Springs weekend. Even if we don't say it, even if we still haven't gone to HR, I can no longer deny we're a couple. I guess the truth is... I don't want to deny it. He's at my place every night and it's hard to imagine not having him there.

He appears in my office early in the evening, the way he always does. His eyes drift over my face in that way of his—languid and possessive at once—and I'm immediately picturing his head between my legs. Alas, it's not to be.

"You can't come over," I tell him. "I have to do some shopping."

There's been no time to get gifts for Victoria's kids because Ben's always around, and I've put it off for as long as I can.

His full mouth tips into a filthy smile. "I don't mind shopping."

"It's not sexy shopping," I say with a roll of my eyes. "I think you're picturing sitting in the dressing room of La Perla while I try on lingerie."

"I wasn't, but now I am." He glances toward the door, then leans down to let his lips brush my neck. "I'll come anyway."

I make him drive me to the Target over on Beverly Boulevard. "Are we here to finally make your apartment look less creepy?" he asks.

"I like my creepy apartment." I push a cart toward him and get one of my own.

"Liar."

I laugh. Fine, I don't like my creepy apartment. "I'm not decorating my place because it's temporary. I'll be a whole new me in a year or two."

"Right," he says. "Widowed veteran or whatever."

"Veterinarian."

"Do you even like animals?"

I pull the kids' letters from my purse. "Stay on task. We're toy shopping." I hand him Phillip's list.

A single brow arches as he looks it over. "I wasn't expecting your shopping lists to contain quite so many Nerf guns."

I smile. "It's this kid I know. Just...pick some stuff. Not twenty Nerf guns, but maybe two of them, and then some other things."

"This is an odd way to tell me you've got kids, Gemma," he says.

I roll my eyes. "They belong to a friend. Money is a little tight this year."

Money will be tight every year for Victoria, for the rest of her damn life. It bothers me. Those kids could become anything they wanted, and I'm not sure they'll ever get the chance. Sure, I put myself through college and law school, but I also spent my childhood surrounded by people who'd made it, and who'd assured me I would too. They don't have that.

I leave him studying the Legos and head to the book section for Lola. Delight stirs inside me as I browse the covers, just like it did when I was a child, combing through books at the library every Wednesday afternoon.

I'd forgotten it until now...my mom was right. I *was* a

really happy kid. I guess, actually, I'm kind of happy now too. I freeze for a moment, shocked by the realization, and stare at Ben as he approaches with an entirely full cart.

I'm happy for the first time in six years because of you.

"Picking up a little reading material?" he asks, grinning at the vampire book in my hands.

I laugh. "Yes. Because I have so much free time these days to read about vampires." I look at his cart. "My God, Ben. Did you buy *every* Nerf gun? You've got to put some of that back."

We finish our shopping. Ben insists on paying for all of it, silencing my argument. "You can get it next Christmas if you make partner. But I wouldn't bank on it," he adds with a grin. "Craig's a pretty strong candidate."

"Someone's asking to get shot with a Nerf gun when we get home," I reply.

We carry everything up to my apartment, and I'm sweating by the time the final trip is completed. "I need a shower," I tell him.

"Are you going to explain how you made friends with someone who can't afford toys for her kids?" he asks.

I bite my lip. He's still a partner, and I'm still explicitly defying Fields' orders on this matter. But he helped me, and against all odds I have faith in him.

"I did some pro bono work for her a while ago," I reply, carrying one of the bags to the coat closet.

"Victoria," he says, and I come to a sudden stop.

"How do you know about her?" I demand. If Fields knows... it's a wonder I'm even employed.

"When I arrived at FMG—" a hint of a smile creeps in at the corner of his mouth "—an associate suggested you were still doing pro bono work after Fields told you to stop. I went to check."

If that's true, then I should have been fired two years ago. I stare at my feet. "So..."

"So I watched you in court," he says, "and then I told the associate in question he'd be fired if he mentioned your name again, but I'd make it worth his while if he didn't. You deserve to take those cases."

I stare at him in complete shock. *Craig.* He's been throwing Craig work for two years for me.

"That was nice of you," I whisper.

His smile is so gentle I can barely stand to look at him. "It was nicer of you."

I excuse myself and walk into the bathroom, shutting the door behind me. I lean over the sink and weep silently, and I'm not even sure why.

34

The office is jovial the week before Christmas—there are constant treats in the break room and carols playing on Terri's computer. I guess I'm kind of jovial too. Ben convinces me to get a tiny tree and we decorate it together, though we sort of half-ass it because Ben's only in his boxers and we keep getting distracted. We watch *It's a Wonderful Life* one night and he pulls me against him with a quiet laugh when I tear up at the end. "I knew you'd cry," he says, pressing his lips to the top of my head. He says it, though, as if it's a good thing.

I'm only going home for the weekend, though it's more for my mother's sake than mine. She'd have felt guilty asking for days off during the post-season rush, and guiltier still if she'd gone to work knowing I was waiting at her apartment.

I have a meeting Friday afternoon, and by the time I get back to the office to grab my suitcase, most of the staff, including Ben, is gone. On my desk sits a beautifully wrapped present, one I'm certain is from Ben though we agreed not to exchange gifts. It's a pair of navy Louboutins I've been lusting after for months: leather that is made to look like denim and what must be nearly a five-inch heel. I have no idea how the hell he knew I wanted them.

The note says *It's as much for me as for you; therefore, not a gift.*

Even his romantic gestures involve argument, but I clutch the note to my chest. It's like he's slowly prying me open after years of being shuttered closed, and I'm emerging into the sunlight at last, remembering how good it all is.

It's really going to hurt if I have to give it up again.

I TAKE the red-eye to DC and arrive early on Christmas Eve. My mother makes brunch for us, and I set the table. She's still using the same plates and glasses she took when she and my father split up. I find that infuriating.

"God, Mom," I say, "you've only got three plates left. I should have gotten you dishes for Christmas."

"It's just me," she says. "Why would I ever need more than three plates? Besides, I already know what I want to ask you for."

I glance at the clock. It's noon and the mall probably closes in a matter of hours. "I hope it's a new blender," I say, taking a sip of the margarita she made me. It's half ice.

"It's not something you have to buy," she adds. "First, I want you to come to mass with me today."

I have to stifle a sigh, though I'd anticipated this one. My mother operates as if God is taking attendance and will dole out His goodness to those who show up most. I bet my dad hasn't been to mass once in fifteen years, but she's not one to let facts ruin things for her.

"Fine. What else?"

"I want you to go see your father on your way out Monday."

My face falls. "Are you serious? *Why?*"

"Because you might not like what he did, but he's still your father. He deserves to spend a few hours with his daughter on Christmas."

I groan. "Mom, do you have any idea what efforts he's made so that *you* wouldn't see me? He's spent over a decade trying to cut you out. I don't understand how you can be so forgiving."

"I'm forgiving, honey, because I see so much of him in you."

I know she isn't wrong, but it hurts anyway. "That's pretty much the worst thing you could have said."

"I didn't mean it as an insult. You're brilliant like he is, but you're also more stubborn than is good for you, and you're so busy looking for the worst in people that you don't always see the best. Instead of thinking he tries to control you because he's punitive, is it at least possible that he loves you also? Couldn't it be both?"

"It's easier just to write people off," I whisper.

She clasps my hand. "I know, Peaches. But that's not a reason to do it."

My mother and I exchange gifts and spend Christmas Day watching Hallmark movies I don't pay much attention to. I used to love them as much as she does, and now...I don't know. It's all well and good, throwing a Christmas dance in a haunted mansion with the ghost you're in love with, but I think I sort of prefer wandering the aisles of Target with Ben, arguing about Nerf guns.

The next morning, I hug my mom goodbye and take an Uber into the city, back to the house where I grew up. The car pulls into my father's driveway, and resentment for Stephani flares anew. She's torn out my mother's willow trees in front. There are cheap planters there now, a showy mailbox. As I walk to the door, I consider subtle ways to let her know her taste sucks, but they're all some version of *you can't teach an old whore new tricks*, and that's probably not in the spirit of what my mother is asking me to do here.

I ring the doorbell, and my father answers with Stephani lurking a few feet behind him, her smile strained and wary. As it should be—the only thing I hate more than a homewrecker is the husband who cheats in the first place. I've never been especially nice to her.

"Gemma!" he shouts. "Come in, come in." He ushers me toward the family room, as if I didn't spend the first fifteen years of my life here. "Steph was just whipping up some mimosas."

I nod reluctantly, and Stephani goes to the bar my father installed across the room. The cabinet is full of new glassware while my mother is still using the same shit she left with over a decade ago. I'm irritated all over again.

Stephani sets the drinks in front of us. "I'll let you two talk," she says.

My father barely notices her, as if she's a servant quietly ushering herself out. *And that's why you don't sleep with your married boss, Steph. Because eventually you'll be the wife he's bored by too.*

"So how are things at FMG?" he asks.

"Great. Busy."

"I saw you're taking on Fiducia."

I stiffen. He always wants something. It's entirely possible Fiducia or their counsel has asked him to lean on me a little.

"I am." My voice hardens. "But I'm not discussing the case with you."

He sighs. "I wasn't trying to get you to divulge secrets. For Christ's sake...can I not even ask you a simple question about work? What's it going to take for you to forgive me?"

"Well, you could stop asking me for things that will hurt

Mom, for starters. You could stop making everything you offer contingent on something else."

"Is that what I was doing?" he demands. "Because I thought I was just asking my daughter about her job, in the hopes she'd finally realize that working for me would be far better than working for FMG."

I set my glass down on the table, intentionally ignoring the coaster. Let Stephani go buy a brand-new table for ten grand because this one now has a water ring. Maybe it'll help make up for the fact that her husband no longer notices her. "Is that what this is about?" I ask. "Convincing me to join your firm?"

"No," he says heavily, and for a moment he looks his age. I can see who he'll become over the next decade or two and it almost makes me sad for him. Except my mother will age, too, and she won't get to do it *here*, with a full set of plates, an extra cabinet of glasses, and the man who promised to cherish her for as long as they both lived. "I'm asking what it will take to make you forgive me. If you don't want to join my firm, fine, though God knows why you're so hell bent on remaining in LA. Tell me what it will take for me to ask you a simple question without you jumping down my throat."

Time travel. Go back in time and don't screw my mother over.

It's the petty answer of an angry teenage girl, though, and pragmatism wins out: if he's willing to strike a bargain, there's definitely something I want.

"Give Mom the money you should have given her in the first place."

"The court—"

"Are you seriously going to try to convince *me* that it was a completely impartial decision?" I explode. "That she had a chance against the fleet of sharks you hired to crush her? I do this for a fucking *living*. It's insulting you'd even try to pretend otherwise with me."

He's completely unperturbed by my outburst. As an attorney, I admire it. As his offspring, it makes me want to kick him in the face.

"Then tell me, Gemma," he says, leaning back in his chair, "what you think she was owed."

"Five million." His mouth opens to object and I keep going. "She'd have walked away with more if she'd had your team in place, and that money would have doubled by now. *More* than doubled, and I'm sure it has, only it's done so in *your* accounts."

"That's ridiculous," he begins.

I stand up. "You asked, I answered. Thanks for the drink."

"You want your mother to get that money?" he asks from behind me. "Come to my firm."

I still. A part of me can't believe he's doing this. Can't believe he's asking me to give up everything I've built in LA before he'll do what he should have done in the first place.

"Mom would never accept that."

He shrugs. "She'd never have to know. I'll tell her I realized I was wrong. You'll forgive me and come to the firm. It makes absolute sense."

My mother won't take a penny from me, but she'd take that money. And he's right. She'd never even have to know. All I'd be giving up is nearly everything I care about. And God I hate him for asking it of me.

"You're doing it again," I tell him, opening the door. "You're incapable of giving without getting something in return."

I walk out. But I'm already wondering if *not* considering it makes me every bit as selfish as him.

35

I text Ben the minute I land. I've spent the past six hours thinking about what my father said and how that money would change my mother's life. I've never wanted to turn down an offer more, and I'm not sure how I can, especially if I don't make partner.

Weirdly, it's the idea of leaving Ben that bothers me most.

He's waiting outside my apartment when I arrive, wearing jeans and deeply in need of a shave. And here I thought he couldn't get better looking.

I pull him inside the door. He grabs the suitcase I've forgotten in the hallway.

"I get the feeling you missed me," he says as I slide to my knees.

"You wish." I slip the belt loose. His lids lower and he runs a hand through my hair.

He's hard as steel as I pull him free from his boxers, groaning when I take him in my mouth. "You don't have to admit it," he says. "But I will. I missed you."

I pretend I haven't heard him. One part of me wants him to stop talking and one part wants him to say it all again.

"Fuck," Ben groans. He arches against me, his fingers pressing to my hair, that subtle pressure begging for more. I don't give it to him. Instead, I savor him, like he's ice cream in a time of famine. Using my hands, my tongue, and the back of my throat on occasion, I don't stop until his inhales grow sharp, and come fast.

"You're killing me," he rasps. He sinks to the floor and has me flat on my back in seconds. "I need to be inside you."

I missed this, I think, as he pulls off my jeans. I suppose I sort of missed him too.

THE DAYS between Christmas and New Year's Eve are quiet. Most of the staff have taken the week off, and even Ben and I aren't working our normal hours. In the morning we take our time, sharing the paper and sipping our coffee, my feet entwined with his beneath the table. We leave work each night at a reasonable hour. The little Christmas tree is still flourishing, which is either a miracle or Ben's watering it.

We're in bed when he mentions New Year's Eve.

"We should go away this weekend," he says.

I roll toward him. Suggesting a weekend away seems like a big step for someone who won't even invite me to his house.

"I'm surprised Drew isn't hosting some magnificent gala on a yacht or flying you all to a private island somewhere."

He grins. "She is, but I'd prefer to spend it with you."

He's missing out on a night with his friends because I'm the asshole who won't go to HR. I refuse to feel guilty about that. He's never even invited me into his home. I tip my chin up to look at him. "You know where we could go? Your place."

"It's a disaster," he says, though he could have built an entirely new house in the amount of time it's taken. "How about one night? We'll go somewhere nearby for New Year's Eve and come back the next morning. Catalina, maybe."

My breath stutters. Kyle booked us a room on Catalina Island for my twenty-third birthday. We'd already chosen a ring by then—I assumed he was going to propose and spent money I didn't have on a new dress. Then Josie flaked out, as always, and he canceled. I'd seen so little of my friends by then that going out with them wasn't even an option. I spent my birthday sitting in my apartment alone.

"I'm not really a fan of Catalina," I reply.

His tongue glides along his bottom lip for a moment, observing me, as if he knows there's more here. I'm scared he's going to ask for details, and the time is coming when he will. Eventually he'll push a little harder to know what happened at Stadler and why I'm prickly about so many things. "I'll figure something out," he says, and I'm so relieved I don't even argue.

We leave work on Saturday just after lunch and drive up the coast to a cottage in Santa Barbara. A porter unlocks the door for us, and while Ben sees him out, I just...stare. I'd expected he'd choose something nice— king-sized bed, room service— but this is another level entirely. It's got two rooms, both with French-glass doors that open wide to a terrace larger than my apartment. A fire blazes in the hearth already, several bottles of wine waiting for us on the mantel. I step outside, passing a pergola to my left, and go to the railing, staring out at the Pacific, ethereal in the distance.

"It's where John and Jackie Kennedy spent their honeymoon," Ben says, walking up behind me and pulling my back to his chest. "It seemed like the kind of thing you'd like."

I can't put into words how much I love it, so naturally I don't admit it all.

"It's less terrible than I anticipated," I say with a grin.

He swoops me up, throwing me over his shoulder as he

starts to carry me inside. "Admit it's the coolest overnight trip you've ever taken."

"Top twenty this year, for sure," I reply, laughing as he throws me down on the bed. I try to crab crawl away from him and he grabs my ankles, pulling me back down the mattress.

"Gemma," he says, pinning me with ease, "we both know I can force you to admit anything I want."

I'm breathless, eager. "Coerced confessions are inadmissible."

His finger trails down my sternum and over my stomach. "Ah, but we're not in court, are we?"

He pulls my t-shirt overhead, then tugs my jeans to the floor in one long pull. I squirm in anticipation. I love how determined he gets when I won't give him what he wants.

"I slept in an ice hotel once in Sweden," I tell him as he grabs his shirt by the neck and pulls it overhead. "*That* was amazing."

He stops suddenly. His eyes narrow, his nostrils flare... and he reaches for his belt.

My breathing grows uneven as he grabs my wrists in one hand and wraps the belt around them, securing it to the headboard. He's held my wrists overhead before—always just before he comes, when his restraint is nearly gone. There's something desperate in his face in those moments, as if a part of him he won't acknowledge just wants to make sure I stay.

Goose bumps crawl over my skin as his hot breath grazes a nipple. His fingers slide over my panties but don't venture inside them. My skin starts to heat everywhere. Having no control—no way to push him to do what I want, no way to stop him—has my heart beating hard. The ache between my thighs is unbearable.

His fingers continue to torture me, and when I try to arch my hips for more contact, his free hand pins me in place.

"Fine," I gasp. "It's cool. It's the coolest place I've ever stayed."

His teeth skim over my skin. "Better than the ice hotel?"

"The ice hotel sucked," I tell him. "I was so cold."

He laughs. "I'd have fucked you even if you hadn't admitted it."

I smile. "Does that mean you're going to untie my wrists?"

He pushes my thighs apart and slides lower on the bed. "No, Gemma. Not a chance."

Good.

LATER, we curl up on the terrace with a bottle of wine, watching the sun set over the Channel Islands in the distance.

"Did you come here, growing up?" I ask. "I mean, not this hotel, but the area?"

He laughs. "No. Your family is more likely to have come here than mine, rich DC girl."

I shake my head. "My whole life was ballet, and a vacation like this would have meant a week away. My parents would have had to drag me kicking and screaming, and it wasn't worth the effort."

"Ballet?" His mouth curves slightly, as if he's just solved a puzzle. "What happened to that?"

"My mom had to move out of the city after the divorce, and she was killing herself trying to work school and all my activities around an entry-level job. So I quit."

He pulls me closer. "You're still upset about it."

I give the tiniest shake of my head. "That was almost fifteen years ago. It just makes me mad."

I can't imagine having to work for my father's firm after everything he did, and my God but he'd use it to his advantage. It wouldn't simply mean doing work I hate—it would mean having him as my boss, demanding I appear by his side at charity functions, sending me out of town on Mother's Day or my mom's birthday.

"He—" I take a deep breath and start over. "My dad used to call my mom all the time when it was going on—God, the shit he said to her. He'd just left her penniless so he could shack up with a twenty-four-year-old, but anytime he didn't get what he wanted, he was telling her she was a loser and worthless, and a terrible mother. And you know...he's good at what he does. He's convincing. A part of her believed every word of it."

"Is that why you went to college early?" he asks quietly.

"Sort of." I rest my face against his chest, oddly soothed by the smell of his soap, the feel of him there. "My father went back to court and won custody, just to punish her. My mom would have let me live with him full time if I'd wanted it. She'd have gone out of her way to make me feel like it was okay. He just did it to prove he *could*."

I really can't believe, after everything he's done, and after everything I suffered to defy him, that he might win all this in the end anyway.

"I'm so sorry," he says.

I shake my head. "What you went through is so much worse, yet somehow I'm the only one of us who hasn't recovered."

He laughs unhappily. "Drew thinks I haven't recovered either, if it makes you feel any better."

"Oh?"

"She says I only date women I can't care about because I'm scared of getting attached to someone. She's probably got a point."

It feels like a knife to the heart. I never *wanted* him to care about me, but it hurts anyway. I sit up and set my wine carefully on the table, needing distance. "That's the kind of thing you should probably keep to yourself when you're with a female."

He pulls me against him before I can rise. "Gemma," he says with a quiet laugh, "I would have kept it to myself if you were one of them."

I look up, studying his face. His eyes are soft and sincere. I want to believe him. I really do.

"How can you not already know that?" he asks as he presses his lips to the top of my head.

Because you never know. You never know until it's too late. I'm starting to think Ben might be different, though, and that's terrifying in its own way.

36

Ben and I are at the office late the following Tuesday, comparing the expense reports Fiducia provided us against the receipts acquired from the strip clubs. If they falsified reports, we can have them charged with fraud. But we will also need to somehow prove these were company-sanctioned events, not one or two rogue employees billing the company for their shady extracurricular activities.

We're sitting at the table in his office in front of a mountain of expense reports when my mother calls.

"Hi, Mom," I say, with a cautious glance at Ben. I haven't told her about him, and don't really want to. She'd just get her hopes up.

"Derek is married," she says, before I ask if I can call her later.

"Who's Derek?"

"The neurosurgeon on *Grey's Anatomy*. Poor Meredith finally gives him a chance and then his wife shows up. Can you believe it?"

I laugh. "Mom, I haven't seen it, so yes, I can believe almost anything Meredith and Derek do. I thought we were talking about real people. How's everything else? You're home kind of early."

"Ed, my boss, made me leave. He was worried about my car making it down the hill—we're supposed to get freezing rain tonight."

My chest tightens. "Did you salt the walkway? Because you know that asshole apartment manager isn't going to do it."

She sighs. "I hadn't even heard about the rain 'til Ed told me, so I don't have any salt yet."

I climb from my seat and head for my laptop, still sitting on the chair by Ben's door. "I'll call the front desk. They're liable for any injuries that take place on their property if they can't show they took proper precautions."

"Gemma, don't. Suzy in the main office has hated me ever since you called last year. She won't even tell me when I get a package now."

My fists clench. "Document it, Mom," I growl. "Document everything she's done. She doesn't get to treat you like that."

I can hear the rage in my voice. It's the sort that would turn to tears as soon as I hang up the call, if Ben wasn't here to witness it.

"Honey, stop. You're just going to make things worse. I don't want Suzy to get fired. She's doing her best, and she's got problems of her own."

Stop being so forgiving, I want to scream. *Stop letting people walk on you. And stop assuming the best of others when no one will extend that same courtesy to you.* I'm angry at her. I'm angry on her behalf. I'm so angry, and I'm so *tired* of being angry all the time. Maybe I wouldn't have to be if I accepted my father's offer —but then I'd be angry about other things instead.

"Okay," I tell her, swallowing hard.

When I hang up the phone, I'm still upset, and considering my options. I'll play along for now, but if she falls, I'm suing them for everything they're worth.

"What was that about?" Ben asks, walking up behind me.

I shake my head because it's easier not to talk about it. "Nothing. Just my mom."

But then he turns me to face him, his hands cradling my jaw, forcing my gaze to his. I sense what it's meant to convey: *tell me, let me in.* How many times now has he held me when I'm upset, patiently waiting for me to open up to him, getting nothing in response? Too many.

"They're expecting freezing rain tonight," I say quietly. "My mom's apartment complex is supposed to shovel and salt the walkways and they never do it. She fell last year and sprained her wrist."

"She didn't want to sue?"

"She said it would just cause more problems and I—" My voice cracks and I have to stop talking about it. I have to.

"You what?" he asks softly.

"I could get her a better place, but she won't let me help her. And nothing in her apartment works. The towel rack came out of the wall, she can't reach the light on the front porch, and there's no place to keep a ladder so it's always burned out. It's just so unfair. She did everything for me, she did everything for my father, and this is where she's ended up. And now people take advantage of her and I can't fucking stand it."

He pulls me closer and presses his lips to the top of my head. "You want to burn the whole world to ash, just to make sure every path she walks is cleared for her. I know the feeling."

THE FOLLOWING DAY, I locate Lauren, the employee Leona told us had been invited to the strip clubs but only if she got on stage. I convince her to meet with me—she can attest to being sexually harassed at work *and* name employees who participated in the strip club outings—but she insists she won't testify.

Even though she's no longer with the company, and doesn't even live in the area, she still can't afford to piss them off.

Ben enters my office just as I'm hanging up the phone.

"You look way too happy," he says. "Let me guess: some guy you're taking to court just sent a dick pic to a small child?"

"Even better," I reply, and he laughs. "I located the woman who was harassed at Fiducia and she's willing to talk to me. I'm flying to Seattle on Friday."

"Let me see if I can move some stuff," he says, pulling out his phone.

I lean back in my chair, bracing for a fight. "I think I should take this one on my own. It's hard for women to discuss harassment with men, especially if it was bad, and she's really skittish."

His tongue prods his cheek and his nostrils flare. He's still my boss and this is *his* case. Of course he wants to be there.

But—astonishingly—he puts his phone away. "Okay," he says. "We'll celebrate when you get back."

"I don't even know if I'm going to get anything from her."

He laughs. "Of course, you're going to get something from her. You're Gemma Charles. You always figure it out."

I smile. He didn't even remind me I haven't made partner.

Later that evening a notification pops up on his phone while he's in the bathroom. He's made a reservation this coming Saturday at Ardor, an insanely expensive Michelin-starred restaurant. *Romance Package for Two.*

It's too much. Too serious, too romantic, and the idea of eating dinner at a table strewn with rose petals while everyone stares at us makes me wince. Yet a little thing in me just... relents. He believes in me in a way no one else ever has. He supports me, and he has waited. If he still wants to go to HR, to sign the form and have the whole goddamned office gossiping about us, then so be it. I'm ready.

37

On Friday, I wake before he does to catch my flight to Seattle. In the shower, I plan out what I will wear to Ardor—maybe the dress I wore to the retreat, with the Louboutins he bought me for Christmas. Perhaps, for once, the night will end at his place rather than mine. And when it does, I'll tell him we can go to HR. He'll be pleased by that—I suspect he wants it more than he lets on.

I perch on the side of the bed when it's time for me to head to the airport. "I left a key on the counter so you can lock up," I tell him. I guess that's a step, too, giving him a key. Doing it this way makes it feel like less of a big deal. "I'm not sure when I'm getting back, so maybe I'll just plan to see you tomorrow? Hopefully there will be something to celebrate."

"Oh." He blinks up at me, still half asleep. "Let's do it Sunday. I've got a family thing tomorrow night."

I freeze. "You're seeing your *family* Saturday night?"

"Yeah." He isn't quite meeting my eye. "The pains of being a local."

Is he lying to me?

How could he not be? That reservation at Ardor was not for

us, and the *romance package for two* sure as hell isn't a *family* thing. The brunches he didn't invite me to, the friends I didn't meet, the house he never wanted me to see...were those lies too?

How could I have been so stupid? How could I have been so stupid *again*?

I rise, holding myself stiffly, as if my bones will crack with any sudden movement.

"Okay," I tell him. I can't help the iciness in my voice, and why the fuck *should* I help the iciness in my voice? "Don't forget to lock up."

He nods. "I'll catch up with you later."

"We'll see," I reply. Which is easier than telling him this is done, but it definitely is.

It hurts in ways I never expected it to.

I'm tempted to storm dramatically into Ardor tomorrow night, but what could I even complain about? We aren't official, at my insistence.

I barely notice the ride to the airport. Keeley calls while I'm waiting for my flight. "Convince me a five-thousand-dollar purse is a good investment," she says.

"Well, Birkin bags hold their value," I reply listlessly.

It's the best I can do. Keeley wastes too much money on garbage. She's never going to be able to retire with the way she spends.

"Your heart really is not into helping me blow five grand on stupid shit the way it normally is."

"My heart is never into that, Keels," I say quietly, resting my face in my free hand. "I worry about you."

"What's wrong with you today?"

I hold a hand to my throat. It's hard to get the words out.

"That reservation I told you about?" I whisper. "It wasn't for me. He told me he has a family thing tomorrow night."

"For *two*? That fucking asshole," she hisses.

I squeeze my eyes shut, trying not to cry, because it isn't what I'd hoped she'd say.

I wanted her to tell me things might be different than they appear. I wanted her to craft an entirely plausible explanation for that reservation, for the lie.

I'm as bad as my clients, the ones who believed their cheating husbands' ridiculous excuses for not coming home, who rationalized a sudden desire to get in shape and the way he started walking outside to make phone calls.

"I'm sorry," she says. "I thought he was different."

Yeah. I did too.

I ARRIVE in Seattle and take the ferry out to Bainbridge Island where Lauren now lives. She has a pretty sweet gig, working from home for a tech firm. The sun comes out as we approach the harbor and I picture moving here too. Putting LA behind me, giving up on everything. I doubt working with Ben will even be possible after this—it's gone too far for me to detach as if it never happened.

Except if I'm going to give up on everything, I should probably just work for my dad. I'm not going to be happy either way, but at least my mom would come out ahead.

I meet Lauren at a café in town, and we manage to get a table outside in the winter sun. She's small and blond like Keeley but orders herself a green juice and a vegan quiche, which Keeley could not be paid to eat.

"I can't believe you flew all the way up here," she says. "No offense, but you look like you need some sleep."

I try to force a smile and find, to my horror, that I'm on the cusp of tears. "Oh, God," I whisper. "Sorry."

I reach for the napkin that came with my lunch and press it to my eyes. I've never once, in my entire life, cried in front of a client or a potential witness.

"I'm so sorry," she says, blinking in surprise. "You're gorgeous, obviously. I just meant you look tired."

I give a small, strangled laugh, which sounds like a sob too. As if I'd cry because someone said I look tired—I've probably looked tired for the past fifteen years straight. "It's not that. My boyfriend is seeing someone else."

I have no idea why I've told her this, or why I'm suddenly calling him my *boyfriend*. It's the most unprofessional moment of my life.

She leans forward. There's nothing like a cheating story to make women unite. "Fucking men," she groans. "They're all the same. I dated a guy who claimed he was picking up overtime because he was saving money for a house, and then I ran into him at a restaurant with his *wife and kids*."

I sigh. "I guess it could have been worse then. Here, let me get out my notes so you can get back to your daughter."

"Take your time," she says. "I never get to eat lunch out anymore."

I pull myself together enough to ask her the questions on my list. She tells me the same story Leona did about the strip clubs and names a slew of men who went to them, at least one of whom was a vice president at the time. I'd hoped I could push her into testifying, but I don't have it in me today. When the meal concludes, I simply hand the waitress my credit card and thank Lauren for her time. Maybe it's for the best the reservation at Ardor wasn't for me, since there won't be much to celebrate.

"So is Fiducia going to get away with this crap?" she asks as we stand to leave.

"I'm not sure," I reply. I'm too disheartened for optimism today. "Men will call you *weak* if you're soft, and they'll call you *abrasive* if you're not soft. They've set it up so there's no way for us to succeed, and they get away with most of it."

She bites her lip. "Will Fiducia have to apologize, if Margaret wins?"

"Yes," I reply with grim certainty. "I'll make sure of it."

I walk down the hill to the ferry. I haven't even climbed on board before Lauren texts to say she'll testify.

I got exactly what I came here for. It doesn't feel like much of a victory, though.

38

I get back to LA early Friday evening. I have no intention of seeing Ben, but he just shows up at my door, having gotten my flight info from Terri.

I want him to go away, but it feels like I'll either scream or burst into tears if I try to address this in person, which means it's better left to email or text—somewhere I can remain in control.

He kisses me, and if he notices how stiff I am as it happens, he doesn't say so.

"I was just about to go to the store," I lie. "And then I'm going to bed." In truth I was planning to eat a handful of chocolate chips and reevaluate my life, but I need to get him out of my apartment first.

He says he'll come with me and I immediately regret the lie. I don't feel like going through the ruse of shopping in addition to the ruse of not being mad at him.

He asks how the trip to Seattle went and I answer, but I'm growing steadily angrier as we walk to the elevator. How can he be the guy who shows up at my apartment the second my flight lands, and also be the guy who lies to my face? How could he push so hard for me to let him in, to lean on him, when he never intended to stick around?

We walk into the store and he grabs us a cart. He's talking about deposing Lauren quickly before she changes her mind, and I'm thinking about him holding me after I talked to my mom the other night. He should never have gone down this path with me in the first place, should never have pushed me to invite him over and take a trip out of town with him. It's utter bullshit that he led me on the way he did.

"What should we make?" he asks.

I thought I could do this, but I can't. I'm not letting him back into my apartment, making dinner by his side as if nothing's gone wrong.

"Some marcona almonds and a little manchego. I don't feel like cooking." I'll claim to have a headache as we leave and send him on his way.

He raises a brow. "Don't you think you ought to learn how to make a few meals for your widowed veterinarian?"

The widowed veterinarian. *Yes.* Someone who won't cheat, who won't trade up, who won't claim he's seeing his family when he's taking another woman to a Michelin-starred restaurant.

"I kind of pictured him doing most of the cooking," I reply, feeling vicious now, more myself. "Or I pictured becoming the kind of person who enjoys cooking."

"Do you have a timeline for when this magnificent transformation will take place?" He smirks. "When you suddenly want to take time off work and cook?"

Rage is turning me into the woman I become in court sometimes—ruthless and without mercy—and I welcome it. *The Castrator* wouldn't weep like a child over some cheating asshole. She'd just remind him she has all those extra teeth. "It won't happen overnight," I reply. "The widowed veterinarian has to teach me how to slow down and smell the roses first."

"Right," he says a little dourly. "I want to see how many shoes you throw the first time a man tries to provide *you* with advice on how to live."

"It will be different with him. Because he'll be wise. Like Dumbledore."

"I guess that explains why you're taking those walks in the country," he mutters, "because I don't see you begging Dumbledore to fuck you harder."

He's jealous of a hypothetical future husband while planning to take out a very non-hypothetical woman tomorrow night. What gives him the fucking right?

"*He'll* be so good at it," I reply with a bitter smile. "I won't even have to ask."

He stops suddenly, in the middle of the produce section. "I'm leaving," he says, fury stamped on every feature of his face.

I stare at him in shock. This is what I wanted, and now I also…don't want him to go. "What?"

"You heard me. Call your widowed veterinarian and have him tell you a bunch of patronizing shit about how to live your life better. See how well you like it."

And then he heads out the door, leaving me behind.

I stand frozen for a moment before I walk stiffly toward the exit, barely holding myself together. I put the cart back, but by the time I reach the elevator, I'm crying. My sadness feels ancient, as if these are tears I should have cried years ago, yet they've got nothing to do with Kyle.

It's Ben, and how disappointed I am that after two years of wanting him, he's breaking my heart, just the way I knew he would.

~

IT'S NEARLY two a.m. and I've cried myself to sleep when I hear a key in the door.

Ben enters the room, taking slow steps toward the side of the bed. In the dim light, he seems exhausted, his shirt untucked and wrinkled, circles under his eyes. He strips down to his boxers and climbs in beside me, pulling me against him. He smells like bourbon. I know I'm being weak, letting him stay. It was weak to ever allow this to begin in the first place. I just want one last night of pretending he's mine.

"I'm crazy about you, Gemma," he whispers against the top of my head. "I don't want to be, but I am."

My hands slide over his back, memorizing the feel of him, his shoulders blades, his spine, the breadth of him. My God, he's so perfect I want to weep.

It's not just an expression. I *do* want to weep. I'm struggling not to. I roll away, letting him tuck me tight to his chest.

"Then don't go tomorrow night," I whisper. I'm begging and it's fucking pathetic, but I can't help myself. "Please just don't go."

I wait for him to answer. To apologize, to tell me he made a mistake and swear he'll fix it.

Instead, his breathing just grows deep and even as sleep overtakes him.

39

I'm sick to my stomach as I head to the office on Saturday. Ben stumbled out early, unhappy again and oddly quiet, seeming to regret he came over at all. I wanted to ask for my key back but I just couldn't do it. I knew I couldn't get the words out without bursting into tears.

I meet Keeley and her newest boytoy at a bar that night. I don't like the guy and I don't like his friends, either, but it would be hard to focus on much tonight anyway, given the circumstances.

Ben is at Ardor by now. I wonder if he's asking her if Malbec's okay, if they're talking as easily and animatedly as we did. If he'll whisper, *"maybe I just want to be someone you trust"* when he kisses her. I thought it was different with us, that I wasn't like every other woman he takes out. I now have no idea why.

"Give me your phone," Keeley says, draining her glass and setting it on the table. "I'm finding you a date."

I blink. "I don't want a date, Keeley."

"The first thing to do when you fall off a horse is climb back on. Ben wasn't what you wanted anyway."

I nod, but she's wrong. I'm pretty sure he was exactly what I wanted, even if it took getting hurt to recognize it, even if I knew better.

"You're welcome," she says, handing me my phone.

"What did you just do?" I demand.

She waves a hand at me. "It's just coffee. You don't have to bang him...although you probably should."

My jaw falls open. Going out with a stranger is the last thing I want to do, especially right now.

"Gemma," she says softly, "think about it. How are you going to stand to work with Ben all week, knowing he's moved on if you haven't at least tried to move on too?"

And I still desperately want to tell her to cancel it...but she isn't wrong.

I HAVE butterflies the next morning as I walk toward a coffee shop in Brentwood to meet a guy named Kevin, and they're not the good kind. It feels like I'm nine again, shoplifting hairspray on a dare, knowing I'm going to get caught.

I have to remind myself I'm not doing anything wrong. Ben and I are not together. We have not exchanged promise rings or made an oath of fidelity. And for fuck's sake, he just took some girl to Ardor last night. For all I know, they wound up back at the house he was unwilling to ever let me see then took her to the family brunch this morning, the one he never invited me to. I owe him nothing.

He texts as I near the coffee shop. I'm tempted to ignore him, but I don't need him turning up at my apartment later because I didn't reply.

BEN

Brunch ended early. Are you at home?

A thousand angry words come to mind. *How was dinner, Ben? Did you bring her with you to meet the family, or was the whole thing about brunch with your family a fucking lie all along?*

I bite the inside of my cheek, willing myself to be cool, disinterested.

No. I have plans today.

Later, I will write him and say something distant and impersonal: *this just isn't what I want and it's run its course.* And then I'll need to figure out how to work by his side on the Lawson case without it destroying me, without letting him know how much I hate him for having failed me.

Kevin is waiting at the table when I arrive. He's cute. If it weren't for Ben, I'd probably be interested.

He rises from his seat and gives me a hug. "It's nice to meet you."

I glance at the line inside. He's already got a drink.

"You too. I'm just gonna—"

"Oh, yeah," he says. "Do you want me to—"

"No, no," I say, waving him off. "Just sit. I'll be right back."

Jesus. I'd forgotten how uncomfortable first dates are.

The line takes too long. I mouth an apology, and he shakes his head, as if it's his fault. I don't want to be here, and I'm not sure why I am. I'm not the kind of girl who can revenge fuck someone hours after she was with someone else.

I return with a latte I don't even want. I take a big sip and burn the shit out of my tongue.

"So..." I say, "you're a farmer?"

To my surprise, he says yes. He's not *also* a struggling actor, not doing it as a stopgap while he decides about grad school or gets his dumb tech start-up off the ground. He proceeds to tell me all about organic gardening.

He's exactly what I want, and spending time with him bores me out of my fucking mind.

I RETURN to my apartment when the interminable date is over and come to a dead stop as I walk down the hall. Ben is sitting outside my door. He doesn't smile when he sees me. Just silently rises, his eyes dark as night.

"What are you doing here?" I ask, shifting my keys from one hand to the next. "I told you I had plans."

"Were you on a date?" he demands.

I have no idea what to say. A part of me wants to throw it in his face, and another part of me still feels like I did something wrong.

"*What?*" I ask.

His nostrils flare. "Were. You. On. A. Fucking. Date?"

I shove my hands into the pockets of my cardigan. "Would it matter?"

His mouth falls open, his breathing uneven. "Yes, it fucking matters."

He turns and unlocks the door with the key I'm about to demand back and marches inside. I follow him in, slowly unbuttoning my sweater and trying to pretend I'm as ambivalent as I *should* be. I hang it on the hook, ignoring him, and then draw my shoulders back. In sneakers I feel way too small standing here before him.

"I'll take your non-answer as an answer," he says with an angry laugh. "Though I should have known when you said you had *plans*. You never make plans that aren't work. Until today, that is."

I blow out a breath. "Is that why you're here? Because I said I had plans?"

"No." He stalks toward me. "I'm here because I fucking *saw you* walking down the street with a guy on what definitely looked like a date, and I was hoping you'd tell me I was wrong."

"So what?" I ask, and all the rage and pain I'm not supposed to feel seem to take possession of me. "If you can take a girl out to Ardor for dinner when you're *supposedly* hanging out with your family, I'm not going to apologize for having coffee at noon with someone else."

His eyes go wide. "How'd you even *know* about that?"

I laugh. I sound completely unhinged—I *am* completely unhinged—but how goddamned typical of a man to cheat and then complain about my invasion of his privacy. "The notification came up on your phone last week, Ben. Don't flatter yourself into thinking I was snooping. And sorry, but no, you're not going to convince me dinner for *two* was a family event. Now get the fuck out of my apartment and leave the key."

He shakes his head, his jaw grinding. "I did not eat at Ardor last night. I made a reservation for my brother, who was proposing to his girlfriend. And then there was a party at my mother's house afterward to celebrate."

I've been here before—the elaborate stories, the spinning of lies, the explanation for everything no matter how outlandish. "Key," I repeat, holding out my hand.

He holds his phone in front of me instead, where someone named Mandy has texted him a photo of a big diamond ring.

MANDY

You knew!!!!! Thanks for setting this all up for us.

I swallow, my stomach in knots. I fucked up and I've probably ruined everything. *But* the lawyer in me argues, *this isn't all my fault. Yes, I shouldn't have jumped to conclusions, but maybe if Ben hadn't been keeping me at arm's length, away from his family and friends and his home, I wouldn't have.* Why didn't he tell me his brother was getting engaged? Why didn't he want me at the party? Would it have been so goddamned hard just to include me a little?

"You can't fault me for misunderstanding," I whisper, and I'm suddenly so very, very tired. Tired of worrying, tired of hurting, tired of thinking I need to protect myself from everything.

"So you decided you'd fuck someone to get even?" he demands.

My head jerks upward. *What?* "For Christ's sake. I met him for coffee and we walked down to the bookstore." I'm angry that he'd even *think* I could do something like that, but then again, why wouldn't he? I thought it of him, and he wasn't the one refusing to admit we were in a relationship.

In *his* shoes, I'd have thought the same thing. I'd have thought worse.

He steps forward, still livid. His hand curves around my neck, tangling in my hair, tilting my face to his. "And did you like him? Did he kiss you?"

My heart thuds in my chest. I wonder what he'd do if I said, "*yes.*" I'm tempted to lie and say I did, because this is all fucked up and I don't ever want to live through another forty-eight hours like the ones that just passed.

"You want the truth?" I demand. "He was a farmer, and *sweet*, and he should have been perfect for me. But I was bored out of my fucking mind. So you were right. Are you happy now?"

"Did. He. Kiss. You?" he demands.

"Of course not!" I shout. "Why are you so obsess—"

His mouth comes down on mine, hard and fast. Angry, demanding.

I don't let myself think about what this means. I just give in.

His hands go to my jeans, and he flips the button and shoves them down. "Take them off. Take it all off," he growls.

I kick off the jeans while he pulls his shirt over his head and lets it fall to the floor. His hands grip my hips, and he walks me backward to the couch, where he pushes me flat, spreading my thighs as he climbs between them. He's forcing me to give up control, and I both hate and love how turned on I am by this—I'm soaked and he hasn't even touched me. He undoes his pants and shoves them down to mid-thigh before he leans over, grabbing each wrist and holding them above my head with one hand in a punishing grip.

I shiver in anticipation as he grasps himself, his eyes on my face as he pushes inside me...for once without a condom. I should resent it, but instead, desire unfurls in my core at the way he is taking without asking.

The sex is harder and faster than normal. For once, he is not concerned about me coming first. I get the feeling he might enjoy making me do without. It's selfish and indulgent and so fucking hot—his recklessness, his quiet groans, the desperate way he moves inside me, his free hand sliding from my breasts and downward, as if he wants to be everywhere at once.

I try to arch, and he presses his weight down, immobilizing me as he pistons in and out. I should hate this. I should. But I'm already close.

"Holy shit, Ben," I beg, breathlessly. "Slow down."

"Jesus," he says, nostrils flaring as he looks at me. "You fucking love this, don't you? Admit you love being held down and fucked."

I do, but I'm not about to give in that easily. "Not as much as you love doing it."

"I'm so goddamn close," he says. "Keep running that smart mouth. Maybe I'll just go ahead and come, and let you wait until later."

I can't. I can't let him do it. I'm *so* close. "I love it."

His grip tightens around my wrists and a jolt of pleasure shoots through me. With his free hand he pulls up my knee, changes the angle, hitting the right spot.

"Oh, God," I gasp, feeling my stomach tighten, and he grabs my hair tight in his fist.

"No more dates," he growls in my ear, and I explode, crying out. "Fuck," he hisses, thrusting faster and faster as he starts to come. "Fuck."

I shift, and he presses harder, breathing heavy. "Stay like that. Just stay. I'm not done."

He's still inside me, still pulsing softly. Once, twice, three times. In a minute he's every bit as hard as he was. He sits up, still inside me, and his gaze holds mine.

"Are we clear now?" he asks. "You've got to stop assuming the worst of me all the time, Gemma."

"Yes," I whisper. I want it to be true, but I'm not sure it is.

Because the problem with telling yourself to ignore that voice in your head—the one that sees danger everywhere—is that sometimes that voice is absolutely right.

40

My graduation from law school was full of smiling faces, but none of them were there for me. I didn't invite my father, and my mother couldn't afford to fly out. All my friends were at Stadler, and I'd seen little of them since I started dating Kyle, who was in the middle of a trial back in New York.

I've never felt more alone than I did on that stage, knowing not a single person was there to see me or knew who I was.

Kyle sent roses, and though he hated to text, that night he sent a picture of him and his daughter with ice cream cones in hand, saying he and Izzy were celebrating my graduation.

I was already thinking of my reply when I noticed something. I stared at the photo for a long moment. Blinked. And then I zoomed in on the background of the image, right over his shoulder and stared again, my stomach sinking.

In the mirror to their left was the reflection of the woman taking the photo. It was Josie, smiling and happy. And she was very, very pregnant.

∾

I STRUGGLED to find any alternate explanation, but nothing worked. I wanted to believe she was pregnant with someone else's kid, but if she were, he'd have told me. And surely it would have come up during one of his stories about her drinking.

His stories. *My God.* When I began to put together the size and depth of all his lies, it made me physically ill. I'd made so many excuses for him: for his insistence on keeping it a secret, all the canceled visits, the way he muted his phone when we were together. I'd actually *admired* him for calling from the sidelines of Oliver's soccer games or while waiting for a children's birthday party to end...when he was probably just capitalizing on some time free of his wife. And when I got upset about the situation, he'd persuaded me he was ready to go public because he knew I'd back down if my job was at risk.

He'd been lying to me—and he'd lied so very, very well—but I'd been lying to myself too. That suspicious voice in my head, the one both he and my therapist had long been telling me not to trust, had been right all along.

Had he ever planned to leave? Had they ever been separated at all? Was he happy with her? I knew he wouldn't tell me the truth, and even if he did, I wouldn't believe it. I had to see for myself.

I friended Josie on social media under a fake name. The first thing I saw was a picture of them, taken on my birthday weekend. They were smiling behind a big blue cake. The banner overhead reading *It's a boy!*

She'd posted pictures of them at various places: a Christmas party, a baseball game he'd called me from, a family trip to Florida he'd told me had just been him and the kids.

And I had no one to discuss it with because who was ever going to believe I really hadn't known he was married? Who was going to believe that I, of all people, had been *that* naïve?

I ignored his calls until evening.

"Where the hell were you all day?" he demanded when I finally answered.

"Just sitting here," I replied, "trying to figure out when your wife is due."

There was the longest silence, and my breath held. There was still a part of me hoping he had an explanation.

"I was going to tell you," he said.

And it was then that I knew, without a doubt, he would lie. And had been lying all along.

41

Ben leaves the following weekend for a trial in DC. He expects it to go quickly, and I hope he's right: depositions for Lawson are set to begin in two weeks, and I want him by my side when they occur.

I've never felt quite as apathetic about work as I do on Monday. There are no strawberries at the morning meeting. Fields is civil to me, nothing more, still holding a grudge over Webber.

I meet Walter for lunch to go over the mountain of work he needs FMG to handle. I can rope in a few of the junior associates to help while I'm dealing with Lawson, but he shouldn't be giving us all this work in the first place.

"I've said this before," I tell him with a smile, "but you really ought to just hire someone in-house. You easily have more than enough work to keep a full-time attorney busy."

He cuts into his steak and spears a bite with his fork. "You trying to get rid of me?" he asks with a grin.

"Of course not. You're still my favorite client. I just don't like to see you wasting your money."

He points his fork at me. "And that's why I like you, Gemma.

Because you tell me the truth even when it does you a disservice. I want to introduce you to my oldest boy, one of these days."

I blush, remembering Ben above me, growling, *"no more dates"* in my ear. "I'm, uh, seeing someone," I reply. "And even he'd tell you I'm no one you'd want to set up with your son."

Walter smiles to himself. "Bet you keep him on his toes."

I laugh. "That's one way of putting it."

More like he keeps me on mine.

On the way back to the office, I read the texts Ben sent during lunch. He's in the middle of jury selection. I write back, encouraging him to select the juror who came in wearing what she *claimed* was an invisibility cloak.

BEN

You just love to fuck with people who really want out of jury duty, don't you?

How dare you? But also, yes.

I wish you were here.

I'm still smiling over that twenty minutes later, when Sophia Waterhouse walks in.

"I'm glad one of us is happy," she says, setting a manila folder on my desk. "My husband just cut off my credit cards to keep me from going on vacation. You told me he had to pay for reasonable expenses."

"He'll be forced to reimburse you," I tell her. "Do you not have anything you can use?" I know I warned her about this. I tell every client to get a credit card in her own name because this *always* happens eventually.

"Yes, but it only has an eighteen-thousand-dollar limit," she replies. "That won't *begin* to cover the trip. I need my platinum card back."

I still. "I said *reasonable* expenses, Sophia. Your husband isn't a millionaire, so the court isn't going to consider a trip that costs more than eighteen grand reasonable."

"I thought you were supposed to be the lawyer who believes in women," she says. "Right now, it feels like you're on his side."

I sigh. She isn't the first client who's accused me of hating women the minute I tell her what she doesn't want to hear.

I straighten the files in front of me. "I'm not on his side, obviously, but you can't draw blood from a stone. A trip that costs more than eighteen grand is a big swing for most people, and even if I get you half his income for the next five years, that's two hundred grand, before taxes. Which means it's a big swing for you too."

"*If* you get me half?" she asks, clutching her Chloe handbag, as if I plan to take it from her next. "I thought that was a certainty. I can't raise two kids in LA for less than that."

"You won't have them all the time," I remind her. "And he'll be paying tuition."

Her eyes narrow, as if I've insulted her somehow. "I want full custody," she says. "I don't want his little whore around my kids."

Evan Waterhouse might not have been the greatest husband, but he seems like a very involved father. I just no longer have it in me to exact revenge on an innocent man for my father's mistakes. "That isn't what we discussed. And you would have to prove he'd done something very, very wrong to get that."

She tilts her head to the side, studying me. "What would be considered very, very wrong?"

"If he was abusive, or violent," I reply, comfortable in the knowledge that Evan is neither of those things. "If he was an addict and refused treatment. It would have to be pretty extreme."

"Okay," she says, taking the manila folder back. "Give me a week."

I watch in dismay as she walks out of the office. I've long wished my mother had been more vindictive, more cutthroat on her own behalf. I've long been cutthroat on my clients' behalf. But right now, it feels very much like I'm on the wrong side.

"I think she's going to fabricate an accusation," I tell Ben when he calls that evening. "She said, '*give me a week*'. There was no mention of abuse at all when she first saw me, and I *asked*. I'm just not sure I want to be a part of this anymore."

I half expect him to encourage me to fire her. He's given me the sense on more than one occasion that he thinks family law won't make me happy.

"It's not the time to be jettisoning clients," he warns instead, after a moment's hesitation. "You need all the hours you can get until Fields has made you partner. Especially when he's still mad at you for threatening Webber."

It's the first time he's admitted that I'll be the one to make partner rather than Craig. I wish I had time to gloat but the topic at hand matters more.

"I can't just keep charging her money if I'm not going to continue with her case."

"I know. But she hasn't done anything wrong yet. Just leave it for now. We'll figure it out when I'm home."

I smile, even though he can't see it. I love not being alone in everything anymore. But I especially love that *he's* the one in my court. There's no one I'd rather have here.

"You're still coming back Friday, right?" I ask, a little embarrassed by how needy the question is. He's only been gone for a day and it's already too long.

"Why?" he asks. "Do you miss me?"

"I'm very hungry. There's been no one here to make sure I eat."

After we hang up, I go to my room and clear out two

drawers for him. I guess I sort of want him to feel like he belongs here.

ON TUESDAY, I place an order for a bigger television since Ben hates mine. On Wednesday, I go to my favorite home store and buy décor: throw pillows, a new duvet cover, matching lamps for my nightstand and Ben's. I replace the plant I killed off months ago—Ben will water it, even if I forget.

On Thursday, the defendant in Ben's case decides to settle. In theory, this means he can be done with the whole thing on Friday, but there's snow in the forecast. The mere idea of his flight getting canceled steals my breath. I hadn't realized, until this moment, just how much I was counting on seeing him.

"Try to get back," I tell him. "I don't want to prepare for the depositions all on my own."

He laughs. "And you're hungry," he reminds me.

"I am. I'm extremely hungry."

I leave work early and drive to Santa Monica because seeing his house makes me feel closer to him, even if he won't let me inside it. The work trucks are gone. So is the construction permit. I wonder if he'll finally invite me over. On the way home I buy groceries. He mentioned once that his favorite food is homemade chicken pot pie. I suppose it won't kill me to try to make him one.

When I wake on Friday, the first thing I do is check the weather in DC. They got three inches of snow, but so far, Ben's flight is still leaving on time.

I call my mom as soon as I arrive in the office. "I heard about the snow. Are they shoveling?"

"Honey, you worry too much," she replies, sounding oddly...happy.

"I don't worry too much, Mom." I begin to pace the floors of my office. "For God's sake...how will you even work at the bar if you sprain your wrist again? Or what if it's something worse?"

"It's all been taken care of," she says. "Look."

She texts me a photo of her parking lot, where not a single thing is shoveled, aside from the path to her car, which has also been cleared of snow.

"They only did *yours*?" I ask.

"You can't ask questions about it," she replies primly, which immediately floods my brain with worst-case scenarios: a creepy apartment manager offering her special favors, an obsessed customer, following her home at night.

"Mom, this is fucked up. Of course, I'm going to ask. Who did this? Is it someone you even know?"

"I know him *now*," she says with a quiet laugh. "Your friend Ben did it. You never mentioned how handsome he was."

"Ben?" I repeat incredulously. "Ben from *work*?"

"I can't believe you said he was 'really old'. I've been picturing a middle-aged man for the past two years."

I exhale, exasperated. "Mom, how the hell did you meet Ben?"

"I heard someone outside this morning, so I went to the window and there he was, shoveling my path, wearing a *suit*."

I perch on my desk, legs suddenly weak. "A suit?"

She laughs. "Yes. No one was more shocked than I to discover it was the terrible Ben Tate, of whom I've heard so much."

My eyes fill and I swallow down the lump now firmly lodged in my throat. He drove all the way out to Manassas before he went to settlement. He must have left before it was even light out.

"How?" I whisper. "I mean, he's staying in a hotel."

"I have no idea. But he brought a shovel and salt, and he did the whole thing then came in and fixed my towel rack and the shelf. I've got to tell you, Gemma...he didn't seem to dislike you nearly as much as you dislike him. In fact, I'd venture to say he likes you an awful lot."

I close my eyes. "I don't dislike him, Mom."

She laughs again. I've never heard her laugh quite so much in one phone call. "Yes, honey, I know. And I'm glad. If you ask me, he's a keeper. But he swore me to secrecy, so don't tell him I told you. That boy might be my son-in-law one of these days."

"He won't be," I reply. My voice cracks.

"My sweetest girl," she says with a sigh. "You think you can see the future, but all you're really doing is choosing it for yourself in advance. And I wish you'd stop choosing the things that can't make you happy."

When we get off the phone, I lock the office door then sit with my face in my hands, trying not to cry.

I love him.

I love him so fucking much it terrifies me.

WHEN BEN'S flight gets in that night, he comes straight to me from the airport, dropping his suitcase in the foyer and wrapping his arms around me, as if it hurt him to stay away. The apartment smells like smoke from the chicken pot pie I accidentally set on fire, but he doesn't seem to notice.

I don't tell him I know what he did for my mom. I don't tell him I'm ready to be official. But I finally admit something that's been true since the beginning. "I missed you," I whisper, pressing my head to his chest.

42

Work, in the days leading up to the first depositions, is frantic. In theory, we're getting ready to go to trial, but our hope is that we can scare Fiducia into settling. It'll be a lot faster and cheaper for everyone involved.

Ben and I are working out of his office night after night and over the following weekend. It's stressful but it's also...fun. I've never enjoyed getting ready for a trial, until now. I didn't even realize it was a possibility.

At the moment, he's preparing questions for Ryan Venek, a manager who got promoted despite several fights at work. I'm working on the questions for Rick Sandburg, the vice president who charged two of the strip club outings to his corporate card. I yawn and look up to find him watching me.

"What?" I ask.

"Can we go away when this is done? On an actual vacation. Not just a weekend somewhere."

"I'm gonna have a ton of work to catch—" I begin, and then I see how much he wants me to just say, *"yes"*, how much he wants me to just be *in* this thing with both feet. I bite the inside of my cheek. "Where would we go?"

His face settles into the kind of relieved smile you get at the end of a race you've spent ages training for. "Fiji. An overwater villa. Clothing optional."

I had something like that on my Pinterest travel page once upon a time. I think of all the things I once pinned: the trips I wanted to take, the books I wanted to read, the home I wanted to build. It's a revelation, discovering I still want those things badly, that they're not something I've entirely left behind. Maybe *future Gemma* isn't an impossibility. Maybe, in a small way, she's already here.

"We can't have sex the entire time," I warn, as if I would *ever* complain if that was the case.

He leans across the table and presses his lips to my forehead. "You can bring as many books as you want."

THREE NIGHTS before the depositions begin, I stay at the office while Ben has dinner with Fields. He was tense when he left, but wouldn't tell me why.

I'm yawning, waiting for him. When my eyes can't stop falling closed, I text.

> I'll meet you at the apartment.

BEN
> I'm exhausted. Have to be in early tomorrow, so I think I'll just head home.

Exhaustion has never stopped him from staying at my place before. I want to suggest I can come to him. To say, *"since I know for a fact your house is done"*, but I don't. I don't say a word. Is this progress, the way I'm trying not to jump to conclusions? Or am I silencing a warning voice I should be listening to, just like I did before?

The next morning, his face is strained when I walk into his office. He looks like he's barely slept.

"How was last night?" I ask.

He rubs the back of his neck. "It was fine. Just a little difference of opinion."

I raise a brow, meaning, *"tell me what happened."*

He raises one back, meaning, *"you know I can't do that."*

I come around to his side of the desk. The door is open so I can't touch him, but I'm drawn toward him like a magnet anyway. "I was thinking," I venture tentatively, "that if we're going away together for a real vacation, then we probably need to go to HR."

I expect him to be pleased—he was the first one to mention it, after all—but a shadow comes over his face, a wariness flickering in his eyes.

"Sure," he says, sounding anything but. "Let's just wait until the Lawson case is done."

It would take us ten minutes at most to go to HR and get the paperwork signed. Two days ago, he was talking about a week away in Fiji, and now it's like he doesn't even want to be in the same room with me.

I'd like to be the version of me that no longer jumps to conclusions, who doesn't assume the worst, but I'm struggling right now. It feels like whatever was discussed with Fields has changed everything.

I take a deep breath. "Is something wrong?" I hate how weak, how vulnerable, it makes me feel, needing to ask.

His teeth sink into his lower lip before he shakes his head. "Just tired. Between this case and the class-action, I'm beat."

We work late and return to my apartment. He falls asleep

while I'm brushing my teeth, but when I wake in the middle of the night, he's pulling me close, and there's a tension in his grip that suggests he's been up for a while.

"Are you okay?" I whisper, rolling to face him.

"Sorry," he says. "I didn't mean to wake you."

I pull him on top of me. I know if I ask, he'll tell me he's fine, though he's clearly not, and all I can do for him now is this.

He moves inside me, slowly and silently, coming with a single sharp gasp, his mouth buried in my neck, and for a moment it feels like we're okay again.

He collapses beside me—his head on my pillow, his palm curving over my hip.

"Are you sure you don't want to talk?" I whisper. "I can tell something's bothering you."

He moves to his own pillow and rolls onto his back, staring at the ceiling.

"What happened at Stadler?" he finally asks.

I stiffen. I'd expected him to ask about Stadler again, but not like this. And not like he already knows. "Who told you about that?"

"Fields said something last night. That you stalked someone there."

My stomach drops. It hurts so much to hear him bring this up to me, to know that same fucking story is still circulating. I sit up with the sheet held to my chest. "And you believed him?"

He rolls toward me. "Of course not. That's why I'm asking you what happened."

"If that was true," I reply, throwing the covers off and swinging my legs to the floor, "you wouldn't even have to ask."

He grabs my hand. "Don't fucking run off, and don't act like you're mad just so you don't have to tell me the truth. I know you didn't stalk anyone. I just need the real story."

I want to refuse because I shouldn't have to defend myself to anyone. But he isn't wrong—part of my desire to run off and hide behind my anger is just that...because I want to hide. What happened wasn't all my fault, but it doesn't make me look great either.

"I was dating a partner there in law school," I begin. "Kyle. He was based out of the New York office. He told me he was getting divorced—he'd even shown me the separation agreement—and it was all a fucking lie. I didn't have a clue he was still with her until I found out she was pregnant. I'm not sure he was ever even planning to leave."

"So what happened?" he asks, his voice neutral, emotionless, giving nothing away. It's the voice I use with clients I don't entirely believe.

"They turned the whole thing around on me to protect him. They marched me out of the building like a fucking criminal, and everyone watched. All these goddamn male partners, protecting their own when every one of them knew it was bullshit."

"Jesus," Ben whispers, pulling me down beside him and wrapping his arms around me. "No wonder you're so obsessed with making partner."

"If I was a man, you wouldn't call me *obsessed*," I reply. "You'd just call me ambitious."

"Craig's been there as long as you," he says. "And I don't worry he'll set the building on fire if he doesn't get what he wants."

"Exactly," I reply, digging my nails into my palms. "Because Craig has no ambition whatsoever. That's why he shouldn't make partner."

He presses his lips to the top of my head. "I'm sorry. I'm so fucking sorry that happened to you."

I say nothing. It's no longer just the male partners at

Stadler, protecting their own. It's the men at my own goddamn firm, discussing this behind my back. Mischaracterizing me and spreading lies whenever it suits them.

I can't believe that after all this time, I'm still the one paying the price for what Kyle did.

43

When I confronted Kyle about his wife, he continued to lie.

I listened to him spin new stories like the master he was, but I listened from a distance, as if I was watching this take place between two other people. He told me he'd slipped one night, after they split. "I don't even know that the kid is mine," he said. "Either way, I'm leaving once the baby comes."

He told me he'd only found out recently, that he was as horrified by the situation as I was. I didn't bother asking him about the gender reveal party they'd held *months* before, or the trip to Florida, or all his stories about her drinking. I already knew exactly who he was: someone who could lie easily, without a shred of guilt.

He'd been building a castle out of a deck of cards, one he had to know would collapse on me eventually. But he just kept building.

"I don't believe a word out of your mouth," I said, my voice flattened by shock.

"If you tell anyone," he replied, "I'll fucking ruin you."

They were the last words we ever exchanged.

I spent that night reeling. Torn between shock and rage, torn between fearing the damage he might do to my career and feeling like his wife deserved to know who he was. It was because of my mom that I did the right thing. She'd given up so many years of her life to a man who didn't deserve her. I couldn't give her those years back, but maybe I could prevent it happening to someone else.

I messaged Josie from the fake profile I'd created and told her the truth—not that we'd chosen a ring and had been looking at houses, because it seemed like too much—but simply the bare facts, with enough detail that it would be hard to doubt me.

When I went into Stadler the next day, security escorted me into the managing partner's office, where I learned my employment offer was being rescinded. Kyle told them I'd been stalking him, and was now harassing his wife.

I argued, of course. I told him we'd been dating since the previous September and that I hadn't known Kyle was still with her.

"If you were dating him, you'd have informed the firm," he replied, which is when I knew I was screwed: they were either going to fire me for not telling HR about our relationship, or they were going to fire me for stalking. "And one of your colleagues has corroborated Kyle's story." He slid a print-out toward me of my text conversation with Meg: It was me joking about joining Equinox to stalk him. Suggesting I might buy an all-red wardrobe after learning it was his favorite color. She'd been just as bad, and had often been worse, but that didn't matter. She'd selectively shared her texts, and that's all Stadler wanted—*proof*, even if taken out of context.

"I've been here for three years," I pled. "You don't seriously believe all this?"

"It doesn't matter what I believe, Miss Charles," he said.

Because Kyle was the one making them money, so Kyle was the one they'd protect as long as they could.

He gave me a choice: allow security to escort me out and cease all contact with employees of the firm, or be fired for cause and struggle to ever get hired somewhere else.

I knew I could probably prove my side of things. I could show them my versions of the conversation with Meg, I could get proof of all the calls Kyle had made and text messages he'd sent. But I'd be blowing up any chance of salvaging my own career to do it.

I let myself be escorted out, under all those disdainful gazes. Meg's eyes met mine and I summoned all my hatred into that final look I gave her. She was just a pawn, but I'd never forgive her for it. I'd never forgive any of them.

Men with power had made this happen. Men just like my father, and the lawyers who railroaded my mother. They helped each other, covered for each other, did whatever was necessary to keep their little circle closed.

And they're apparently still doing it.

44

Ben's in a rush the next morning, the day before our first round of depositions. He's fully dressed while I'm still blinking myself awake.

"Do we need to talk about the thing from last night?" I ask him. He swings yesterday's jacket over his shoulder. "Yeah," he says, giving me a too-small smile, "but not right now."

When I get into the office, I go to my Pinterest travel page. I *did* have a Fiji trip on there. The link shows me an open-air villa with a large white bed, an entire open wall facing the sea.

Two days ago, it felt like a real possibility. Now, I'm not sure.

I open my email and discover Sophia has sent me photos of what is supposedly her diary, each entry detailing an incident of abuse. She says Evan hit her one night and that he threatened to kill her and the kids more than once. *I'm so scared of him,* she writes in one entry. *I just want the kids to be safe.*

Except it's dated two weeks before the trip she took to an Arizona spa, and you don't leave your kids for the weekend with someone you mistrust to that extent. She'd certainly have mentioned some of this before now.

I'd like to discuss it with Ben, but everything has to be

tabled until we get through tomorrow and he's so busy it's early evening before I even see him.

"Sorry," he says. "I didn't intend to be gone for so long. You probably haven't come up for air once."

"I took a little break to look up trips to Fiji," I tell him with a nervous smile, testing the water.

He winces. It's a half-second at most, but I see it. I turn away, distractedly shuffling through files. Inside, though, more bricks are added to the wall I wanted to rebuild the night he slept at his own place, the one I started building in earnest last night when he suggested I'd stalked someone.

I could ask him if the conversation with Fields has changed things between us, but why would I bother? It's obvious it has.

THE DEPOSITIONS BEGIN EARLY the next morning in a conference room at the Ritz-Carlton.

The first witness, Michelle Mitchell—Fiducia's only female manager—has clearly been coached, so she doesn't offer us a single useful word. Every question is answered with, *"I don't remember"* or *"Not to the best of my knowledge."*

Next up is Ryan Venek, who acknowledges he was in a fist fight with another employee and still got promoted. He also admits that yes, there'd been some trips to strip clubs on the company's dime.

Lauren is next. She attests to the strip club outings, and says she was told she could only come if she was, *"willing to take it all off."*

I produce receipts from two of the clubs, which show the charges billed to a corporate card. "Were these two of those nights?" I ask, and she says they were. She names every employee she remembers attending. It's a long list.

I've already warned her that Aronson is going to do his best to make her doubt herself, but her shoulders sag as he asks about her affair with another employee, references a party where she drank too much, an inappropriate comment made about her boss's attire. I complain about the relevance of the questions to no avail. Nonetheless, Aronson is a lot less smug when it concludes.

Our final witness is Rick Sandburg, the vice president who charged $15,000 at Magnolia's Adult Playhouse.

We ask the basic questions about his role, his length of employment. I'm already smiling because I can feel it coming: the moment when Aronson realizes how much worse this is going than he thinks.

I ask about the company outings to Magnolia's. He claims not to remember until I produce a photo of him getting a lap dance there.

"I charged it to the company card," he then says, "but I paid them back."

"So, if I were to subpoena your bank records," I continue, still smiling, leaning forward, "I'd find a check to Fiducia for over fifteen thousand dollars? Let me remind you that lying under oath is a felony with a prison sentence of up to five years."

"Miss Charles," says Aronson, "you're intimidating the witness."

I *am*, and it's worked. Sandburg's gaze veers wildly from opposing counsel to me. "I'm done," he announces, rising from his chair. "I want my own attorney present before this continues."

Aronson looks furious as Sandburg walks out. I'm smiling like I've just won the lottery.

"Funnily enough, none of the strip club outings appears in the expense reports we were sent," I tell him, sliding the hotel receipt someone clearly forged for the same amount. "How *curious* that it came to us as this instead."

He rises, looking only at Ben. "I need to talk to my client."

I REMAIN in the conference room until midnight with Ben, Craig, Fields and another partner, hammering out what we will ask for. Aronson called Ben to say they want to settle. He refuses to speak to me. Perhaps he finds me *shrill* and *abrasive*.

There's a number that could be arrived at based on what Margaret actually lost: what she'd have earned over the course of ten years as a manager and what she's lost in this past year of unemployment.

"That's a lot of money," Craig says when we calculate the amount.

"No," I argue. "I want to nail Fiducia to the wall over this. They falsified records, for fuck's sake. Accusing them of a crime will show the world just how shady they are."

"We can't," says Ben. "Margaret's our client. We're here to serve her, not to reform the system."

"But—"

He runs a hand over his face, tired of my arguments, though he can hardly fault me. When *he* wants something, he's like a dog with a bone too.

"Gemma, that they falsified records is the only leverage we have. With it, we can get them to double the amount they'd have paid her, and that alone will draw a shitload of negative attention. Every story about them for the next year will be about what they've done to change, and isn't that what you want?"

I hate when he's right.

"Fine. But it has to be accompanied by a formal apology," I reply. "Fiducia has to admit they made a mistake."

"Fine," he says with a tired smile. "We'll make them apologize."

We finish up so late that there's no point in Ben coming to my apartment—he'd barely let his head hit the pillow before he'd have to wake up and drive to Santa Monica.

"Get some rest," I tell him when we reach our cars. "We'll celebrate when we win tomorrow. I'll even attempt to cook."

He looks away. "Let's save your cooking for a time when we're feeling more ambivalent about our lives. I have plans tomorrow night, but we'll celebrate soon."

I freeze a little. That word, *plans*, is the cheater's version of a long *um*...the pause during which he comes up with some detail to sell his lie.

"Just a little family dinner," he adds, while something sinks further inside me. "But they tend to run late."

I've agreed to go to HR, I've agreed to go on a trip with him, but he's still shutting me out. He's gone from being a hundred percent in to acting like a guy who's counting the minutes until he can end things.

And it's going to hurt a thousand times more than my break-up with Kyle when it happens.

45

W e meet opposing counsel the next morning at the Beverly Hills Hotel. Ben arrives a few minutes late because he had to talk to Fields first, and remains in the background during the negotiation, letting me do the work. They give us a number slightly lower than Craig's until I remind them that Fiducia falsified records. "The last time a CEO was prosecuted for falsifying records, he wound up in jail," I tell them. "You might want to discuss that with your client before this conversation continues."

They leave to discuss it, and return with an amount more than double the one they came in with, along with a formal apology. In exchange, we will not accuse Fiducia of fraud.

"You can call Margaret to tell her," Ben says when we're done. "This was your victory, not mine. You were amazing in there."

There is something more muted about him than I expected. "Yet you don't seem happy."

His smile is small and forced. "I'm fine," he lies. "Just tired."

I call Margaret from the car. She cries when I tell her the outcome, and it's so much better than almost any moment I've had in court because no one has been *broken* by what occurred today. Fiducia might wind up a better company for it. Margaret will have enough to live off, and might even be able to get another job now.

I turn to Ben, who's in the middle of sending a text. When he finally glances at me, he looks uncertain.

"You're still seeing your family tonight?" I ask.

"Yes," he says, biting his lip. "It's my stepdad's birthday."

"I'd like to meet them sometime," I say, forcing myself to be this new version of Gemma, the one who is open and communicative and doesn't freeze him out the moment I feel a glimmer of fear. "Just to make sure you were born and not spawned."

He smiles but there's some discomfort in it. "I'm not sure meeting them would enlighten you any. My brothers are worse than me."

He avoided that a little too well. I stare out the window, trying not to be upset by it, but all the ways I used to console myself—*this doesn't mean anything, we aren't really together*—are no longer true, are they?

"If you're willing to tell HR we're a couple," I reply quietly, just as we arrive at the office, "then maybe you ought to be willing to introduce me to your family." *And your friends. And invite me to your home.*

"We need to talk later," he says. My head jerks toward him in surprise. He's already climbing out of the car, in a hurry. "Not now, though. Fields wants us all in the conference room. He's making a big announcement."

My heart begins to race as I accept his outstretched hand. "A big announcement?" I ask breathlessly.

He winks at me. "A big announcement," he repeats.

Suddenly it seems so petty, my complaints about Ben not inviting me along tonight.

We take the elevator upstairs and walk to the conference

room, where the staff is gathered. It's standing room only and there's a large cake on the table. I guess someone at the firm was a little more certain than we were the settlement would be a success.

"Let the heroes of the hour in here!" shouts Arvin, from the other end of the room and everyone claps. Once it's quiet, he continues. "I've got a little announcement to make, and it's been a long time coming. Ben, get up here."

Ben gives me a quick glance, a *worried* glance, and then goes to the head of the table.

"Some excellent work was done today," Fields says, "and we give credit where it's due." He pulls down a sign to reveal the new name of the firm: Fields, McGovern, Geiger, and *Tate*. "Say hello to our first name partner in two decades, who will be leaving next month to head up the San Francisco office with our newest junior partner, Craig Stanley."

The noise is suddenly deafening, and I'm the only one who isn't making a sound, who's standing stiff and stunned, watching as the partners surround Ben.

His gaze finds mine across a sea of people, and I see worry there, but not surprise.

Because he knew this was coming.

Of course, he fucking knew. They wouldn't be announcing it if he hadn't agreed. This is why he's been so weird the past few days. Why he no longer cares about going to HR, why that trip to Fiji doesn't matter. Because they offered him a big fucking promotion and he knew he was throwing me under the bus to get it. Maybe it was always the plan, he just didn't know it would happen so soon.

If he'd ripped my heart out of my chest, I doubt it could hurt more than this moment does. Every fucking thing I've worked for has just been stolen from me, and he helped make it happen.

I can barely hear over the rush of blood in my ears, my

breath coming too fast. My hand clings to the nearest chair, struggling to stay upright.

"I almost forgot!" shouts Arvin over the noise, and my breath holds. "Debbie, start cutting that cake! It's not going to eat itself."

I want to throw a fist into the middle of that fucking cake. I want to climb on the table and scream about what an absolute farce this is.

My legs tremble and my jaw aches with the effort it takes to hold it together. People offer me embarrassed smiles, wincing a little as they congratulate me on the case someone else has gotten all the credit for. I catch Terri's eye and her expression mirrors my own. Shock, anger, disbelief. I push past the crowd, out the door, walking blindly down the hall.

Someone runs out behind me, and I want it to be Ben. I want him to tell me it's a misunderstanding and that he really thought I was making partner, but I turn to find Terri instead, still looking as shellshocked as I am.

"Gemma," she gasps, "this is bullshit."

It is. I cannot believe I just won one of the biggest gender discrimination settlements in the country, and did nearly all the work, and I'm not going to get any fucking credit for it. Ben and FMG will get the credit. Ben—who just screwed over a female colleague—and FMG—which doesn't have even *one* female partner—are now positioned as champions of women in the workplace.

But the worst part is what Terri doesn't know: that Ben was *in on it*. That I'd convinced myself he was everything, but in the end, he was every bit as cutthroat and Machiavellian as Kyle or my father. He made me believe I was being paranoid, thinking the worst of him. That I was damaged—and maybe I *am* damaged, but if so, then he just made it a thousand times worse. I don't even care about making partner right now. I just want to make sure I never lay eyes on Ben again.

I turn to Terri, blinking away tears. "That's it," I tell her softly. "I'm done. I'm out."

"Gemma, don't do anything rash," she says. "You were still part of something amazing. You'll be able to write your own ticket anywhere."

I nod, numbly. I want to have a tantrum, but isn't that exactly what they will expect of me? And then behind my back they will make jokes about how it must be *that time of the month*" and how much it would suck to *"be married to that."* No way am I giving them the satisfaction.

I'll wait until I'm calm to resign, but I can't stay here in the meantime. I need to be back home with the one person I know I can trust.

I go to my office and grab my laptop and purse. From the elevator I look toward the conference room, where a bunch of men in suits celebrate, alongside a bunch of women who won't ever make partner.

Six fucking years. And my life hasn't changed a bit.

The first time Ben Tate walked into FMG, my breath caught.

I'd been curious about him, before that first meeting—no one really understood why he'd come to us when he'd already made partner at a more successful firm—but that's all it was: curiosity, easily satisfied.

And then I saw him—younger than I'd expected, and taller, and lovelier—and he was already looking at me when I entered the room as if I was exactly what he'd been waiting for.

When our eyes locked, his smile was sheepish. A moment later, I was the one sneaking a glance. He caught me; I blushed to my roots. I'd sworn off men like him, but in five minutes' time, I was already trying to make an exception.

We all introduced ourselves to him after the initial meeting. When it was my turn, I started to tell him my name and he stopped me with an embarrassed smile. "I know who you are," he said. "I saw you in court decimating a partner at my last firm."

He said it as if impressed, and I blushed again. "A few of us are going to the bar across the street tomorrow night," he told me. "If you're free." He held my eye. It felt like he was asking something more.

I was terrified—of how badly I wanted to go, of how much I wanted to see his uneven smile again, and as soon as possible. I opened my mouth to reply, but Fields was there, dragging him off. I'm still not sure what I was going to say.

When I found out, the very next morning, that he'd stolen Brewer Campbell from me, the first emotion I felt, even before rage, was relief. As if I'd been spared a much worse fate, as if being able to hate him would make my life easier.

If only I could have kept hating him, because I'm never, ever going to recover from Ben Tate. I think I knew I wouldn't, even that first day we met.

I do not sleep a wink on the red-eye to DC. I want to cry, but I'm too stunned. Where do I go from here? The last six years of my life have been spent working toward one goal I didn't achieve, and the only thing I actually *loved* about my job was the man who just made sure I didn't achieve it.

My mother hovers over me from the moment I arrive home. I summed up what happened, but she's struggling to believe Ben is a man like Kyle, like my father. Little surprise, that. Her picker has proven, historically, to be every bit as bad as mine.

"Here," she says, sliding a glass of something bright green, flecked with brown. "It's a kale and spirulina smoothie. Just try it. You're probably low on Vitamin D, which causes depression."

"Everyone is low on Vitamin D," I argue, glancing at the kitchen counter. Since when does my mom shell out for spirulina? You can't even walk into Whole Foods without spending more than she makes in a day. That's when I notice the five-hundred-dollar blender sitting on her counter.

"You bought a *Vitamix*?" I ask. This is my mom, who thinks she's okay with nothing but three chipped plates, after all.

She bites her lip. "I've always wanted one," she begins. "And

I've been meaning to discuss it with you, once you weren't so busy. Your father called out of nowhere and said he wants to make things right. He sent me a very, very large check."

"He *did*? And what did he demand in exchange?"

She smiles. "Nothing, hon. He said you spoke to him and he realized he'd been wrong."

I push a hand through my hair. "Mom, he doesn't do anything out of the goodness of his heart. Did he make you sign something? Was there any kind of verbal agreement?"

Her laugh is quiet and unhappy, as if it's sad that I'm so suspicious when what's actually sad is that she *isn't*, after everything he's done. "No, Gemma. Nothing. Isn't it possible that he wanted to do the right thing? Or maybe just wanted to earn your respect?"

"It would take a lot more than that," I reply, and my voice cracks. He didn't even tell me he was doing it and he didn't try to force my hand at all. Maybe he finally heard me when I exploded at him on Christmas, or maybe this is just a ploy to get me to come to his firm. "Why are you still working two jobs, then?"

She shrugs. "I like my jobs, and Ed says—"

"Who the hell is Ed?" I'm instantly suspicious. My mother is fragile, and she's got very little experience with men. A child could take advantage of her.

"*Language*, Gemma," she scolds. "He owns the bar. You know that. He—" She blushes. "I told him about Ben coming here to shovel and he was so upset. He's been coming over ever since to take care of things and I guess we've sort of begun—"

"Fucking?"

"Gemma! Jesus, the mouth on you. *Dating*. But anyway, he says I should take my time and decide what I really want to do with my life, so I'm just sitting tight for now." That's actually really sensible advice from *Ed*, if that's really his name. But that doesn't mean I trust him.

"I'm going to need to meet this guy," I warn.

"You act like he's a stranger, Gemma," she says. "I've known him for a year. He was just too shy to ask."

"Or too much of a sociopath," I suggest. "Too busy trying to get rid of the teenage girls he trapped in his basement."

She frowns at me. "I've been to his house. He doesn't have a basement."

"Fine," I say with a sigh. "Maybe he's shy."

Perhaps my mom is getting her Hallmark movie ending after all. I'm going to need to make a radical change to get my own, however.

I look out the window: the morning light is still gray and sunless, the trees are bare, and less than a mile away the traffic on 66 is at a standstill, crowded with angry, stressed-out commuters.

I didn't especially like growing up in DC, and there's nothing about it I like now, but I need a new playing field entirely, and I suppose the logical one is here. My father did the right thing, at last, and would it be so bad, working at his firm? I'd enter as a partner, I'm sure, and I'd be an equity partner soon enough.

It's not the work I want to do, but I'm not sure helping the Sophia Waterhouses of the world lie to get custody is much better. I might as well do whatever it takes to get ahead, just like Ben did.

"Would you be mad if I took the job Dad offered me?" I ask, studying her face as she studies mine.

"Of course not," she finally says. "But why? You love living in LA."

"Not so much anymore," I reply.

She hugs me for a long time and tells me it will all be better after I've had a nap, as if I'm a toddler. And I suppose things can't get much worse.

When she goes to work, I climb into bed, staring at the bare ceiling of her guest room, wondering what's next. Yesterday seems almost too terrible to have occurred the way I remember. I keep wanting to make excuses for Ben, the same way I did for Kyle six years prior.

I snuggle deeper into the pillow and pick up my phone. I've ignored every sound it's made since leaving the office, not ready to deal with what Ben has to say, and apparently there's a lot: notifications from him cover my home screen. Taking a deep breath, I open the message app and scan the last few texts he's sent.

> **BEN**
>
> Please answer the goddamn phone.
>
> Gemma, this is fucking ridiculous. We need to talk. NOW.

He sounds more irritated than conciliatory, just like Kyle did. I throw down the phone and pick it up again.

> Tell me something. Did you know this was going to happen all along? Did you sleep with me for months, knowing they'd promote you and Craig but not me, knowing you were MOVING? Don't bother replying because the answer no longer matters. I know everything I need to know. Tell Fields once he's done celebrating my victory that he'll be very lucky if I don't bring a similar suit against FMG.

I hit send and immediately regret it. I don't know if I'll really bring a suit against the firm, but I haven't done myself any favors by telegraphing the possibility.

I turn off my phone and lapse into an exhausted sleep. When I wake, the dim afternoon sun is coming through the windows. I slept for at least six hours, but I don't feel any better for it.

I shower and get an Uber to drive me downtown, to my father's firm. The Law Offices of Adam Charles now occupy two entire floors of a massive building on K Street, but it otherwise feels a lot like FMG did. Soulless and corporate.

My father greets me enthusiastically, congratulating me on the Lawson case as we walk down the hall. "Let me show you the office you'll have if you come aboard," he says, opening a door. It's as big as Fields' office back in LA. In the distance, I can make out the Washington Monument and the top of the White House.

He tells me the salary, and it's double what I make now. In two years, I'll be an equity partner and get a share of the firm's net.

"I'm not sure how soon you can get started," he says, "but I have the perfect case for you. A legislative aide has accused one of our clients of sexual misconduct."

Something inside me deflates. "I assume your client is a congressman?"

He nods with a gleam in his eyes. "It's going to get a ton of press."

That's all he sees right now—the attention this case will bring the firm—while all I see is that I'm about to become someone like Aronson. I'll be the person *defending* Fiducia. It will be me sitting in a deposition implying Lauren is a slut to cast doubt on her testimony. But how much worse is that than taking custody away from Dennis Roberts or telling Sophia Waterhouse how to make sure her ex loses the kids?

I ask my father for the weekend to think about it and he agrees, as if he already knows I'll say yes. I suppose I already know this too.

"You're welcome to stay with us, by the way," he says as I'm leaving. "I'm sure you'll want your own place eventually, but in the meantime...that commute from Manassas will kill you."

And so it begins. He's already finding ways to make this

more than a job. I wonder if giving my mom that money was simply another of his tactics, if he gambled on me coming to the firm in response to his show of goodwill.

The air outside is bitingly cold as I walk to the parking garage, the sky solid gray and unyielding. DC goes from one extreme to the next: six months from now it'll be so humid I won't be able to walk down the street without my clothes sticking to me. I'll miss the weather in LA. I'll miss other things even more.

It takes an hour and a half in traffic to get back to my mother's apartment complex. I groan quietly when I hear voices on the other side of the door. I suppose Ed is here. I'm not likely to make the best impression today.

I force myself toward the living room...and freeze. Ben is sitting on my mother's couch—jacket off, collar unbuttoned, hair boyishly rumpled.

The sight of him breaks my heart all over again. I loved him so much. I still love him even now, despite what he did. But I'm not the same person I was before—he made sure of that.

"Why the fuck are you here?" I demand.

"Oh, Gemma, be nice," my mother chides. "He flew all the way out to talk to you."

I ignore her. My mother's insistence on being nice to everyone has gotten her nowhere. "You flew all this way for nothing, then," I tell him. "Get out."

My mother slides from the room as he rises, his face as angry as mine. "If you'd just answered your goddamned phone, this would have been over last night."

"I don't want to hear it, Ben! You had your opportunity to talk to me *before* that fucking announcement and you chose not to." My voice cracks and I dig my nails into my palms to hold myself together. "You're a liar. There were a *thousand* signs this was wrong—the way you never invited me over or introduced me to anyone—and I ignored them all, but I'm done ignoring them, so go back where you came from."

I turn to walk away and he grabs my arm. "They're making you partner."

I stare at him blankly. It can't be true and honestly...I don't even want it anymore. Fields intentionally humiliated me yesterday by announcing Ben and Craig's promotions at that meeting, so fuck him. I still want to crush the boys' club, but I'll crush it from the outside in. "Bullshit."

"They weren't going to," he says. "I found out the other night. I agreed to head up the San Francisco office for a year if they made you a partner once we won, but I thought I'd get a chance to discuss it with you first. I had no clue Fields was going to do that. I really thought the announcement was going to be about you."

I want to continue believing it's all a lie, but he's too smart to tell one I could easily disprove.

I shake him off. "You were pulling away. I saw it."

"No," he says, running a frustrated hand through his hair. "I was sick over the situation and desperately trying to figure out how to fix things, Gemma. And wishing I could discuss it with you and knowing I couldn't, not 'til the case was done. You wouldn't even have wanted me to tell you that before we went into the negotiations."

I want to argue, but he's right. If I'd known, it would have unnerved me. Instead, I went into settlement feeling indomitable and it showed.

"You've never once invited me to your place," I insist, as if the whole bit about making partner is irrelevant. And it is. There are too many other pieces of this that don't fit. "You didn't want me to meet your family or your friends, and then you put off going to HR when I suggested it."

"You spin a story in the courtroom better than anyone I know, but the way you narrate your own life sucks," he says, eyes flashing. "Because you *know* why you haven't met my friends, and *I* was the one who brought up HR months ago, so where does that fit into your theory about what a prick I am?"

I laugh angrily. "So did Kyle. Look where that got me."

He pulls his phone from his pocket and starts swiping. "You still need me to prove I'm different? Fine. *This* is my family."

I roll my eyes. If he thinks letting me into some tiny corner of his life *now* could possibly make up for shutting me out of it, he's insane. I open my mouth to tell him exactly that, and then it closes.

The photo is of him, his younger brothers...and Walter, my client.

I blink. "Why is Walter in a photo with your family?"

"Because he's my stepfather."

My jaw hangs open. "*Bullshit*. Why would...why would—"

"I never meant to take Brewer Campbell from you, and Walter's in-house had quit, so I asked him to hire you for a while until I could find another way to fix the situation. I knew if I told you the truth, you'd refuse the job."

He's right. I would have.

My back presses to the wall, trying to make sense of everything. I spent two years hating him over a stolen client, without a clue he'd brought me a better one in its place.

"You should have told me," I say quietly. I've been begging Walter for ages to hire someone in-house.

"You'd have refused to keep working for him if you knew," he says, "and Fields was never going to make you partner without him. I thought it could wait."

He steps toward me slowly, as if I'm a small animal he might frighten off. I'm scared to believe him, but if this is all true... then everything he did, he did for me. I think of the night we spoke about my mom—him saying, *"you want to burn the world to ash just to make sure her path is clear."*

He was talking about me. And he's been clearing my path every day since we met.

"I'm sorry, Gemma," he says. He's close enough now that if I reached out, I could touch him. "If I'd had a clue it was going to go down that way, I'd have refused Fields' offer. You mean a thousand times more to me than any promotion, and you mean a thousand times more to me than staying at FMG. Whether I go to San Francisco or even remain at the firm is entirely your call. But please tell me you understand why I did it."

My eyes sting. I nod, and when he finally closes the distance between us, I allow it, resting my head against his chest. His arms wrap around me and we remain that way for a long moment.

"I'm not going back to FMG," I tell him. "I will never make that firm another dime for as long as I live. But do you lose the promotion if you don't go to San Francisco?"

"I couldn't care less about that promotion," he says. "If you'd wanted to stay at FMG, I'd have suggested we go to San Francisco together. But since you don't...I have a better idea. What if we both left FMG and went out on our own?"

I'm so dumbfounded I can barely find the right words. "You want to *leave*? And start a new firm with *me*?"

He gives a quiet laugh. "Just imagine how many non-paying clients you could bring in if we set up our own shop. And yes, of course I'd leave. You only stayed because you had something to prove, and I only stayed because I was in love with this woman there who loathed me."

"You love me?" I ask.

His thumb swipes a tear off my cheek. "This can't be a surprise to you. I've been in love with you for two years straight. You were the only reason I interviewed there in the first place."

I think of him then, watching me that first day. Saying, *"I know who you are"* with that same tender thing in his eyes I've seen a thousand times since. I narrated our story in the worst way possible, just like he said. But I'm going to tell it a different way from this moment on.

"I love you," I whisper. "And I wanted to make partner, but for the past two years, you were the reason I stayed there too."

He laughs as he presses his lips to mine. "I know," he says quietly. "But I'm glad you finally figured it out."

ON THE WAY back to LA, I call my father and tell him I'm not taking the job, and then I fire Sophia Waterhouse after reminding her that false abuse claims are a felony.

Ben and I spend the flight mapping out how we'd structure our firm, and who we'll bring with us. Terri, of course, and Ben's assistant. I argue that none of the associates are smart enough, *especially* Nicole, and Ben says I'm being an asshole, which is entirely possible.

"So do I finally get to meet everyone?" I ask him.

He laughs. "Yes...my mother, Tali, and Drew have been relentless about this for months. They'll probably show up at the airport if they know we're coming in."

"And do I get to see your place?" I ask.

A flicker of uncertainty crosses his face. "Yeah," he says. "I guess."

"What the hell is in there that you're so worried about? Is it, like, a doll collection? A bunch of mannequins posed on the couch in sexy lingerie?"

He laughs. "That would be slightly less embarrassing than the truth. You'll just have to see for yourself."

Our flight lands and he directs our driver to Santa Monica rather than my apartment. I'm not sure which of us is more nervous about this big reveal. What could possibly be so awful about the interior of a home he's spent two years working on?

The car pulls up to the curb and we climb out. "It's not

much to look at from the outside," Ben warns, grabbing my bag from the trunk. I don't mention that I've driven by it a few thousand times—he's seen enough of my psychotic side for one week.

We walk up the path, and with a deep breath, he unlocks the door and holds it open for me. I step inside...and freeze.

There are wide plank hardwood floors and white furniture, an exposed beam ceiling, a beaded chandelier. Toward the back of the house, in the kitchen, I see butcher block counters and an island painted navy blue.

I gasp. "It's *exactly* like my Pinterest board."

"Yeah," he says. And he sounds ashamed, which is when I turn to him, confused for a moment, and then incredulous.

"I didn't realize what I was doing at first," he says softly. "And by the time I did, I couldn't take it back, and I didn't figure it would matter. It seemed like you were never, ever going to give me the time of day."

I brush at the tears running down my face as I laugh. "That's so creepy. It's so much worse than I thought."

"I know, right?" he asks. "But...imagine how much more of our money you could blow on shoes if you lived here instead of your apartment."

"*Our* money?"

He rests his hands on my hips. "I have waited for you, Gemma Charles, for two years. Every day of two fucking years. You don't really think I'm letting you go after all that?"

I smile like a pre-teen who just got asked out for the first time. It's so goofy I want to hide my face from him, but I don't. I just go up on my toes and press a single kiss to his mouth. "Fine. But I don't really believe in marriage."

He grins. "Sure you don't."

EPILOGUE

FIVE MONTHS LATER

Ben appears in my office at noon, tapping his watch.

I glance up from my laptop. "Did you need something?" I ask.

He raises a single, stern brow. "Gemma, you *promised*."

It's been eight months from that first night we were together in his office, and he's insisting we celebrate with a weekend away. Weekends off are hardly unusual for us—I find myself putting work on hold at least once a month for one of Drew's lavish trips, which haven't abated at all even now that she is very, very pregnant. But this is different. It's just us this time, at his insistence.

He's also insisting the destination be a surprise, even though I hate surprises.

I grin. "I know. Give me five more minutes. I'm trying to get Lola into that magnet school Victoria likes."

His gaze softens. He's been with me to Victoria's a few times now, and even if she hadn't won Ben over, which she did, the kids would have. Phillip's drawings of "me and my friend Ben" now hang all over our refrigerator.

"Five minutes, Gemma, and not a second more," he warns, doing his best to look threatening.

I finish up my appeal of the school board's decision, send it off then bolt for the door, purse in hand. I smile at the sight of Ben standing there chatting with Terri, newly grateful he's making us do this. It's been at least forty-eight hours since I've gotten the chance to peel a suit off him, and that's forty-seven hours too long.

"Don't get her pregnant!" Terri shouts after us as we walk out. "She doesn't have time for that!"

Ben laughs under his breath. "No promises."

I have no idea where we're going, though I know it won't be Fiji—there just isn't time. Thanks to the attention we got from the Lawson case and our pre-existing clients, we have more work than we know what to do with. I just placed an ad for two more associates this morning and eventually we'll get caught up...but it won't be today.

We pull out of the parking garage. I can see the Pacific Coast Highway from our new office, but he heads inland instead, up the 405.

"You're sure you want to go this way?" I ask. I was hoping we'd return to the cottage where we spent New Year's Eve, but this is definitely *not* moving us toward Santa Barbara.

He grins. "Yes, I'm sure."

"There's nothing but woods up this way, though," I tell him. "Oh, God. We're not camping, right?"

He laughs. "I think I know you a little better than that, Princess. Stop asking questions."

Eventually, he veers onto the 5 toward Bakersfield, which continues to be a direction I'm not interested in exploring. I manage to hold my tongue until he cuts off onto a nameless side road.

"I can't do it, Ben. I can't not ask. Where are we going? Because we're in the middle of fucking nowhere."

His eyes cut to mine and return to the road. "Do I need to define the word *surprise* for you?"

"This looks like a place you'd go to dump a body. If that's your plan, I told people about this trip so you won't get away with it."

"Yes, I figured you would," he says. "I guess I'll have to bide my time."

I pick up my phone to text Drew.

> You don't happen to know where Ben is taking me, do you? I know he probably swore you to secrecy, but I have legitimate reason to think he might be planning to kill me.

DREW

> He wouldn't take a whole weekend off to kill you. He's way too busy for that.

I laugh.

> So you don't know anything?

> I don't know a thing. But make sure Keeley comes to Tali's party next weekend. My brother-in-law wants to meet her.

I turn to Ben. "How much do you know about Josh's brother?"

In true lawyer fashion, rather than just answering the question, he raises a brow. "Why?"

"He's interested in Keeley, apparently," I reply. "He's in a band, right? You know Keeley would eat that up, so I'm assessing the situation first."

He shrugs, failing to answer once again. "You know, Graham asked about her too," he says. The admission is reluctant, as he is staunchly against getting involved in his brothers' personal lives.

I bark a laugh. "Your *brother*? Never."

He glares at me before his gaze returns to the road. "What's wrong with Graham? I've already heard plenty about how attractive you find the men in my family."

I laugh again. He heard me tell Keeley *once* that his brothers were hot and he's been quietly bitter about it ever since. "They are so, *so* hot. All of them."

"You can stop now," he mutters.

I smile. "Nothing is wrong with Graham. But can you imagine him with Keeley? Mr. Responsibility with Miss 'Lucky Charms is a health food and retirement planning is for dorks'? His head would explode."

He shrugs and then frowns. "Shit," he says under his breath, pulling the car over to the shoulder and coming to a stop.

"Did you finally realize we've been driving the wrong way for two hours?"

He gives me a dirty look as he pops the hood and climbs out. "No, but thanks for letting me know how you feel, *again*. The car's making a noise."

I sigh loudly. Even if he *does* hear a noise and even if he knew, inexplicably, how to fix it, what's he going to do—carve a new part out of wood? There's nothing but trees for miles.

"I think it's the alternator," he announces, climbing back in the car.

"The alternator? How would you possibly know that?"

"I didn't always work in an office," he says.

I'm pretty sure he *did* always work in an office. I picture him being born in a tiny suit and tie, immediately demanding a higher quality formula than the one offered by the hospital.

He examines the map. "We'd better get someone to take a look. I wouldn't want you stuck in *the middle of fucking nowhere*, as you so charmingly referred to it."

It all seems really unnecessary. His BMW is barely two years old—the odds that something is seriously wrong are slim.

He drives us a few miles away, to a tiny town that barely appeared on the map.

"Is the name of this place *actually* Hickory Hills?" I ask, as we pass a carved wooden sign on its outskirts.

He's on his phone, looking for the service station. "I guess. Why?"

"Because it's so...Hallmark. I mean, it even looks like a town in a Hallmark movie." I'm practically hanging out the window to get a better look. We are on Main Street, now, which also seems to be their *only* street. There's a cute little coffee shop, an ancient drugstore and a retro diner but little else.

Ben's ignoring me, frowning at his phone. "I'm gonna drive down to the gas station and get them to take a look," he says, stopping beside a small cafe. "You want to run in and grab us some coffee? I'll walk back and meet you in a few."

"Sure," I reply, kissing him on the cheek. "It'll all be fine." I really hate surprises, and nothing about this experience is proving that wrong so far, but I imagine he's a lot more stressed than I am. He's wanted this weekend away for a while.

My heels catch in the divots in the cute brick sidewalk. I guess I should have changed before we left the office, but I had no idea he was going to be depositing me in Backwoods, USA.

I enter the coffee shop and a tiny bell over the door announces my arrival. A cat lounges in the window seat, which I assume is a health code violation. "Well," says the woman behind the counter, "I can tell you're not from these parts." She nods at my outfit.

I force a smile. "No," I reply. "Can I get—"

"Los Angeles, I'm guessing?" she asks.

"Right," I tell her. "I guess the suit gave it away. Could I get—"

"My sister used to live in LA. Silverlake. You ever go there?"

"Um...sometimes?"

"There's a cute little Thai place there," she says. "If you go, tell them Amy said hi."

For fuck's sake. Yes, I'll drive all the way to Silverlake for Thai food, and I'll be sure to tell them a complete stranger said hi. "Sure. Could I just get two coffees?"

"Why don't I make it a latte?" she asks. "You could use a little fattening up."

Ugh. Commenting on my weight, good or bad, exceeds the limits of acceptable small-town quirkiness. "I'm fine thanks. Just the coffee. To go."

"Take a seat and I'll bring it over," she tells me.

I do as she says, and it takes her several minutes to bring me two cups of coffee, which are *not* to-go. I'm thanking her as the door opens and three small children spill in, followed by their harried mother.

Amy swoops one of them up and gives him a kiss on the cheek. "How are my grandbabies?" she asks.

"Trouble as always," answers the woman, who drops into a seat near mine.

One of the kids plops on the floor and starts rolling his toy car into my shoe. Once is an accident, but by the third time I realize destroying my shoe is his chosen activity for the next few minutes.

"That's Jarrett," Amy explains. "He loves cars."

I love unscuffed Jimmy Choos, but I guess we don't always get what we want. I lift my feet and Jarrett glares at me like I just entered his soccer game and stole the ball.

Meanwhile, Amy continues her running commentary about her grandchildren—their likes, their dislikes, their favorite books—and is still going strong when Ben walks in.

I jump to my feet and he waves me to sit. "You might as well get comfortable," he says. "It looks like we're stuck here."

BEN'S CAR needs a new part, one that won't arrive until morning. We check into a bed and breakfast, all wallpaper and chintz, with creepy dolls on every shelf, and a proprietor named Julie who stays slightly too close as she leads us through the house. She asks us to remove our shoes and warns us that the toilet isn't great. "Call down to me if you need a plunger," she says. "You probably will."

The room smells like moth balls and history. "Don't lose the key and don't come in after ten, please," she says.

"What would we even find to *do* here after ten?" I ask, and Ben steps on my foot to shut me up.

She stops at the door on her way out and looks Ben over, from head to toe. "And I should warn you that the bed squeaks and the walls are thin."

I raise a brow at him once she's gone. "I think she basically just told us not to have sex."

"She'd need to try a little harder for that to succeed," he says, wrapping his arms around me. He looks at the bed. "So what do you think?"

"I think that quilt hasn't been washed once since someone made it in 1972 and is probably covered in bodily fluids."

"We'll remove the quilt," he says. His mouth slips into a sly smile and he loosens his tie. "Look at the headboard. That's the kind of bed we need at home."

By which he means the kind that wrists can be tied to. I squeeze my thighs together in anticipation.

"I bet she's standing right outside listening," I whisper.

He crosses the room and opens the door. "I think you're being paranoid...Oh, hi, Julie."

She scurries away and he turns to me, his shoulders sagging. "Maybe we'll just go for a walk, then."

I change into shorts and sneakers, and we stroll through the town, hand in hand. Ben asks someone if there are any good hikes, which sounds like a lot of work to me, and we are directed to the woods at the edge of town, where there's a path and a *"pretty little lake".*

As we walk, I start talking about our new gender discrimination case and he stops me. "This is a no-work weekend, remember?"

"Well, if Julie wasn't standing outside our room like a creep, I'd tell you exactly how to take my mind off work."

He nods at the trees overhead. "Try to enjoy nature."

"I've seen trees before," I reply, kicking a branch out of our way. "Unpopular opinion, but nature is boring."

He laughs and pulls me toward the stupid little lake, which was not worth walking a mile to view. We sit on a bench, and I rest my head on his shoulder.

"What do you think?" he asks.

"I think they ought to drain this lake and make it a big Target Superstore," I reply. "That would make it worth the one-mile walk. But I'm glad you're here suffering with me."

"Because you like having me around," he asks, "or because you want me to suffer?"

I grin. "Can't it be both?"

He laughs, pulling me to my feet, and we head back. My cute white Vejas are no longer white by the time we near town, and they're giving me a blister. He gives me a piggyback ride to the bed and breakfast, where we have furtive, silent sex in the shower before changing to go to dinner. It's only four p.m., but there's nothing else to do.

The diner isn't as cute and retro as I thought. Tap water is delivered to us in cloudy glasses. We decide we aren't thirsty.

"It smells like forty-year-old cooking oil in here," Ben says, leaning forward to avoid anyone hearing.

We share a sandwich and fries, and when we finally get outside, I turn to him. "I can't wait to get out of this town, Ben."

He pulls me against him with a soft smile on his face. "So, life in a small town isn't everything you thought it would be?"

"No," I say, laughing into his t-shirt. "It's so boring here. I'd go crazy."

His lips press to the top of my head. "I know," he says. "That's why I picked it."

I blink. "*What?*"

His shoulders shake with silent laughter. "There's nothing wrong with my car. It's parked in back of the barbershop and we can leave right now. I just wanted you to get your whole Hallmark experience."

"You—" I sputter. "But...I can't believe...I mean, how did you even know what the towns in those movies were like?"

He shrugs. "It mattered to you, so I watched a few of them the last time you went back to visit your mom."

I abandoned the Hallmark thing quite a while ago, but tears sting my eyes. "I can't believe you," I say, and it comes out a little broken.

"Don't get me wrong...I did a lot of fast-forwarding because they're ridiculously boring, but yeah." He stops suddenly. "Are you crying?"

I nod and press my face to his shirt. "This was both the nicest and the cruelest thing anyone's done to me in a long time."

"Amy was in on it, by the way," he says. "From the coffee shop? I called her yesterday and asked her to be as nosy as possible."

"And Julie?"

He shakes his head. "No. She's just weird. But this whole trip has inspired me. I think I've got a movie we could pitch to Hallmark—"

"It can't be about two lawyers. One of us needs to be a good person."

He laughs. "They can branch out this once. So, these two

lawyers are crazy about each other and refuse to admit it until he fingers her in his office. And then he takes her away somewhere like Santa Barbara and proposes because they're too busy to go to Iceland."

I fight a smile, my heart beating like a drum. "No one gets fingered in a Hallmark movie."

"What about the rest of it?" he asks, pulling me closer.

"Yeah," I whisper, as hope begins to expand in my chest. "The rest of it sounds pretty good. I'd have hated Iceland."

He laughs. "I know."

All those dreams and plans I had were...nonsense. They were fantasies—the more unlikely, the more impossible the better, because it kept me that much safer from having to contend with something real.

He rubs the back of his neck. "So," he begins quietly, "we have a reservation in Santa Barbara if you're ready to go."

He's so nervous. So sheepish. Just like he was his first day at FMG, trying to casually invite me to join him at the bar across the street.

I wrap my arms around his neck, my smile ridiculously wide. "I'm ready."

Because something real is no longer terrifying. And I can't wait to say *"yes"* to Ben Tate.

THE END

ALSO BY ELIZABETH O'ROARK

The Devil Series:

A Deal with the Devil

The Devil and the Deep Blue Sea

The Devil You Know

The Devil Gets His Due

Waking Olivia

Drowning Erin

The Parallel Series

The Summer We Fell

ACKNOWLEDGMENTS

Thanks, first and foremost, to Katie Foster Meyer. If it wasn't for Katie's encouragement back when I was getting started, I'd probably never have published anything. She's the first person I show stuff to, and the last I check in with before it goes to print. Katie: thank you, thank you, thank you. I've got the job of my dreams and I wouldn't be here without you.

Next, a huge hug and thanks to my wonderful beta readers: Nancy Ames, Michelle Chen, Kimberly Dallaire, Christine Estevez, Katie Meyer, Jen Wilson Owens and Tawanna Williams. Your enthusiasm for this book thrilled me and your suggestions were pure gold.

An extra shout-out to Christine and Jen for helping me this year in too many ways to name. My sister Kate listened to me rant endlessly about the process and also came up with the company names here so I don't get sued. Samantha Brentmoor —you knocked another audio out of the park and I feel so lucky to have found you. Entirely Bonkerz, your stories and reels have made me laugh countless times this spring and I'm so grateful for all your support.

Sali Benbow-Powers, thank you for caring about my characters as much as I do. You've taken a part of the process I used to dread and made it a highlight. Many thanks to Kelly Golland— I learned so much from your edit—and to Julie Deaton, who caught all my last-minute typos.

Nina Grinstead, Kim Cermak and the whole team at Valentine PR: I continue to be amazed by how freaking *on top of it* y'all are. Releasing a book makes me want to crawl in a dark room and sleep—thanks to you, I *can* and it'll still be okay (but I won't, I promise).

Finally, a special shout-out to the unbelievably generous and kind authors, reviewers and readers I've encountered along the way. To the members of Elizabeth O'Roark Books, the Parallel Series Spoiler Room and everyone who's posted on IG or made a TikTok about this series and others: you make Book World a wonderful place to be.

ABOUT THE AUTHOR

Elizabeth O'Roark spent many years as a medical writer before publishing her first novel in 2013. She holds two bachelor's degrees from the University of Texas, and a master's degree from Notre Dame. She lives in Washington, D.C. with her three children. Join her book group, Elizabeth O'Roark Books, on Facebook for updates, book talk and lots of complaints about her children.